ECHOES OF THE STORM

Published by Gone Feral Publishing
1625 Market Street
Galveston, Texas 77550

www.goneferalpublishing.com

ISBN Number 978-0-615-46689-7

ECHOES OF THE STORM

A Galveston Hurricane Mystery

Amanda Still

For Ian who loves me and encourages me, for my daughters who put up with me, and all those people who dream they can write a book and don't just stop at a dream.

Acknowledgements

My editor, Mickey, my agent, Andrea, and my critique partners, the Yahoo Mystery Group, as well as those friends who contributed their time, knowledge, and inspiration, including Ann Haugen, Paul Kieniewicz, and Cheryl Robbins.

Author's Note

In September of 1900, Galveston, the Queen City, was one of the largest ports and most successful towns in the United States. All that was washed away on the 8th of September. A wall of water from the Gulf of Mexico rose to over fifteen feet and pushed a wall of debris across the island, taking lives and destroying property. The bathhouses on piers broke apart and the roof of Ritter's Saloon fell in, killing almost all the businessmen within. The Catholic Orphans Home fell under the waves, killing nearly 100 children and the nuns who tried to protect them. Eventually, the waters of the Gulf and of Galveston Bay met and the entire island was submerged while the wind howled overhead.

Since whole families were washed away, no one can be sure of the death toll, but estimates place it between 6,000 and 12,000. Many sources hold with 8,000. Outside of war, this was the most devastating event in American History.

Contents

Galveston, Texas, April 1901

Chapter 1

I grabbed my jacket from the wall hook. "I should be back before anyone misses me." I patted a bit of astrakhan trim back into place on the charity-shop jacket and shoved my hands through the puffed wool sleeves.

Evangeline, my stenographer and typewriter, looked at the watch pinned to her work apron. "Miss Dash, your next appointment's in five—"

"Yes, yes." I buttoned the coat around my tight shirtwaist and heard the creak of a seam giving way. I looked up.

Evangeline heard it, too, and she stared at me with what appeared to be disapproval in her black-brown eyes.

"I need to get this over with." I bolted to the office door of carved walnut before her frown could emit more words, and I would end up explaining that this summons scared me for no reason I could explain.

I pushed open the heavy building doors and leapt over loose bricks. I landed on a slippery spot of the crushed-shell road, and grabbed a bent lamppost before smacking to the ground. I forced a deep breath to relax, but my jaw clenched and muscles tightened with nerves I didn't understand. I looked across to a small row off two-story offices with shops on the ground floor with their broken windows and jetsam piled against the doors.

I'd seen hundreds of bloated bodies before, everyone in town had. Back in September, I'd identified my neighbors and their children, so this request from the police shouldn't bother me. When the telephone call came into my office about a naked woman found with my calling card, I was fine, but now as I stepped over stray roof slates and sand in the street between my office and the morgue, I grew all-overish. What if I embarrassed myself? I might turn apoplectic in front of the police or worse, scream.

A respectable woman, I repeated to myself. The widow of a prominent citizen, I now worked for a living. *I can do this, I can. And not come up all banshee in front of the police.*

Remnants of yesterday's rain puddled around a building I remembered this brownstone from before the storm when it was a dry-good warehouse. Now, black paint covered the bays of high windows to convert it to the cooling room of the permanent morgue and a ghost of dirt showed where an ornate sign once hung over the now nameless building. Just above the waterline mark, a policeman rested his hand. The floodwater had been around five feet.

I didn't want to go in there, but couldn't ignore the police who summoned me.

How did a naked, drowned woman have my calling card?

Maybe when I saw the body, I'd have an answer to that.

A half-hearted drizzle swirled through the street and brought out the smell of dead fish and lost hope that haunted the city. A man in clothes and beard as gray as the day stepped into my path to offer a handbill emblazoned with "Galveston's Flood; a City Cursed for Arrogance," but with a look at my face, he turned away to examine a loose pile of bricks at the curb. Even beneath a mourning veil, I could manage a glare that let him know I was not a superstitious ninny who believed in curses. The city had been hit by the wind and waves of the worst hurricane in history. Our disaster was meteorology, not metaphysics.

I clutched my dripping veil tight to keep my fingers from trembling and made rapid steps through the muddy street to the morgue. I passed the skeleton of a building where once a three-story monument to commerce stood. I looked up at it and wondered how many had died there. Had I known any who perished there? With so many dead, I would never know.

To dispel a shudder, I whispered, "I'm used to this."

In September of 1900, those of us who survived in Galveston had tramped through make-shift morgues to find a loved one or neighbor. The Great Hurricane had been the deadliest natural disaster in American history and thousands of bodies had littered the beaches. Even now in April, the shadow of the storm spread over Galveston Island. Everyone had lost something in the storm from property to loved ones. A swell had caught my house and carried it off its foundation, but spared the fifty or so people—most of them strangers—sheltering with me. My husband had not come home, and his body was never found.

The brass handle on the iron-studded door felt cold through my gloves, but I pulled it open and strode into the building. Forcing a fast, firm walk, I stepped up to the desk that separated the black and white squared floor of entryway from the black-painted zone beyond. In an alcove, three policemen smoked. First one, than another, and then the last slipped a glance at me, but then went back to their conversation. To the young man behind the desk, I slipped a smile and my calling card. He craned over the small card sitting on his desk to mouth what he read:

> Mrs. Gallagher
> Legal Assistance

My mother always said a lady never goes anywhere without her calling cards. She would be aghast to know mine advertised my business, but she would approve the nosegay engraved on them.

"Yes," I said. "But go ahead and call me Miss Dash, everyone does." I waited for him to ask about such a funny name, most people did. It was short for "Dasha," which was the diminutive of the Russian name, "Daria."

He said nothing. Young, he looked as though he played dress up in his daddy's police hat and uniform. He shook his head and slid his hands to the edges of his desk, a pencil-gouged barrier to the land of the dead beyond.

A few yards behind him, a man in a lab coat steadied a woman with yellow hair. Another slid a sheet-covered gurney toward them and uphill from where green tile sloped to a drain in the floor.

In the alcove, one smoking policeman and then another glanced at the boy cop and me. Heck, those older cops glanced at us more than they did the dyed-haired woman.

She stood over a body that lay revealed on the gurney. She fought with her shawl to keep from revealing all of her buxom form.

"I was asked to come here." I rolled back my veil for a moment to show my face of high cheekbones and short, straight nose. With big hazel eyes and a wasp waist, I was pretty. Some would say, beautiful. A few had even said gorgeous. My appearance came in handy when dealing with men. "I got a call on the telephone. A woman drowned. She had nothing, not even clothes, but she had my card." I gave an energetic little shrug. "I don't know how, but she did."

Of course I had no idea how a naked woman could end up drowned holding my card. Beyond the physical difficulty of where she would have held it, how could I have known the sort of person who could end up drowned and "clothesless"? Yes, clothesless was the word the policeman made up on the telephone when he did not want to say "naked" to a lady over a party line. As an attorney, I might have a man's job, but I was a lady, a respectable lady. Oh yes, and a mother.

A thrill of nerves went through me at the thought of being a mother, a role that pleased, but scared me. Although not officially one yet, I would be a mother as soon as a judge signed the adoption papers. Then, my girls would be my daughters, rather than just the orphans who lived with me after the flood. That call from the courthouse may have already come into my office.

The clerk looked up to my face, but his gaze wandered down to my dress.

Yes, it was that bad. I had attempted to dye it last night in the darkest part of the evening and because I wanted to get on with the important business of braiding my daughter's hair, I figured I wouldn't look so bad. The black was blackest on the lace and seams, and there still varied. Black, blue, and purple vied across my figure where my efforts to dye the cloth had turned to a mottled mess that drew up the fabric around the neck until it threatened to choke me. I looked like a bruise.

He frowned at my dress. "Come back with a male escort."

"I was summoned here. I want to get in, get out, and get back to my office. I'm late for a client."

Well, the client was late for me. She was always late, and I had bolted from the office so she would be left to swing her feet under the visitor's chair in my office's front room for a while.

He looked at me as though waiting for me to say something or at least something interesting.

I leaned forward and caught the sweet, sharp smell of what I believed to be ether. "A couple months ago, women weren't stopped from coming to the morgue. When they existed, at least." My throat constricted at the thought of this and my eyes began to water. Most of us had no chance to find out loved ones. The fear of disease led the authorities to close the morgue and loaded the bodies onto barges to dump them at sea. I thought of the bodies I had seen near my ruined house that had washed back to shore. Tears stung as I wondered if my husband had been among those gathered with animal corpses and burned on a fire of storm debris.

Maybe I could just turn and run out before he saw me get emotional. No, word might get back to the courthouse that I was a hysteric and that might interfere with the adoption. .

His narrow face gathered into a frown and he shook his head until the loose hat threatened to rattle free.

I took a deep breath and adopted an urbane pose with pursed lips and a raise of my arched eyebrows. "What female in Galveston hasn't seen a body?" *Offer him money?* No, he was probably too green to take a bribe.

He was so young, his parents had probably locked him in the house to keep him from seeing the bodies burned in the street. "We don't allow ladies in here without an escort. Leastwise not anymore."

I gave a soft "ahem" and motioned down the hall with a tilt of my head and bounce of arched eyebrows.

He turned to look at the dyed-haired woman standing over a morgue table. She shouted, balled her fists, and smashed them against her cheeks.

He whipped back around to me. "No respectable lady without an escort."

"Thank you." I smiled. "But I assure you, I'm not squeamish. My father made sure of that." I remembered a rapid blur of faces; old women and a couple old men, a stunned pair of parents who had called my father, the town doctor, because they could face the idea of their beloved having died, but not the permanence of death. My father often had me along because a child's face, he believed, offered comfort even if I didn't speak much English then. "He was—"

"Then ask your dad to come."

"I can't. He's dead, as is my husband." I plucked at the sleeve of my dress to show it was mourning attire and not an affliction. This gesture left smears of black dye on the fingers of my not-quite-black gloves. "I'm—"

"Some man to come with you in case you feel the vapors." He meant someone with a knife, who could slice me out of my corset in case I needed more air or room to vomit. Even with the new health corsets pushing the front forward and behind back rather than cutting into the midsection, women sometimes had moments of trouble.

I turned my glare on him. "Look kid." Oh dear. That prettiness thing wasn't working for me and I was losing out on charm as well. "Don't worry about me."

"I'm not worried about you." He slapped a piece of paper from the blotter into a basket on the corner of the desk. "I don't cotton to you making a fuss like this when you know I'm not going to let you in, not alone."

As a female attorney, I negotiated contracts and reviewed legal briefs for larger firms rather than trying cases or joining that Bar Association like the men. Still, I had a legal status. "As an officer of the court, I cannot ignore a summons by the police."

"Then come back with a man."

I inched away from the desk. My mind sorted through the few men I knew and did not hit on anyone I would like to ask to join me for a stroll down to the morgue. There was one man, but since I had never dared speak to him beyond a "hello" how could I ask him for this favor?

I pulled the veil back down over my face, raised my skirt over the gutter and crossed the street to head back toward my office on the Strand.

As I walked through the muddy, sandy street, I reviewed the list of men I knew for a prospective escort. None of the fellows at church would be charmed by a request to come see a dead body with me, and I wouldn't want any of them to know I was acquainted with someone who drowned and did it while naked. Because of my profession, I was probably seen as somewhat peculiar and this would make it a certainty. I could ambush the milkman tomorrow morning or bribe the hobo who sometimes sold newspapers out in front of the grocer's, but neither of those seemed like good ideas.

I neared the pier and saw stevedores unloading bundles of cable from a high-masted ship.

More unloading. People still sent rebuilding supplies and even charity items. Those castoffs were the source of my wardrobe. My skill with a needle enabled me to update the out-of-style items. From now on, I would have to do something other than dye them myself, but that something would have to come without taking money away from what I would spend on my girls.

I thought of the girls. My housekeeper would be dropping them off at school about now.

Maybe my housekeeper dress up in a man's suit. I found several of them old men's suits I had found in the upper closets of the house I got when my mother-in-law died. No, these were police. They were probably trained to notice that sort of thing, and we were a little too late to say it was a Mardi Gras costume.

I looked in the arched window of the bakery on the first floor of my building and smiled at Mrs. Hulpke behind the brass counter.

I stopped mid-wave. I realized my landlord was the only suitable male I knew, my landlord, my ramrod straight, stern-faced, fearsome landlord. Well, he counted as "man I knew of," since after I signed the lease, what I saw of him was a shadow behind the office with 'L. Barker, Consulting Detective" etched on the glass of the door. I hadn't even dared to speak to the formidable fellow when I sat across the desk from him and signed the rental agreement for my office.

I opened the cathedral-sized front door.

There he was, upstairs in the open and striding across the landing between our offices.

Behind him, Evangeline, my stenographer and typewriter, looked out from my office door.

He must have been in my office. What was he doing there?

Barker turned to me. His intense blue eyes bored into mine.

I looked away from him his face before he could turn me to stone or get me to confess to some unsolved crime and gave Evangeline an imploring glance. "Mrs. Dorfman?"

"She never came." Evangeline's black-brown eyes knitted creased with concern. "Never called."

Larisa Karparova Dorfman had never missed an appointment. That naked dead woman, could she have been my client? I had a premonition she was the body, an image in my mind of her pretty face bloated and decaying, that was why I dreaded seeing the body. I hadn't seen that of a friend or family member since September. The storm was not gone from the city even if the winds and waves had stopped. I had thought the misery was over, but still had to look death in the clouded eyes.

I took a deep breath to dispel this thought since waterlogged bodies were still being found, especially on a day like this after a storm jogged them loose from the depths of the sea. My rain-drenched veil slapped against my face and I tucked it into the crown of my wide hat.

"Mrs. Gallagher." The tall man in a three-piece sack suit marched down the stairs toward me. He stopped beside the bronze of Joan of Arc at the newel post. "Chuffed to see you're here, at last."

So that I wouldn't take a step back from having a man so close, I grabbed the railing. I imagined his pronouncement was positive, since he smiled to show straight teeth in a face I would describe as "strong" with a square jaw, prominent nose that was just short of too large, and clear blue eyes with the slight crinkle of crowsfeet at the edges. This sounded promising for me to ask him to leave his busy detective agency and come with me to the morgue. Still, it sounded strange--and not just because of that accent that rolled through phrases, but cut off the ends of words--coming from a man I had heard say nothing more than, "Good day," "Hello," or that one time he said, "Perhaps you ladies could wear some form of rubberized petticoat and not track in so much rain," since he rented to me an office across the landing from his. This was probably the best opportunity I would get. I ventured, "Mr. Barker, I fear I need your help."

Chapter 2

"Yes, Mrs. Gallagher, we can discuss that later." Barker slipped his arm beneath my elbow to guide me up the great staircase of carved wood. He was not so forward as to touch me, but urged me up the stairs with the insistence of his gaze and am energy that vibrated through him, as though electricity had returned to the city in the form of a tall man of athletic build and an accent from one of those places I always thought spoke English better than in America, but I would never admit that aloud. "Can you still speak Russian?"

My foot slid off the step. He caught my elbow, but released me almost as soon as his hands touched my sleeve. "How did you know?" No one ever knew unless I told them and I sure-as-shooting hadn't told my landlord that I was once a Russian orphan who got adopted at nine-years old.

"You have an accent, but that isn't important now. If you still speak the language, I would appreciate some help with a family—some prospective clients—in my office." His rapid gait took him three steps farther than I could go without jumping, so I lagged back.

He turned back and waved his hand in an encouragement. "They have shown a marked tendency to speak to each other in their own language rather than to me."

"I sound as Texas as anyone." I thought of his accents with sudden stops before the words ended and rolled 'r's. "More than anyone." Gees, I was a step behind on the stairs and in this conversation. I trotted to get beside him.

"To most ears, I'm sure." "I would appreciate your not telling the Karparovs you speak their language."

"Spying?" I felt a grin spread across my face. "You want me to . . . hey, Karparov. That was my client." My hands flapped toward my office where she should have been. "The one who missed her appointment—her maiden name. Can't be many of those around. Could she be in with your folks?"

"No one named 'Dorfman', I fear." He continued his progress toward the closed door of his office.

"How did you know her name was Dorfman?"

He scowled at me and then forced a smile that was even more insulting for the patronizing voice that came with it. "You said her name when you arrived."

He started to open the door, but I tugged at his plaid suit sleeve. I whispered, ""My client is at the mercy of criminals." I made an expansive gesture to demonstrate the whole of a criminal underworld gathered around one petite woman. "Hence, I fear for her. She missed an appointment this morning and that is unlike her."

The gesture released him to open the door to his office. Barker frowned at my dress.

I looked down. The drizzle had made the dress an even greater travesty of mourning with pale spots on the dress that I was sure made dark spots on my underclothes and skin.

Barker plunged inside and did not stop until he was beside a roll-top desk, placed in a corner to take advantage of the light from the windows at the back and side of the room. On the desk, papers resided in tidy folders within the cubbyholes. The only decoration to break up the surface of smooth, dark wood was a framed newspaper etching of a slender woman with wide eyes.

I stepped in and looked around the room. His office was big, bigger than mine, but that was no surprise since the successful detective did own the entire building. A rounded window with curved walnut trim would still show the ocean even after the rubble and empty lots had been turned back into shops and apartments. Inside this office, moss green wall paper depicted ferns, columns, and books. The wainscot was carved to look like acorns and oak leaves, two plush, green chairs sat on either side of a small settee. On the settee sat a young woman with pale hair and wide-set brown eyes and beside her sat a man with shoulder-length silver hair. In the chair beneath the side window sat a woman swathed in gray. Beyond her, a small desk that must have been for the office man who worked for Barker and a door ajar to what looked like a large closet or small laboratory. The framed photograph on the roll-top desk was the only personal item decorating the room.

The young woman looked at my dress with a start. She wore a lace bodice that ended in cuffs, gloves, and a fashionable hat. It was big and round, covered with fripperies, but she failed to manage a rakish angle with it and the hat sat atop her head like a manhole cover topped with confetti and debris left from a passing parade.

She was a very slender girl who probably only wore a ribbon corset beneath her clothes, which allowed her to slump something fierce. She clutched the arm of the old man beside her.

His silver hair flowed over his shoulders from a face led by a wandering nose. He had the look of someone artistic and in charge, such as a conductor, one of those conductors who specialize in avant garde music and shouting at the string section. He did not stand up when I entered the room.

"Is this your secretary, Barker?" His accent was similar to the ones I remembered from childhood and similar to the one my Russian professor had in college, but only in the way vodka is similar to water. His accent held a force and snarl much greater than anyone else I had ever heard.

I extended a hand and said, "Hello, I'm Mrs. Gallagher, an attorney maybe all y'all could find useful." I whipped my head back to Barker to see his reaction.

Barker stood tall, made even taller by the best posture I ever saw. His deep blue eyes were shaded by thick black lashes, so I could see no expression in them, but he had not told me to leave so I hoped I had no blown my chance to have him escort me to the morgue.   "Mrs. Gallagher, this is Mr. Karparov, Mrs. Karparova, Miss Karparova." He gave each a slight bow.

Impressive. He knows Russian names for women take a female ending.

They each acknowledged the roll call with a nod. Yes, they really were here, one of the wealthiest families in the country, perhaps the world. He had made his money in railroads and shipping across the Caspian. He may have gone beyond the work entrusted to him by the company and ruled his area as a king or evil despot, depending on who you asked.

I extended a visiting card.

The parents looked at me as though I'd offered them a case of leprosy. Only the girl reached forward and took the card.

I said, "I'm the attorney for Larisa Dorfman."

The woman in the veil pressed a gloved hand to her heart at the mention of her daughter's name. This woman's black dress with gray piping fit tight over an hourglass figure that had been thickened by the sands of time.

"Larisa?" the father questioned and said in Russian, "Dead." He might have meant "Dead to me," it was not a language of subtleties.

The young woman said in English, "Your client is estranged from my father." Her hand fluttered, but never caught flight, and landed back on her lap. The sleeve fell back to show a scratch—no, a series of scratches—on the back of her hand above her short glove.

She did that to herself. I closed my eyes to not slip an alarmed glance to Barker. I had seen women like that when I apprenticed in my husband's law firm. They were always in trouble and nervous, but those were poor women, not the daughter of privilege sitting before me.

She smoothed her sleeve back over her hand. "And she is estranged from me." She shifted the card from hand to hand until her mother snatched it away and dropped it in her steel-mesh purse. She said in Russian, "What do we do? We need the detective to help us, but we don't want her knowing our family business."

Barker gave a wave with one of his large hands toward me. "Please, make yourself comfortable." He scraped his chair across the wood floor, took a file from his drawer, and sat reading it without looking up at the visitors before him. He was a detective and a famous one. I'd bet he didn't have any idea what was in that file, but wanted to get a glimpse at these people without them knowing. I doubted a man would do that with people he trusted.

"Let her stay," said the father, a Russian bear in kid gloves speaking in his native language. "I would have let your sister come, why not her friend here?"

I looked at Barker. He tilted the chair back toward the window and reached over to the desk. Now that he had aligned his pencils from shortest to longest, he arranged them in the water glass serving as a pencil holder.

"We should not do this," said the veiled mother said in the Russian of a Muscovite. "We do not need to find it. The casket is cursed."

"Cursed?" The daughter gave a dry laugh. "I don't believe in magic."

"No one does," the father said. "Yet, everyone does. They need my magic"

English or Russian, this was weird.

He straightened his cuff that bore his monogram in Cyrillic letters. "Like those businessmen I met the other night, they did not believe in magic, but wanted its power. I need it back."

"Do you think Larisa would dare to take it?" the girl asked.

"Larisa," the mother said. "She is smart." She sneered this out in a way that indicated she thought the absent daughter was the only one with anything on the ball. This snide comment made me want to punch her in the veiled nose on behalf of all mothers and daughters. "She would not steal from her father."

Their conversation lapsed into silence and Barker looked up as if he noticed them for the first time.

"Any time you're ready." Barker pulled out his pocket watch and gave it a glance. "We have twenty minutes left in your consultation."

The mother looked out the side window near her chair. "I just don't know if we can trust these people here," she said in Russian.

Her husband gave a single mocking laugh and demanded, "What? Do you think the famous detective is some ruffian to steal from us?" At least, it was a word that I thought was ruffians. My Russian might not be as good as I had led Barker to believe.

"So, what did you want to see me about?" Barker asked. He circled in slow sure steps, like the kid who had just tripped the only other contender in a game of musical chairs.

"Something was stolen from my home," Karparov said in English. "Something very old, a . . . a box. With clasps on it. A casket."

"How old?" Barker sat at his desk, licked his pencil and poised it over the tablet of small, square papers.

"Old," Karparov said. "Centuries old, but none know how many." His gloved fingers, lumpy with rheumatism, flicked through the dust motes and memories. "Gold once covered the entire face of the thing, but now only slight flecks about the edges of the carved stone. It is . . ." He held his hands high and then wide to indicate something smaller than a cotton bale, but not by much. "I need you to find it. It was stolen from a room in my home probably a couple days ago, but I do not know exactly."

"I'll need to see where it was stored," Barker said to his note pad.

"At my home." Karparov waved dismissal. "I will have the servants let you in sometime."

Barker leaned forward with his knuckles on the desk. "I do not care if you have a trained monkey who can work the door. I need to see the scene of the crime and expect no one to disturb it between now and then." His accent made "Do not care" come out as "Dinna care."

Karparov looked at Barker as if he would growl.

I tucked a loose wave into my hairstyle and blinked big eyes him. "Were there any, oh, identifying characteristics about this casket?"

The Karparovs turned every penny of their attention to me.

I smiled. Sometimes, that worked for me. "Quite a lot of caskets out there in the world. Just wondering if there was some way Mr. Barker could tell this one from that one in the window of Al and Frank's Second Hand Store and Livery Stable—the second hand part, of course. " *Oh! I was babbling.*

Those velvet brown Karparov eyes remained open, unblinking, and on me, yet the Karparov mouths closed.

"Yes," Barker said. "Anything special you can tell me about this box?"

The Karparovs turned to him with such experience in unison head movements, that I suspect they frequented tennis matches.

Outside the office, I heard the voice of Evangeline, my typewriter and stenographer. I had no appointments other than Larisa this early and I doubt she knew anyone with a telephone. I turned my attention back to the Karparovs who now stared at Barker.

Karparov dropped his head to one side and shrugged in the gesture which reminded me of a felon I had once seen protesting he had nothing while hiding a weapon from a policeman. "It is something of no great monetary value—just an antique cask, we long ago lost the knowledge of how to open it—but it has great sentimental value to me."

In Russian, the young woman said, "You don't need the thing, do you, Papa? It seems more trouble than it is worth."

"Don't you dare say such things!" Karparov hissed in the way I always envisioned the witch, Baba Yaga used when uttering a spell.

The young woman shivered.

The mother's gloved hands grabbed the bottom of the veil and she threw it back over her hat. The face was Larisa's: slanting brown eyes, heavy lashes, and narrow nose, but it had lost its beauty beneath a puffy layer of years and worry. "The thing can mean great trouble to anyone who has it. Only my husband can control it."

"Stupid to tell," Karparov muttered in Russian.

The girl bit the end of her gloved index finger.

"What makes you say that?" Barker turned to the mother with a smile and a bland enough voice to sound as though someone came into his office and complaining of accursedness happened to him every other Tuesday.

A knock sounded so slight, I could not be sure it as at the door or simply my heartbeat. Evangeline's dark auburn head poked through the open door followed by her apple cheeks of dark olive skin and ready dimples. "Pardon me, but I heard you in here, Mrs. Gallagher. You need to come. Please." She shot a glance of black-brown eyes at Barker. "I'm danged sorry about this, Mr. Barker, but I'm sure you understand."

Chapter 3

I sidled past Barker. He nodded at me. At the door, I bobbed with a "Nice to meet you," to the Karparovs and closed the door behind me.

Evangeline turned away without meeting my eyes.

I looked out the oval window surrounded by sinews of wood carved into vines and trees. The stevedores had returned to their work of hauling huge coils of wire off a steam ship. I wondered if that dock had been where they found the woman. I looked down to the green marble stairs and saw water on the steps.

"Mr. Barker is dashing," Evangeline said. I knew this behavior; she filled the air with talk until she worked up to a point she was reluctant to make. "I heard he rode with Teddy Roosevelt and the Rough Riders." She walked into our office.

My office had trim of whitewashed wood and walls painted the color of an old rose. The walls sported small oil paintings of pretty flowers and dubious skill, photographs of Clara Barton, Abraham Lincoln, President McKinley, and my new daughters—they felt like my daughters even though the court had yet to appoint someone to sign off on the paperwork—in their school uniforms and church clothes. Evangeline's desk with typewriter was toward the door, while mine angled beneath the back window.

Evangeline stood with her hands folded. She frowned at my dress. She said, "The city is full of death.

Seeing so many women in black just gets dreary. Maybe wearing a little color would help the—"

"You called me in here," I said.

"You got a call on that telephone," she whispered. She must have just gotten in when the call came since she only now put on the apron she wore to protect her clothes from ink and pieces of typewriter ribbon. "It was your ring—two short, one long, so I answered it."

"The courthouse?" My heart raced. Some clerk would have called this early before court started. Maybe they made sure the girls were indeed orphans and finalized my adoption.

Although she nodded, a frown clouded Evangeline's face. "They want you to come." She handed me a page torn from her notebook with the name of a clerk and room number.

I smiled. Someone had been assigned. I would get my daughters all legal-like. They would always know we were a family and belonged to me. I dashed from the door. But if that were true, why did Evangeline look as though she would cry?

I raced away from Evangeline and to the stairs. On the first step on the stairs, my laced boot hit a puddle. I skid like an uncoordinated ice skater. I screamed and flailed in a frantic attempt to regain balance. A man stood below me. His hand caught my arm. I slid further and felt my hand scrape against the skin, but his tight grasp kept me from plunging down the stairs.

Still with his hand on my arm, I turned uphill to him and said, "Thank you."

I recognized the man who gripped my arm so tight. The hooded eyes, the long nose, and tidy brown goatee belonged to Larisa's husband, Viktor Dorfman. I had never met him, but I had seen him in the society column a friend of mine wrote for the newspaper.

"I can't believe I did that." I walked up to his step.

He blinked at me a couple of times. They were deep set dark eyes, and his narrow cheeks were pale beneath a deep flush. He gave a timid smile with his eyes meeting mine. The smile was shy, but nice enough to make me hope the rumors that he and Larisa were estranged were not true.

"Marble can be slippery." He released my arm and placed it at my side with a gentle pat.

"Oh, dear." I caught his hand back.

On his wrist, a gash that was not deep, but looked painful and now filled with beads of blood.

"I did that, didn't I? I'm so sorry; I didn't mean to scratch you."

"No," he said. "It just opened back up. I had been gardening the other day."

"Oh, well I'm still sorry. I've never injured a man and—"

Barker's door swung open. He stood in the doorway and said, "Heard screams, but you look all right, Mrs. Gallagher. Glad you could make it. Mr. Dorfman, I presume?"

"Yes," Dorfman said. He gave me a quick nod and finished the last stairs to Barker's office.

Miss Karparova poked her head out the door and whined in Russian, "Viktor, you are very late, Papa is furious."

"I was in Houston." He said in English. "For a bridge that is fixed, the train stops often for washouts. Larisa, is she here?"

Miss Karparova shook her head and led her brother-in-law into the office.

Barker stared at me.

I walked away, but clung to the banister to keep my balance over further slicks and forced myself not to turn back to see if Barker still stared. I hoped her understood that I needed to go. I needed to get the adoption finalized.

Chapter 4

No loveliness remains in a dead body. No matter what romantic tales may say of fallen princes or maidens slain in the blossom of youth, still with beauty's glow on their face even after rigor mortis sets in, death is ugly and dead is the worst anyone will ever look. The skin goes pale yet blotchy and the muscles go slack, so all strength of jaw or softness of cheek is obliterated. One who met her death in water is bloated.

I turned to Barker at my side and smiled at him. "Thank you for doing this for me."

"You're welcome." He looked at the table before him and not at me or anything else in the disused warehouse turned morgue.

I also looked away from him and down at the green dress I had brought up to style of narrow sleeves and gathers above the waist after thumbing through Harper's Bazaar. "I had to ask you because of the police, but don't worry. I had no intention of getting sick in this dress." I straightened the crepe ribbon around my arm. Why shouldn't I show my mourning as a man does? This was more efficient than ruining clothes in vats of black dye. My eye went down my dress to the instruments in a pan. They were cleaned and waiting to be used, but the order was all wrong for a living patient. The sponges were the closest, the scalpels the farthest away, and the retractors between.

"You did offer me some help yesterday," Barker said. "And I expect you to give me the information when you are . . . collected."

"That makes me sound like an overdue bill." I
forced a laugh. I was certainly of sound-enough mind that I
could have told him what the Karparovs had said, but then
he wouldn't need me anymore and I suspected I wanted
him to need me for a little longer. "I'm sorry I had to leave
so suddenly." Also sorry at what the courthouse had held
in store for me. I raced up to the clerk's office, expecting a
stack of signed papers and a reason to celebrate. Things
used to run like that in America's wealthiest seaside before
the storm played havoc with the city's filing systems.
Instead, I got bureaucracy and a delay.

The clerk told me a judge had been assigned to the
case, but just assigned and wanted to review the case. That
was why Evangeline had been so grim. She knew how
important getting the girls recognized legally was to me.
She knew this setback would sting.

I forced my mind back to the present and to the
body that the doctor would be wheeling out.

I reminded myself that my daughters were fine at
school, they had not been the victims. I did not have to be
so upset. But still, someone's daughter had died and that
made me feel all empty inside for the mother who might be
gardening or crocheting because she did not know.

"I expect that what we see won't throw you a
wobble." He punctuated the remark with a determined nod.
His eyes slid over me, marking the edge of the space I
consumed, as if expecting me to be in constant danger of
jittering off the edge of the earth and into some land of pink
cakes and silly songs. "Since you helped your father who
was a doctor."

That announcement did make me wobble. "How
could you know that?" I asked.

"I deduced it," Barker said. He seemed to swell until his muscles threatened the seams of his tan plaid suit. "You looked at those instruments, ken how they should be laid out, and your hand raised in to rearrange them, but you did not, you mentally deferred to the doctor, even though we have not met him. That means you worked with a doctor in your past who made a fearful great impression on you. Since you are not in a medical field, I determined you did not work for the doctor officially. You are in an educated profession, indicating that your parents valued that. Your father was a doctor." He looked at his watch. We had waited five minutes and I saw no one approaching us with a body to identify. I prayed Barker would not leave me here alone to be escorted out.

"Deductive reasoning," he said.

"Inductive reasoning," I said.

"Excuse me?"

Oh, I had his interest now. He would not bolt. "What the ancient Greeks called 'inductive reasoning' to use clues available to infer what they cannot see. In this instance, my father, who went to his rewards years ago. Therefore, inductive reasoning."

Still no doctor. No police around us either.

"So, what else have you got?" I asked. "What else do you know about me?"

"Your missing client was being blackmailed. Aye, I see from your face that's true enough. Her background and your state of unease."

I could have managed a look of outrage that was prettier than the open mouth with curled lip that I fixed on Barker.

He did not notice. "She hasn't told you what she wanted you to do about the blackmail, so your energetic temperament leads you to do anything you can, even talk to her parents."

I nodded.

"I deduced—"

"Induced," I supplied. I needed to stop doing that.

He said, "I knew that as a woman you would treat your clients in a way that could be considered nurturing. Also, that you would be prone to irrationality and assume one missed appointment meant she was lying in a ditch, unable to call to you."

"You don't like me much," I said. "Do you?"

"I don't dislike you," he said. "I'm not a man who seeks the company of women or knows much about your sex."

"You barely know me, so I wouldn't expect you to, well, get too upset if I took the next train to Anna Karininaville." *Why couldn't I stop talking?* "Not that I would, but—anyway—my point is that I can't help thinking you've made some sort of judgment about me."

A man in a white coat wheeled out a battered gurney with the remnants of white paint. On the gurney lay something that looked like a log under a blanket. He put blanket and burden on a silver table that had all the shine scratched away.

I fanned the air with my hand to dispel some of the morgue air, stale and scented sickly sweet with preserving chemicals, but this action only evoked more of the rot that still clung to the city.

Barker put his arm around me without touching my back. He held my elbow between index finger and thumb and led me forward to the table.

"Hello," the man said. He looked at me, gave a frown and said his name to Barker. I did not hear what it was. "Doctor Something." He flipped the blanket back to reveal the body.

Her eyes were clouded and now sagged rather than slanted beneath the thick lash clotted with gulf mud. Black hair swirled and tangled over the blanket and clung in sandy masses to the naked skin of her shoulders, where white, water-wrinkled skin gave way to darker skin on her lower arms. That must show the angle her body rested at when the blood settled, slightly forward. The tresses were strewn with pieces of broken hair comb.

I took another look at her face to make sure I recognized her and was not just obsessed with the woman.

A face I knew was once beautiful. White skin now faded to an almost green in a rubber mass, slack over muscles. I recognized those slanting, brown eyes. I knew the hair and the eyebrows of the deepest black. I knew the slight size that had once been so full of energy.

Larisa. My client who missed an appointment would never make another.

I looked Dr. Something in the glasses.

He folded back the rest of the army blanket.

Her round breasts slid free from the soaking corset of yellow, Chinese silk. That and the slight cotton undergarment, also wet, were all she wore. Her small body was clad only in that and the little chemise beneath, which bore rips from what must have been the tide and the rocks since the lacerations on the flesh of her legs bore no redness, but fleshy, white chaff. They must have occurred after death when the body floated.

I winced. "Of course you found it in her corset." I looked at Barker and Doctor Something. "My visiting card. She couldn't exactly have had it crumpled in her hand, could she?"

Barker looked at the hands on either side of Larisa. His hand made a quick stroke over her hair in a gesture I found tenderer than I would have expected in the short time I had known him.

"Because it would have been too difficult for her to have held on to the card after she died."

Barker gave me one of those cranky-librarian "Shush!" looks with his forehead puckered and nose narrowed.

"Do you know who she is?" Doctor Something asked.

"Larisa," I said. "Larisa Dorfman." I turned to Barker and steadied myself on his arm. I looked at my dead client and then at the doctor. She would never have chosen him what with the array of specialists her family must have hired during her lifetime for anything that ailed her. She looked so small. I remembered her throwing back that head of jet black hair and laughing at something I had said, often, I would start to explain that I had not meant it as a joke, but she would silence me by telling me how much fun I was. Now dead, she did not just look petite, but slight and frail.

"Dorfman?" Doctor Something asked with so little interest, the word spilled from only one corner of his pale bottom lip.

I nodded.

"What do you make the cause of death?" Barker frowned at the body and then at the doctor.

"Drow-ning," he said. His whole mouth moved this time, announcing each letter as if for the hard-of-hearing or imbecilic.

Oh, that two-syllable thing is going to cost you, Dr. Something. This man is perhaps the best detective on earth. He knows death. He knows drowning. That's why the insurance companies and shippers have paid him huge amounts to sort out the mess after the flood.

"Aye," Barker said. He smiled. His teeth were aligned with only a couple of crooked ones on the bottom. I could now place his accent. He was a Scotsman.

He looks like an encyclopedia salesman greeting the housewife through a front-door screen. That's probably just a bind. Lure the doctor in to make another goof and feel like a true idiot when he goes for the crushing blow of knowledge.

Barker said, "She shows the signs, doesn't she?"

Hah, he even sounds as though he's asking for approval.

"That and the body was pulled up out of the gulf not breathing."

"That would be an indicator." Barker said with a smile so engaging it might have been needed to sell a full deluxe set of the Encyclopedia Britannica with almanac and atlas or lose employment by the afternoon.

"Signs?" I asked Barker. "You could tell by looking at her that she drowned and wasn't just dumped later?"

Barker turned to me with a closed-lip smile.

"Haven't you seen a drowned body before?" The doctor asked. His glasses filled with heliotrope-patterned barbs from the ceiling lights. "You new in town? Don't remember the flood? Bodies didn't stop washing up until last year."

"You called me in here," I said to the doctor. Before he could mention that my business was done and show me the door, I added in the firm voice I had once learned from a dog trainer, "I want to know what you found out about my client, how you found it out, and why. I want to know what you as a professional did this morning, not what any of us who have seen bodies wash up over the last few years could have done."

"Her eyes are bloodshot to an extreme consistent with a suffocation death," the doctor said. He waved a hand toward Larisa and I noticed his sleeves needed to be cinched up in arm garters to make them at least an inch shorter. "We'll close them—the eyes—people think that looks more peaceful, more like the person is asleep."

You deal better with the dead, who don't talk back, don't you?

I smiled. "Thank you, so you know she died from a lack of air of some kind."

"A lack of air from the ocean—that's where she drowned, in seawater. Look at her face." He flicked his finger around near her short nose. "You can see it's all red from breathing in stuff no one can breathe."

"But 'tis not traumatized enough," Barker said. He took his blue tinted spectacles from his pocket and wrapped them around an ear, over the nose, and around the other ear. "Not like you usually see with silty water like this around here. Interesting"

"And you're Doctor . . .?"

"Mister, Mister Barker." Barker gave a little bow by dipping his ramrod straight frame forward for an instant. "Also consistent with freshwater."

"The state of her lungs was consistent with a saltwater death."

I opened my mouth with a question, but Barker waved me quiet.

Barker arched over the body and then stood straight. "Are you sure she drowned in the gulf?"

Behind the glasses, Dr. Something's eyes rolled toward heaven. "Yes, that's where we found her."

"What kind of water did you find in her stomach?" Barker asked.

The doctor let out a sigh timbered with petulance. "I'm sure her stomach would look the same."

"Show us," I said.

The doctor's eyebrows managed to arch halfway up his forehead in a shape as round as his glasses. Barker just pulled back his head and smirked. They acted as if I'd asked them to unbutton trousers and show me underwear.

"This woman is my client. As her attorney, I have a duty to her family to be able to answer any questions they might have or any suspicions I might have about her death." I smiled at the doctor. A sweet smile, it showed all my straight upper teeth and even some of the lower ones. I even allowed the slightest of head bobbles. "Now I'm sure you kept a sample. You are the only professional at this in the room and we need your help."

Barker let out a puff of air that sounded steam-driven.

Doctor Something frowned. "You think someone might have killed this woman? Who do you suspect?"

Golly. There's the father who wished her dead, the mother whose perfect little world went all catawampus because of this kid, the estranged husband who would probably like to have her money around without the chance of it going to a next husband, and given enough time, I could probably come up with a case against the sister. A regular rogues gallery from the rotogravure, but an attorney should not give out groundless suspicions.

I said, "Mr. Barker seems to think she looks as though she's gone through some sort of trauma indicating foul play."

I looked at him and mouthed to his single raised eyebrow, "Inductive reasoning."

He did not look at me, but his face looked redder than this cold room would demand. He had questioned the cause of death. He suspected something.

Doctor Something's glasses attempted to focus light from the ceiling through his bifocals to burn a hole in Barker.

Barker pocketed his blue specs and took out a fountain pen that he used to move the arm. "That bruise on the forearm and palm and up to the neck." Barker used the pen to indicate the arm and curled, stiff hand. The marks were barely visible on the white flesh transitioning to purple where blood had settled within the corpse. "Classic defensive marks."

"Or from clawing at something out in the water," the doctor said.

"She also has what looks to be someone's skin under her nails." Barker pointed his pen toward the short nails.

"Or her own skin—they do flail in the water," Doctor Something said.

I thought of Larisa panicking in her last few moments of life, turbid water filling her lungs and choking off all air, all life, all thought. "Oh my."

They both looked at me.

I swallowed and stood up as straight as I could. I took another deep breath, winced a bit, and looked at Larisa's head. "Her hair comb is all broken. What in the water did that? Did it . . . did it break her head?"

"No," the doctor said. "Her skull is intact. She probably jumped in at an angle that went slightly backwards and the pressure of the drop did that." He turned to Barker to say this. "Usually, when they jump off a bridge, the force is enough to press their lace underpinnings into their skin. It's printed on their flesh in little bruises over the chest. With her it didn't, so the angle accounts for that. Or she waded in shallow, slipped and banged her head on rocks, knocking herself out."

"Why do you think she jumped?" Barker said.

Doctor Something shrugged.

"Yes," I said. "But you're skilled at this and you know something. What is it?"

Doctor Something rubbed his face. He knocked the glasses askew and for a moment I saw brown eyes with pale lashes blink at me. He righted the glasses and said to Barker, "I didn't want to say this with the lady present."

"Oh that's quite all right," Barker said without any traceable snippiness. "She wants to know all."

Doctor Something said, "She had quite a lot of alcohol in her system. Some cocaine, too. An opiate of some kind."

"So she spent more time at the drugstore than she should have," I said. "And washed it down with a pint of bourbon. That doesn't seem to rule out murder to me. Just makes her vulnerable."

His lips pressed together as if to play a trumpet rather than speak something he loathed to say. "We found semen in her. More than that of just one man."

I glanced at the body below me. She was a corpse now, never to know earthly pleasure again. Now, sex was not the act of love between a man and a woman. It was just the clinical exchange of fluids and friction. Maybe that was all it ever was.

I thought of something. "How could you possibly know that?"

"I can't." The doctor sneered. "Only there's quite a lot of it. More than just one man is likely to produce in an evening and in both orifices."

"Oh," I said. Quick breath. "So she could have been—oh—abused."

"No. No signs of any struggle—"

"Except for that bruise Mr. Barker saw on—"

"No signs of struggle down there. No forced entry."

"Oh," I said. Quick jagged breath. "That doesn't mean she wasn't. She might have willed herself to relax, pretend she wasn't even there."

The doctor shot a look at Barker who shook his head. "I've never heard of it happening." The doctor frowned and looked past Larisa to me. He reached over the body, took my arm in his. I sure hope he hadn't touched that body. He said, "I don't know anything yet, Ma'am and I'll continue to study this, but my suspicion is this woman was leading a destructive lifestyle, knew that, and looked to death as a relief." He released my hand by pulling straight back with his own.

"Thank you." My hand curved in the air over the body. "Truly, thank you. Now, can you show us the sample of fluid from her stomach or draw another?"

Chapter 5

"That was awful," I said to the sky, the boardwalk, and the mule pulling the streetcar. I snapped my parasol open and shoved it toward the sun and walked at a fast pace. I should have taken my bicycle. Images of the bloated and lifeless woman broke through my thoughts like lightning bolts. Larisa's form was joined by others I had seen deteriorating in the water or dead on the planks that had been their homes. I feared I would lose my mind if I did not think of something else, but I needed to know what Barker thought.

Barker strode along the boardwalk beside me. With long strides, straight posture, and arms swinging with loose joints, he had a walk that put me in mind of a cop on his way to have a talk with some miscreants. "I expect the whole thing will get sorted out soon enough. Reporters will be keen to know what killed an heiress and all."

I gasped. I planted my parasol and leaned against it. "Oh no. Oh no. They'll know about my card. My clients. I have to have clients to make a living."

Barker laughed. He strolled past me. "Yes, Mrs. Gallagher, but P. T. Barnum would have told you how fortunate any type of publicity is."

"You don't understand," I said. I darted past before he could see my eyes welling with stinging tears. "P.T. Barnum wasn't a lady." I took a deep breath and said, "I have to be respectable for my clients. Most of them are from groups like the Nonsmoking Society, the Women's Health and Preservation Association, or the Temperance League."

He huffed at that and looked at the saloon on the corner where a bar had been set up in a wall-less vacant lot.

"I'm not a full member. Some of us believe in moderation. Anyway, the suffragists will have nothing to do with me when a scandal like this erupts. They can't afford it and I wouldn't blame them."

Barker walked. His hands in his pockets and his eyes to the sky did not show if he even heard me.

To his back, I said, "The court is going to let me adopt my girls even though my husband is dead because I have a good enough income to provide for them." I held my breath to keep from hyperventilating. "If this isn't solved, it will ruin my business and I'll lose them."

"You see many calamities coming together before they have happened."

"Perhaps you're right," I said. "I have time. They are not likely to find out about any of this until after the funeral. That won't be for a few days."

He turned the corner to a street of brick office and stores. Our office was at the end. "The doctor wanted to protect you," Barker said. He squinted against the sun. He offered a hand to help me from steep curb to street.

I grasped the hand, descended to the boards over the gulley of water drained from another pocket of flood ravaged city, and felt the hand withdraw. "The last thing I need to be protected from is a small vial of reddish liquid."

"People who die in salt water do stew in their own juices as it were." Barker lit noiselessly on the boards beside me. He hooked his hands in his vest pockets and did not look at me as he spoke. He was comfortable in his own thoughts and world, and his Scottish accent got even stronger. "She should have been *malchit*—a mess—but she was clean. The nasal passages should nay have looked like that for someone drowned in the sort of gumbo pot of an ocean this gulf is. The foam in the mouth showed she drowned."

Dang, I hadn't noticed any foam. Yes, there was. I would have to be more observant.

"But the doctor is right that could be explained by storm surge and all the rain on the night she died."

"You know she didn't drown." I gripped my parasol handle with enough force to strike any fool notion from his mind. "Not in the gulf."

"Aye, but she was drowned. She was forced down into water and held under 'til her lungs filled with water." Down sounded like "doon" when he said it, but I soon figured it out.

"Yes, the poor thing." My mind clouded with emotion over yet another person I knew drowning. "But the police will realize that, won't they?"

"The police have restored order to the town, but just. The army 'tis gone and the saloons are back. They have enough to do, have had enough death. Many of the experienced men who would know what to look for are dead themselves. They don't want to deal with another drowning, not of someone whose family doesn't even care about her." Barker stopped walking before the grocer's where tomatoes, pecans, and raspberries filled bins under the painted-steel awning. He reached into his vest pocket and pulled out a small brown shard of filigree.

"When you stroked her hair!" I said. "I should have known you weren't sentimental."

He reached into his pocket again and pulled out a safety match. "If it just blackens, it is tortoise shell." He struck the match on his shoe. "If it burns, it is celluloid." He handed the match to me and held the shard above it.

The shard blackened, but did not burn.

"What does that mean?" I asked. I blew out the match and tossed it in a sidewalk ashtray. The image of the dead woman kept filling my head and my heart. I wanted something other than the suffering of a drowning victim in my mind. I asked to bring another topic.

Barker started off in that cadet's parade stride of his. "Celluloid is much weaker and brittle. If a ship or rock had hit her in the water, it would have broken, tortoise shell would not. She fought while she had life, but the hands that held her down did it with such force, her hair comb crumbled before her body died."

I nodded and took a deep breath to dispel the images that still came at the edges of my mind. "We must find who killed her."

"I regret to inform you, Mrs. Gallagher—"

"Dash."

"Pardon?"

"Dash, please call me Dash. Everyone does. It's short for Dasha, which is a nickname for Daria."

"Mrs. Gallagher, this is your case and not mine."

"But that thingamajig you're hunting may be what got her killed."

"Precisely." He walked fast ahead of me. "My client's case may jolly well be involved. I cannot share information with you. I have a duty to them now that they have hired me." He flicked fingers in what looked like an attempt to shoo me away from him. "You must do this on your own."

I did not look at Mrs. Hulpke in the bakery. To look often garnered a free cookie or a hello just as sweet, but I could not bear to let Barker go yet. He was my only hope. I followed him through the front door. On the stairs, I caught his sleeve. "Please Mr. Barker, I'm an attorney, not an investigator, I don't know how this is done."

Barker stopped along the walnut banister. He turned and stomped down the three steps to stand just above me. "Mrs. Gallagher, if you have the interest in your late friend that you claim, you would follow the trail whether you're a lawyer, laundress, or lady of leisure."

"Didn't you let me find out about this case when you wanted me to listen to their Russian?"

"Mrs. Gallagher, you cannot say that was behind their back. Asking me to consult on this would be."

I followed him into his office where he sat at the roll-top desk beside the window. I wondered about something. I considered asking, but instead I asked another question with an assumption in it. "Because Larisa is a she? That's why you won't help me, isn't it? Because you don't want to get involved with women?" I sat on the stool beside the desk.

"Technically, Larisa is neither he nor she now, but a corpse, and you had best start thinking of her in the past tense."

"So, why don't you like women?"

With two fingers on the edge of the picture frame, he turned the portrait of the wide-eyed woman toward me.

"I saw her once, before she'd killed her last victim. I should have known it was she, but I hesitated. I let myself think 'no, someone like that couldn't be a ruthless killer.' I realize behind the mask of fripperies and curls can lay a diabolical mind—or no mind at all. Either way, your gender distracts from those things I find most important."

"You saw a woman through the window of a passing train or standing in line at the general store." I touched the frame. "A glance she probably did not remember past the next inhale of coal-sodden Scottish air, but you've turned it into the pivotal moment of a lifetime." I grinned. "Why Mr. Barker, you are a frightful romantic."

"Did you hear what I—"

"Yes, and I found it full of romantic notions of feelings so great, they can dissuade you from any logical thought." I slapped the picture face down on the desk with a "smack." "Although I think having her looking at her clients is a little perverse."

He eyeballed me.

"I think you'll find most relationships are not about feeling at all—not the emotional kind, but simple chemical reactions, that's all."

"Chemical reactions?" He frowned with interest.

"Those health-giving juices physical stimulation causes to course through our bodies." My hand flapped in a gesture that did not look as scientific as I would have liked. "Doctors now understand the need for this."

"Undoubtedly," Barker said. "Yet I've no idea what you mean."

I barely did. I just wanted to think of something other than the tangled mass that now was Larisa's nonlife and how it now affected mine. Well, I would have time before the papers found out about her. Even then, they might not make a fuss. I was sure I'd have plenty of time.

Chapter 6

I heard the creak of the front porch and clack of women's shoes out there.

I sat up on the chaise longue and raised the brocade curtain enough to allow only a sliver of light to stab through the room that had gotten dark while I read. Beneath the wooden spindles and corbels, I saw a familiar shape in a feathered hat and yellow suit. She had a narrow frame that looked even skinnier because of her tight checked suit. Her flaming red hair, piled into a topknot was more sparkling than I recalled. In college she had been Mary Jane Smith. I suppose if you grew up a Smith, being a Quackenbush held a luster. Now to the Daily Mail, she was MJ Quackenbush, reporter.

I dropped the curtain, fell back on the velveteen arm of the chaise, and noted the page of I was on in "The Prisoner of Zenda."

"I hear you in there," she shouted from the porch. "I don't care if you're not at home to anyone today. I need to talk to you."

I heard a noise and craned to see through the arched doorway to the entryway to where my two girls in white lace dresses scurried up the stairs and away from the door.

The housekeeper who we had elevated to family and called, "Aunt Cornelia," stood in the foyer, scratching her uncorsetted midsection until I gave as big a wave as I could muster without jostling my throbbing head . She opened the front door, but did not step aside for MJ to enter.

The Quackenbush in MJ's name was a late husband. She was also a widow, but since he was sixty and she was twenty when they married, she was nearly the only one able to walk down the aisle. The rest of us in the dormitory had expected him to have money and I figured MJ thought so, too. When he died, she was left with a few moth-ridden suits, a bohemian crystal chandelier, and tin box full of unpaid tabs at some of the finest bars from Beaumont to Dallas.

I gave a shove to the cat, Dewey, who had worked his way into the big top of my daughters' toy circus and started the process of curling up on the tin lions and elephants. He balanced as best he could on three legs, righted himself from my push, and sat in the center ring, where he could train a baleful glance at me. After the storm, the big, black and white cat had appeared on the porch and demanded food and stitches for the injury that had taken his front leg.

I stretched to my feet and leaned forward to see around the tassels that edged the archway to the parlor. Through the lace-curtain on the window in the door, I could see MJ bobbing. "Yes, I know her. Let her in."

Without a word and with a grunt, Aunt Cornelia jerked the door open, but stood between MJ and the entryway.

"Thanks for the vouchsafe, Dash." MJ gave me a slight bow before she turned toward Aunt Cornelia. "Now step aside Bertha May so I can come in." She walked into the wide and high entry way and looked up to where the girls played on the staircase landing. She gave them a salute with a theatrical click of her heels. Theodora laughed. Eugenia returned the salute that ruffled her short bangs. Her hair had been cut off when she suffered from

scarlet fever in the orphanage. "Good to see you girls
again." She turned to me with a smile that resonated in her
green eyes. "They're charmers."

"Thank you." I felt my cheeks flush with a beam of
joy. I loved being their mother. I remembered MJ was as
well. It just wasn't part of how I pictured her. "How is
your boy doing?" That was something else her husband
left MJ; a son born a few months into her young
widowhood.

She blew out a sigh and shook her head. "Went up
to visit him and my mother had him in ringlets." Since the
flood, the five-year old boy lived with her mother, and MJ
sent a check up every week for his support. "Now I ask
you. What kind of boy wears ringlets?" She shot a glance
at Eugenia's hair that was not long enough to wrap around
a curling iron, but pinched her lips closed.

The housekeeper looked at me and smacked her
hands together to indicate ability and probably desire to
grab the slender woman by her black and white skirt and
chuck her into the rose bushes. Dewey stalked past MJ
with furry shoulders low and the single back foot sliding.

"What do you want, Mary Jane?"

"MJ"

"MJ?"

"An aperitif for starters. Can you work on that,
Beulah? And a whole raft of things with you," MJ blew
the girls a kissed and then looked at me over her narrow
shoulder.

A pair of marble sculptures watching her work,
Aunt Cornelia opened the lower doors of the sideboard
with a yank on the fat maroon tassels and pulled out a
bottle of jasmine and fruit cordial I had made at the end of

last season.   She slapped it into MJ's hand, set a pair of
etched blue crystal glasses on the walnut side table, and
pointed MJ toward the couch with the high carved back and
satin insets the bore the ravages of the storm.

"Thank you." MJ said to her. She sat on the couch
and turned to me. She tipped her head back and to the side.
This was a posture she had assumed for years to make the
bump on the bridge of that freckled nose less noticeable.

"Come on," the housekeeper bade to the girls to
coax them upstairs. "You have more room in your own
rooms." The girls raced each other to their rooms.

I took a sip. Good, full of flowers and fruit. Cheap
gin always made the finest base.

MJ took a sip and made a noisy grimace. "Way too
sweet. Have you got anything to mix in a cocktail, Dasha?"
MJ hung out with men even more than I did.

I waved past the arch to the dining room.   "I think
there's a bottle of tonic water in the kitchen."

MJ walked behind the house to the kitchen and
returned after a few minutes when she dropped a slice of
lime in my glass and filled it with the promised tonic water.

I gave her a sideways glance. "Why are you here?"

"That's sweet, Dasha!"

"Dash, it's what I go by now."

"Dash?"

I took a sip. Yes, even better.

"Sorry." I waved her toward a pair of wingback
chairs. "I've had a presupposing sort of day."

She stood beside the chair. Maybe she had a
petticoat too tight to let her bend. "Yeah, so I've heard."

I stiffened to the point where I needed no stays. Dewey jumped back onto the side table with the big top and knocked over the tin ringmaster.

MJ looked up past paintings of long-dead in-laws and pastoral scenes in stream and river to stare at the light fixture on the high ceiling where electric bulbs lay in hopes that someday this part of town would also get the power back on. "Larisa Dorfman was her name, wasn't it?"

I felt the weight of my pompadour as my head nodded. How did she know so fast? I expected I would have a few days before this got to the press. I reached out and stroked the cat.

MJ glared at the creature.

With claws out, Dewey slapped my hand, leapt from the circus, and ran up to MJ. She glared at the cat and drew her mouth open in a hiss. He ran from the parlor in his loping, tripod gait, but without giving MJ's skirt a swipe in passing.

I picked up the little metal bareback rider and trapeze artists from the floor and arranged them rather than look at MJ. "How did you know?"

"Who doesn't know, Toots? Apparently you made one first-class fuss at the morgue. Everyone was talking about the lady attorney who strong-armed her way past the police so she could get all swoony at seeing her dead friend."

"That's not exactly how it happened."

"How did it happen?"

I leaned my throbbing head back with a sigh. I knew better than to talk to the press, especially a member of the press who was my friend. "You behave like this with your society types?"

"Are you kidding?" She strolled between the wingback chairs, but did not sit. "I can do the 'how's your mother? Brother? Dog?' and avoid getting to the point with the best of them."

"Please don't tell anyone about this."

"Honey." She pulled up the small tete a tete bench and perched on the side before the sofa. "It's the headline for tomorrow's paper and that's not me."

"Can't you stop it?" I stopped myself from taking a gulp of the drink and sipped again.

"I'm the society column, Sweetie. I couldn't stop a rush at the hors d'oeuvre tray." She drained her drink and mixed another in tidy alchemy at the side table. "Wanton woman commits suicide," will make headlines unless that Nicaraguan canal suddenly gets built this afternoon. So come, tell nice Auntie MJ everything you know about her."

I tried to say nothing, but after a few moments under Auntie MJ's glare I blurted, "She wasn't suicidal at all. Maybe if I prove that, people won't mind that my business card was found on her."

"Oh, that's who she was," MJ said with a smile and glass raised in victory. "She's that black-haired, birdlike thing you took to the St. Mary's Orphanage luncheon."

I sat very still. I did not blink. I doubt my heart even beat.

"Yes," MJ closed her eyes and snapped her fingers as though in a party game at a church social and she would win a ham for coming up with answer. "Not Dorfman, that's not her father. That Karpar-Kaparar-Karparov, that's him."

"Oh sugar!" I drained my drink and held the cold glass to my temple. "Be careful what you write. Wild speculation could lose me my clients." And that could lose my daughters since the judge had yet to sign the adoption decree. I looked out into the entryway and saw a pair of small feet jutting through the spindles of the staircase.

Teddie—Theodora—spent so much time protecting Jinxie—Eugenia—a condition I suspect started before they were orphaned. I could offer them a home where they felt secure and knew they would be loved and stay together.

I couldn't let Larisa's murder interfere with my daughter's life.

"Why did she have your business card on her?"

"I have no idea." I took another sip. "Maybe she figured I was the one who could find her murderer."

"Come again?"

"Oh, nothing I would repeat for the press," I leaned back and rocked a few inches back and forth. I set my drink on my copy of "The Black Cat" Magazine. *The only way to make this stop is to find the murderer.*

A knock braced the front door so hard, the crystal rattled in my entryway chandelier.

MJ stood as if she would go and answer the door, but I careened past to get away from MJ, her notebook, and pencil. Near the stairwell, I slid my hand over the green wall cloth and straightened the frame of an oil painting of the Acropolis and eighteenth century tourists.

I hopped over an errant roller skate on the Persian rug of short silk threads. "Eugenia!"

No answer.

"Jinxie, you left something downstairs!"

I heard footsteps above.

I knew the younger girl, Jinxie, had to have been the culprit. Her sister had tidy rows of all her objects within her closet. When I saw Teddie's door before it slammed closed one day, I caught a glimpse of what might have been a clipboard hanging on the door. I imagine it held an inventory down to each aggie in the kid's marble collection. Jinxie tended toward my policy of spew and sprawl.

I opened the square peephole within the door and let out a small cry.

Deep blue eyes bored through the small opening. Barker said, "Perhaps you can come out on the veranda. I will only take a few seconds of your time."

"Mr. Barker, why don't you come inside before the neighbors see and start asking me questions?" I yanked open the door.

Barker shoved his hands in his pockets and ambled through the opening.

I pushed the door closed with both hands and pulled my skirt free from where the flood waters had turned the door into rough, splintered wood.

He stared at me with a frown that held no glint-eyed malice, but a thoughtful concern furrowing his eyebrows.

The silence slew me before him. "I'm impressed with your intuitive powers, Mr. Barker. You somehow used that skill to find where I live." I stepped toward him. I could smell something, something masculine. Yes, soap.

"You put your home address on the lease."

I turned my head away. I could still feel his eyes on the expanse of pale neck above my stiff lace collar and even his breath on the curls that always escaped the series of winding buns of my own hair and mail-order "rats" surrounding my head.

"Hiya, pal," MJ said. She leaned on the mantle and knocked a couple picture of the girls with me askew. She whirled her purse around in the comfortable pose I would imagine one of those procuresses I had heard of on Post Office Street when welcoming customers.

"Mrs. Quackenbush," I said with a quick tip of my head toward MJ.

Barker gave her a nod but concentrated his gaze on the photos just past MJ's arm. "You have children, Mrs. Gallagher."

This was an easy deduction since I could see Eugenia's large green eyes. She slipped down the stairs, grabbed the roller-skate, and darted upstairs before I could make introductions. Theodora stood on the stair landing, but caught sight of me and went to her room.

I glanced back at Barker.

He stood between the mantle and a marble bust on a carved stand. "You only got them after the flood, when your husband died, orphans just like you."

I stepped forward so fast, my skirt caught on one of the plugs that made a hasty repair in the wood floor. Barker caught my arm before I fell onto the pecan boards. I asked, "What do you know about me? And how?"

MJ snickered and strode back to the tete a tete. Perhaps she hoped Barker would join her on the other side of the little bench, but he stood between bust and mantle.

Barker added, "When you moved to this house, sometime after the storm."

"That, sure as shooting, that wasn't in the rental application." I dropped into one of the wingback chairs next to where Barker stood.

Gliding past me and across the room, he mouthed the phrase "sure as shooting," his mouth lingering on the 'g' sound, which most people would omit from the colloquialism. "Simple, really. You have a Russian accent—no matter how slight, it is there—yet your maiden name was 'Darlington'. Yes, this was also on the rental application." He slid his hand over a marble bust of some forgotten in-law who let down her hair to pose some time in the last century as Aphrodite.

"Your daughter looked to be the same age as she is in the picture and has new skates. Although she is the younger girl, her dress is clearly new, not handed down from her sister. Your daughters have new things because they are new to being your daughters."

"That just says I'm extravagant."

'Nay." He sat on the sofa at the end farthest from MJ on the bench, his arm rested level to deny the existence of high, uneven flourishes of artistic woodwork, as though his will could change this bit of Victorian frippery into a man's armchair. "A woman who has a goat trimming her lawn and no maid to answer the door is not but canny with her shillings."

"I just love the way you talk," MJ said. Her cherry lips grew around a smile and made me want to sneak a kiss of crepe paper to redden mine. "Explain some more."

Barker did not look at MJ as she spoke, but at my copy of the "Prisoner of Zenda." He mumbled something that sounded like, "no bookmark" and looked at me. "You honor a memory by mourning." He gestured with a thick finger at the mourning band I wore on the arm of my lace and satin housedress.

"Yeah," MJ said to me with a flick of her finger at my armband. "I like the new look."

"That must be your husband's memory since I do not see any but old pictures of you with him. Obviously, you were not here for the flood, but came after. Your pictures include you with your husband, those are all older shots and none are with husband and daughters. The ones of you with the girls use the modern dry-plate photography."

"Excellent inductive reasoning," I said.

MJ swooped to the sideboard and filled a glass with amber liquor I didn't even know had been in the cupboard, and pressed it into Barker's hand. "Scotch. I heard you owned a distillery over there, so don't expect this to measure up."

"And the house," I said. "How did you know I moved here after the flood?"

After a quick "thank you," Barker said to me, "Your door shows a water line far lower than that on your couch."

I glanced to the door. "I didn't even know that still showed."

Barker hitched his thumb into his vest pocket. "So, that makes me suspect you did not retain everything you once had. Also, you didn't know where the hole was in the floor, so you did not chop them yourself to keep the house from floating away in the storm. This was not your house then."

He took a drink and gave a frown that encompassed both big eyebrows. I imagined one of Lucretia Borgia's fellas might have given his glass that same look just after swilling down an arsenic cocktail.

"So why are you here, Mr. Barker?"

"Permit me to finish answering your last question."

I clapped a theatrical hand over my mouth.

"The original owner died, but that person's house remained intact and was willed to you."

"Yes," I said. "My mother-in-law, I guess she was afraid the house wouldn't hold. She went outside that night. The wind was so hard, it tore her clothes and her hair came loose. Before any of the neighbors could wade out to her, she became tangled in a tree and was sliced to death by the flying roof tiles."

MJ let out a sigh at such a familiar story. Barker just frowned at his drink.

I walked to the credenza in the dining room. "I have a housekeeper." I said. I hacked a slicer through the cherry pie sitting there and set the pieces on flowered plate. "She's upstairs, probably asleep by now." I did not know why I was arguing. He was right: I had adopted after the flood, I was a flood widow, and I was probably every bit a skinflint as this Scotsman.

MJ gave me a wave to decline her piece. Barker's fingers plucked the plate and fork from the tray I held. He said, "The fact that she is not serving pie, but you are indicates either that she is not the most expensive of domestic, or you are one of those souls benighted with what is termed a kind-heart. Either indicates I am right about you adopting after the flood."

MJ howled with laughter.

I sat on the couch, but as far from Barker as I could without keeling over the armrest. I was irritated that he figured out so much about me and angered that being called kindhearted made me embarrassed. "And what did you want from this ridiculously kind heart, Mr. Barker?"

Barker looked at MJ for the first time since he arrived.

My words bubbled with laughter when I asked, "What can you induce about her, Mr. Barker?"

MJ's right hand slid over her left and, through the glove, spun the large engagement ring that was once part of her wedding set and now the only jewelry she wore.

Barker's eyes smiled and those high cheeks got a little flush, perhaps from the whiskey. "Enough to say that our gentlewoman of the press would rather leave than have me talk about her."

MJ gave him a little nod and headed for the door.

As she passed, I offered a hug that she accepted. She was about as cuddly as a folding chair.

After I closed the door behind her, I saw Barker's muscular form perched on the jacquard sofa. "Oh, I left the translation of what the Karparov's said with my secretary. I'm sure she must have left it for you. She would never forget something like that. She's a peach."

"Yes," Barker said in the crisp syllables one uses when speaking to the hard of hearing deficient of brain, or chronically annoying. "She's competent."

I smoothed my skirts and sat beside him, but not close enough for even my skirts to touch him. "I'm sure I remembered everything."

Barker took another drink of whiskey and winced. "I certainly would not doubt a woman who remembers the page number of the book she's reading would have a good memory."

I shrugged with a rustle of taffeta. "My mother always told me a smart girl doesn't need a bookmark. I'm not sure she was right, but some habits stick."

Barker sat in silence for a moment. When I could stand it no longer, I asked: "What did the Karparovs say after I left? Perhaps you heard some more Russian you need translated." I gave a smile that even I knew bubbled with eagerness.

He set his glass on a crocheted coaster. "Nothing I can tell you now that they are my clients."

"But I need your help to figure out who murdered her," I said.

Blue eyes augured into me.

I whispered, "They said 'Magic.' They spoke of 'magic,' and sorcery, casting spells sort of things. Do you think the box actually has that kind of power?"

"Perhaps" He twisted the crystal glass around in his fingers.

"Oh, certainly a man of reason such as you cannot believe in something so far in the realm of Oogie-Boogie!"

"From what you said, you can deduce that Karparov believes it is magic. That is all it needs to be to have a power over them, or a power they can use over others who also believe. The human mind, Mrs. Gallagher, can create its own magic."

I took this in with a frown.

"Thank you for the, uh, drink, Mrs. Gallagher," he said. He stood. "The pie was excellent."

"Why did you come here?" I asked.

"Just to warn you that reporters might be lurking around your office tomorrow. Pay them no mind." He screwed up his face as if he'd swallowed something sour. "Too late to tell you not to speak to the press."

I looked down. I felt the pain behind my throat. I didn't know why, but I was upset and felt alone. "Yes, she died in salt water, but people can make salt water—a fountain, her bath tub, a swimming pool." I blinked and looked up at him. "Larisa, I mean."

"Yes, I knew."

"Anyway, the evening she died, she would have been up late and intoxicated. She would have had the, um, encounter with a gentleman."

Barker squinted at the staircase. "Sexual intercourse with multiple partners."

I nodded. "Whoever dumped her dead body in the sea—"

"Or had her dumped," Barker said.

"May have been a lover, someone upset that she had taken a lover, or someone who took advantage of her preoccupied state to kill her for other reasons."

"Or maybe the wee box worked its spell on her," Barker said with earnest eyes and a big smirk. When I looked at him in open-mouthed alarm, he winked at me.

I stood. "In law, you see, we aren't concerned with motive." I held a hand to my forehead. "But I don't think I can figure out who killed my friend without figuring that out."

"Most likely not," Barker said. "So you need to find out as much you can about the people who had what you lawyers like to call 'opportunity.' Then, find out any reason they might have had. You work on that, and you will find the killer. Just don't come to any conclusions before you do have all those facts." He strode to the door. "So, have you determined where you plan to start?"

"Well, I was thinking I would—"

"I do not need your answer to that." He left without saying another word.

Maybe I was fortunate he hadn't heard my idea. Sure as shooting, he'd find it pretty dang bad.

Chapter 7

Page 3 of the newspaper held only a brief announcement:

> Up From the Sea
>> Yesterday, the lifeless body of Mrs. Viktor Dorfman was pulled from the waters onto the docks near the train station yesterday. This is not another storm victim, but an apparent suicide from the night before.
>> Born Larisa Karparov, she had not been on speaking terms with her wealthy family and was living a separate life from her husband. Why she would choose to end her life is unclear, since she left no note and all she had on her at the time was the most scant of underclothing and the business card of one of Galveston's first lady attorneys, Mrs. D. Gallagher.

No byline was attached, but dollars to doughnuts, MJ had written this.

I slapped the newspaper aside and raced to the train station. Only two trains left for Houston each morning and I was determined to be on the first one.

"Were you invited?" Coralie asked. My sister's voice had more twang than mine. People often guessed I came from places all over the South, but her accent was pure East Texas.

She gave an extra hard tug to the corset strings.

"Even society folks don't exactly send out invitations to a funeral." Which was why I was willing to gatecrash a funeral. Yes, this was a bad idea.

I looked at my reflection in the oval mirror set near the four poster bed in the upstairs guest bedroom at my sister and brother-in-law's house. I didn't need my corset pulled this tight, weeks of bicycling and worry had made me thin, Coralie's work had made my breasts look extra large and my waist willow thin. "And I'm a friend of the deceased."

"I was fond of Queen Victoria," Cora said. "Didn't mean they let me into Buckingham Palace for her funeral."

"I can't imagine they'd throw me out of the church." Even if the announcement in the Galveston Daily News stated "not open to the public." I didn't think I counted as public.

"Church?"

"Yes, the Russian Orthodox one, downtown Houston." I buttoned my corset cover. "There isn't one in Galveston, so the funeral will be there. It's a lovely church. I've seen it."

"So, are you one of those Orthodox types?"

"Coralie! I'm as much a Baptist as you."

"Well, you seem to have changed a lot."

Yes, I had grown some, and I'd avoided on our mother who told me on the day of my wedding that I had always been a trial to her. I figured not seeing me was what she wanted.

I stepped into my black silk petticoat, the only one of mine that passed muster with my big sister. I held up the dress of jet beads, black ruffles, and wide sleeves some ten years out of fashion and sewn for my shorter sister. "The Baptists brought me to America and found me a family. Nobody else did."

She tugged the dress from my fingers. "I didn't mean . . . I mean . . . "

"I met the priest when I was working for a family setting up a donation." That priest had also told me where and when Larisa's funeral would be.

"Yes I'm sure." She tossed the mourning dress over my head with a rustle of moiré and a snap of beads.

"It's little dressy for daytime," I said.

"Dasha, you're not going to wear that horrible thing you dyed yourself."

Well, that was the last thing I had in black.

Coralie stood with hands on her hips. "I will not let my sister go to a society funeral looking like some Holstein cow." The collar of Coralie's loaned black dress was high, but the netting showed décolleté—more on my taller, thinner shape than on hers—before being caught in ribbons and beads. It would have to do for the afternoon funeral. I needed to get a good look at all these people and find out who cared about Larisa's death and who didn't.

Coralie went at the buttons with a hook and I wrapped a black scarf over my head.

No, they wouldn't throw me out of a funeral, would they? I had about forty-five minutes to catch a cab and go see.

The church was a basilica with a large rounded dome covered with mosaics. It was a Greek Orthodox structure because this was a Greek Orthodox Church. The smaller Russian Orthodox congregation used it for one service early on Sunday morning or weddings, christenings, and funerals.

"Thanks," I said to the cab driver and waved him away with a handful of coins.

I walked into the sanctuary. Tiles depicted the last supper and the crucifixion. Within the dome, the resurrected Christ stretched his arms above golden clouds with a magnificence that took my breath away. I tried to keep my pointed shoes from scratching across the marble floor, but my guess was Karparov laid out a fine layer of grit just so he knew who was sneaking up on him.

At the far end of the church, a painted and gilt iconostasis showed the local saints on the bottom layer, New Testament favorites in the middle, and at the top, an image of Christ. To the right stood an altar with the baptismal large enough to submerge a small child and the large, ornate cross. I loved the Russian Orthodox cross with its extra slanted bar at the base and what it meant: the freedom to choose.

I passed my hand over the dress netting and touched the gold cross I wore around my neck. It was something I still had from Russia that I always wore. A woman in the orphanage who thought I was pretty and wanted me to remember what she termed "my motherland" after I left.

I saw Karparov standing near the bier with a tremendous carved wood casket atop it. Great swaths of yellow, red and white flowers circled the casket and two baskets of yellow gladiolas and camellias and gardenias spiked with orchid sprays stood on either side of the dais.

Beside Karparov, stood his remaining daughter, Nina. Beyond her, the mother languished in fashionable gauze. Both women wore black lace veils on their heads, but no mourning veil covering their faces. Nina heard my steps and turned to look at me. This movement drew her mother's gaze as well.

Mrs. Karparova was fine-boned, but had filled that in with weight over the years. The skin now drooped and puffed. This would be reasonable for a mother of two adult daughters, but the yellowness of the skin, the faded eyes, and slackness looked as if she had been a beauty and had aged badly. She turned back around and there it was, a quiver so bad she had to lean on Nina.

This was her daughter's funeral. I knew if Teddie or Jinxie had died before me, I would be paralytic, not just aquiver. But she wasn't paralytic, unsteady was probably her normal state.

Mother and sister did not cry. They moved in what looked like an approximation of sadness, based more on sluggishness than any inner grief I had ever known. As the clutch of men in suits filed past Karparov and then his family, Nina and then her mother extended black-kid gloves to shake hands in civility, but not what looked like warmth for any of these men.

I had seen many funerals over the last few months. Some where women wept for the bodies of children just because no one else was there to weep for them. Those were events clogged with such emotion I know caught my breath and felt tears.

I fought the emotion. It did not belong in this place as bereft of feeling as a city council meeting. Besides, I was not here to mourn as much as I was to see if I could spot a murderer.

I smelled the mustiness of the large, open room and stepped closer until I was about three yards away from the family. In an alcove, I saw Viktor in a gray morning coat standing alone, a silky handkerchief with black trim held to his face. He stood so still and pale with one of the churches banners behind him, he looked like a suit of armor.

I nodded to him and received a small bow in return. I walked toward the family.

These were the people whose life had been the most disrupted by Larisa.

The cluster of men in suits approached Karparov and spoke to him.

"No chairs," Barker's voice whispered in my ear.

"No," I whispered and heard the sound of it etch along the stone walls. "You stand for a Russian Orthodox service. If they're doing a full mass that will be at least an hour and a half." I turned to look at him.

His thick thatch of dark hair freed, he held his black derby hat against the breast of his black suit. His boutonniere of a single small gardenia was the only thing that kept the suit from being all black.

I leaned toward him, but still looked forward. "Did you see Viktor Dorfman standing alone?"

I think I heard an "Mm-hmm?"

"Looks to me as though he isn't close to his in-laws. I know Larisa lived a single life. I wonder if she planned to divorce him and leave him cut off from their money."

"Something to investigate," Barker said. "But perhaps not at this moment."

I looked at the mother again and wondered if her addictions could have led her to murder. Yes, if Larisa had somehow gotten between her and her choice of poison or even threatened to expose her vice. Whatever that vice might be, I couldn't tell.

Barker bent down until his mouth was on the scarf pinned to my head. He whispered, "Alcohol abuse would have left her fatter and not with the rheumy eyes. Appears she's on the hop."

I pulled away to gape at him. "How did you know I . . ?"

"You were staring at the woman. When she stumbled, your head bobbed in concert with her actions, studying her movements. You are reviewing them as suspects."

The priest, robed in red satin with gold trim and a white garment beneath walked in with an incense burner. He chanted in Russian I could not understand.

Beside the iconostasis, a group of women in headscarves sang thrilling, sad notes.

I leaned toward Barker.

He craned his head down for me to reach his ear.

I said: "What I wonder is, would any of them actually kill her. I mean, she was their family. Could, say, Karparov kill his own child?"

"Like Ivan the Terrible did or Peter the Great? Karparov saw himself to be a Tsar back home."

The choir sound soared and dove.

I whispered to Barker: "Do you see the cross?"

He nodded.

"The extra bar at the bottom that slants? Do you know what that is for? It's for the two thieves who died at Calvary with Christ. The one side goes up, for the thief who chose to go to heaven. The other side goes down, for the thief who denies Christ to the end and goes to hell."

"So, 'tis about choices."

"You understand!"

Karparov looked at me.

The priest droned a chant.

The choir sang in a minor key.

The priest led a prayer. At the end, I joined in crossing myself left to right as I remembered from my early childhood in Russia, with my fingers clasped in a reminder of the trinity, or was it clasping a communion wafer? That was long ago, I could not remember. For an instant, I thought of my original Russian parents—always angry and sometimes cruel in my memory—and what little I could remember of them. Did they die or did they just leave me on the street to find my own way? Then, I remembered my American father telling me not to be afraid of those memories. I was safe now and I wasn't that person anymore, but they were part of me and memories make us who we are.

Karparov's watery eyes still bore into me.

I tipped my head in acknowledgement.

I asked in a whisper: "What have your keen powers of deductive reasoning told you about these people?" Barker gave me a sardonic squint. "The same you have seen. None of these people feel a strong sense of loss. At least it hasn't hit yet."

I heard scuffing behind us. I tried not to look.

They sounded like male feet, heavier than female.

Barker looked. He nodded to the owner.

Another priest began a eulogy in Russian. These were generic words of kindness of one who knew nothing of the deceased.

The man walked past. His hair was starting to silver and smoothed back. He had a long nose and hooded brown eyes. He wasn't handsome, but looked, well, as if he knew how to treat a woman badly in the right ways. Maybe I was just lonely after a few months of widowhood and a few years of my husband not touching me after he learned we would not be having children, but he produced a definite "Golly!" inside me. I whispered to Barker, "You know who he is?"

We prayed again. After I crossed myself, I looked for the man and saw he had joined the cluster of male business men who mourned near Karparov.

Barker said, "Arbuthnot. Parents were furriers. He's moved much of his investments in the oil discoveries in Beaumont now."

"Looks like he knows Karparov."

"Yes, they are both investors in oil. I think most of the men here are."

"He looks like someone who would have caught Larisa's eye," *Why did I say that?* Had I seen her look at men? No. "Hey," I whispered. "I've seen the young fellow next to him."

That fellow was young with a wealth of wavy hair, sad eyes, and clear skin.

I closed my eyes to join in the prayer. I saw a memory of a curtained, two-wheel carriage waiting for Larisa. I had not seen much of the man within. A well formed cheek and an arm filling out a suit in a robust fashion. I opened my eyes. Yes, that was the young man.

I glanced at Arbuthnot.

He turned to me with a charming smile and tipped his head in a bow. He gave me the once over a couple of times, with a fraction extra where my breasts threatened the thin black netting.

I gave Arbuthnot a little smile. I would probably want to find out more information from him, but I would be careful, since he wore a wedding ring.

The choir started up a harrowing chord.

The priest led a prayer.

Arbuthnot did not move more than a couple steps toward the great gothic arch of a door, but watched six large men with pale hair and wide-set eyes surround the casket.

I had not seen the pallbearers before. They must have been in another alcove.

Nina whispered something to the largest. He did not look at her in response, but at Karparov. Karparov nodded to him.

The men raised the casket to their shoulders.

The priest with the incense burner started to walk from the church, behind him, the last remains of Larisa was borne on the shoulders of men I would if she even knew.

Before the priest could get out of the building, Karparov stepped before him. The priest looked at this boldness in wide-eyed shock, but Karparov ignored him. He raised his hand toward the small congregation and said, "Gentlemen . . ." He looked at me and I realized I was the only woman here other than his wife and daughter. "And ladies."

"This is the end of my daughter," Karparov said. "She was a great spiritual being, in so many ways larger than her small body. We will miss her, but we will not mourn. Life will go on for us as before. She would have wished this and we will speak no more of her."

Mrs. Karparova's hand grasped out toward the passing casket. Nina grabbed her away and looked around as if she hoped no one would notice. When she spotted me, Nina shot a look toward me with her brows knit in confusion. She must not have remembered me from the day before. She looked up at Barker and a smile came to her wan face. She hustled her slumping mother out of the church.

Behind her, Karparov had the hands-in-his-pockets, squint-at-the-crown-molding look of a man discussing business. He walked out in the midst of the fifteen men in suits, sixteen when Arbuthnot was added.

He gave me a wink and smile as he exited.

"We all grieve in our own ways," Barker said and I saw with the edge of my vision a trace of a grin on his face.

Viktor walked out. He slid his watch from his vest pocket for a quick look and then resumed a stately pace.

Barker gestured for me to go first, but I walked at his side into the bright sun of midday. "Did you hear her father? Your client was absolutely indecent."

"They often are."

"Why would a man say something like that?"

"Many reasons, one of them being he thought that would honor her."

I spotted something horrifying. I took Barker's arm to pull his ear close to my mouth, "Newspaper men, and her."

MJ Quakenbush raced toward me like a bantam rooster spotting something across the yard. Her black hat had been skewered by a great, iridescent bird that looked as though it attempted even now in death to flap away. Her bright auburn hair glistened in the sun; her pale, freckled skin glowed beneath. Her black crepe suit with velvet insets fit her slender body tight. A pair of men in felt hats blocked her path, but she gave one a chummy pat that shoved him out of her path. They started to follow her, but she looked back at them and they stopped.

I pulled my feet together to bring myself to my full height. My eyes came even with her hat brim.

"Hello Dash," she said with a smile. We both leaned forward and kissed cheeks. She opted for the side away from Barker and whispered in my ear, "Good to remind people now and then how impressive your breasts are, Sweets." She pivoted her kid boots to face Barker. She took two fingers to the edge of that hat and made a little salute. "Hi there, delicious."

"Did you want something MJ?"

"Aside from the mouth-watering Mr. Barker?" She looked at me when she said that, but toward Barker, she was doing that thing where she tilted her head back so her nose looked straight and you couldn't see the bump on the ridge. Her green eyes stayed on me. "What is your first name, Mr. Barker?"

"Leucippus Barker." He disengaged his arm from my hand to tip his hat.

"So, everyone calls you 'Lew'?"

"No, Barker."

"So what brings you here? Detecting something fascinating? Do you think Larisa Dorfman was murdered? Perhaps by a jealous lover?"

A smile slapped across Barker's face between high cheek bones and that square jaw.

She smiled and waited for him to say something. Her mouth opened to ask him another question, but then flapped a little before closing for a swallow and then turning to me. "But getting back to you, what do you think of the fact that someone who lived the life Larisa Karparova Dorfman did gets to end up in a church as though she were a good Christian girl?"

"You're asking me to judge?"

"I'm asking you as a woman how you feel about someone who cavorted with men who were not her husband and died in a shameless state of undress getting a service in a church as though she were a decent lady?"

"Of course I think it's where she belonged," I said. "Beneath the symbol of the Russian cross with that second cross there to indicate how each of us has a choice of what to do with our lives. I would never take that from someone. Why do you have a notebook out?"

"Russian double cross," MJ muttered. She licked her stubby pencil and scribbled.

"Mary Jane, if you twist my words, I'll, well, I'll tell your mother."

She frowned at me. "You learned Russian in college, didn't you?" She looked at Barker and jerked her pencil at me.

I shrugged in answer. She continued, "Professor said she was a natural at it." She made this sound as if she were describing a goiter, rather than a talent. She looked out to where the casket was being loaded into the glass-sided hearse. "Did you hear what the live daughter said to that pallbearer? Oh what is his name? I've seen him before."

"I have no idea."

Slav . . . ?" she drawled. "Stan . . .? Stanislav? Yes, but they call him 'Slava.' He's one of the family bodyguards—and I do mean bodyguards in this for-instance since he did carry the body out. Those boys have been keeping us plain folks away from Karparov for a very long time now."

"They are big fellows," I said.

"I think you could take them," MJ said somewhere between Barker and me. Her neck was going to hurt soon, what with her head tipped back at that angle for so long. She said to me, "So you didn't like what Karparov said?"

"Excuse me?" I knew she had not been in the church. She would not have heard him.

"Karparov. You don't think he should honor the memory of his daughter by doing what she would have wanted?"

I don't know how she heard. Maybe those two other reporters hoisted her up behind the azaleas to listen in the window.

The horses with black plumed headdresses pulled the hearse away.

"If you ladies would like me to hail you a cab," Barker said. "I would be obliged."

"Yes," I said. I had to get back to my sister's house, get out of this predatory widow dress, and get on the last train of the day. I had a plan to gain information and that required me to be in Galveston tomorrow.

"Oh," MJ said. "I've found a nice gentleman to give me a ride to the graveside service."
"But the public isn't invited to that," I said.

Barker leaned into the street and waved one of those broad hands to flag a cab.

"I'm not the public. I'm the press."

"Which is why I'm keeping my opinions to myself," I said.

"But you're bothered by what he said." Her narrow, freckled hand gave my shoulder a pair of pats. "I can see it, but you're just going to let him get away with it. I guess because he's rich everyone lets him do what he wants."

"Oh shut your big bazoo!" I hissed. "I've seen plenty of families who faced the death of all sorts of people. None of them—not-one—suspended mourning. They needed it. You should have seen folks after the flood, sitting on porches or even debris piles and crying. They cared about the person who died and couldn't keep those feelings in."

Barker took my arm and steered me across the lawn, to the cab he'd stopped.

I watched MJ to see if she joined one of the businessmen or perhaps Arbuthnot. He would probably give a pretty girl like MJ a ride anywhere she wanted to go.

She walked to a junior priest who looked frightened, awed, and aware that he was part of a religion that did not require a vow of celibacy.

"You defended your dead friend ably." Barker gave an arm to help me into the cab. "But you may not have done yourself any good."

No, but I knew I would do more harm if I didn't find something out before MJ.

He put on his derby and walked away at a near run.

"Train station," I said to the cabbie. "And please make it before the four-thirty for Galveston leaves."

Chapter 8

Broadway Street on Galveston had been one of the most expensive neighborhoods in the country. Now, at least one place down this street held the homeless squatters still lingered in a twenty-five room mansion that would have to be moved out by police once the family returned from Europe. I grabbed my daughter closer as we passed a Negro having a cigarette on that lawn.

This was my plan; bring the girls out on a sympathy call to people who wanted nothing to do with me. Maybe I used them in a way a mother should not, but I spent much time thinking of this last night after I missed the train and spent the night at my sister's place. It didn't seem wrong.

Columns, with the acanthus leaves of ancient Corinth, stretched across the front of the Karparov mansion. Only a conservatory revealed that this was a modern structure and not the home of one of the better Caesars. The conservatory was on the right showed clear glass in almost every pane. Vast repairs must have been performed on the front of this house.

Past the azaleas and a lawn of even green stretched to the gothic revival of brown, rough stone that formed the Dorfman castle. I wondered if Larisa had planted the gardenias around the long windows of the turret. Either an excellent gardener or luck favored these bushes since the bread-plate-sized blossoms would have been big at the height of the season, but immense this early. Each flower pointed out toward the walkway, the sign of a loving gardener. They seemed to have become neglected recently both of the bushes below the windows bore the sting of early death in brown flowers down the inner side.

As unintended as this might be, the flowers were the only sign of mourning in this fine neighborhood of wide roads, rebuilding, and a man in a seersucker suit and straw hat lay in the road.

I secured my basket in the crook of my arm, grabbed a girl in each hand and ran toward the man.

I prayed he wasn't dead. I probably shouldn't have my girls with me to see a body. Well, that was a part of life after the storm.

The girls kept pace with me although Teddie probably got hit with the basket a few times and I know my new silk parasol flapped against Jinxie with each step.

"Mama, do you see that man?" Theodora asked.

"Yes dear." I slowed and gave a relieved sigh when we reached the sidewalk. "That's Mr. Barker, my landlord." I hadn't expected to see him here, and his presence here in the mud could interfere with what I planned to do today. I prayed he wouldn't stop me from what I intended with daughters, basket, and all. "You saw him at the house the other night. Our house."

"Why is he laying in the road?" Theodora stared at the man in a pale suit prone in the wet dirt road.

"He's a detective." My shrug made the velvet flowers and paper fruit of my hat bob from side to side for a moment after I stopped moving. "They do such things."

"I want to be a detective,' Jinxie said in a voice, wistful and breathy.

"He's looking for clues to a crime." I looked at the muddy road before him. The ghosts of wagon ruts haunted either side of this road and could have been years old. Before him the mud showed about a half revolution of one ill-defined wheel.

I leaned forward, cleared my throat, and said, "Hello Mr. Barker." With a gentle hand, I pulled Jinxie back to the curb. "This is Theodora and Eugenia. You saw them last night." To the girls, I said, "I would think any clues would still be here now."

Barker continued to look at the muddy road. "Hello Teddie, Jinxie," Barker said.

I had no idea how he knew their nicknames.

His face stayed pointed toward the muddy ground, but his hand reached up and waved. The other hand held a magnifying glass. This close, I saw that he rested his elbows and knees on a brown oilskin.

"I would have thought this would be your first stop when you took the case." I opened my parasol to cast lacy shade covered my face and his back. "I admit I'm surprised to see you here three days later."

"Hello, Mrs. Gallagher. I'm afraid you're blocking my sunlight."

I flapped a hand at the girls to get them to join me as we inched a few spaces up the road from him until sunlight poured on his peach skin with a few freckles. "I expect the rain we had last Wednesday would have petered out before it got here. So the roads are essentially the same as the night your doodad was taken."

"Mmm-hmmm" he said. "Which is why I am here for a second time. "

"Which, coincidentally was around the night my client died. Do you believe in coincidence, Mr. Barker?"

"I believe in gathering data, Mrs. Gallagher, and then forming a theory about any situation." He rolled to a crouch and pulled a magnifying glass from his pocket to examine a section of road.

"So what do your wagon ruts say?" I moved a little closer to the road. "It looks to have been a heavy wagon, but the milkman's load is heavy, isn't it?"

He plucked a needle sized sliver of wood from a wagon rut and with careful, arched fingers, pulled a silver cigarette case from his pocket and sprung it open. It proved to be empty and probably carried for just such treasures. He set this inside, pressed a bit of felt against it, and snapped the case closed. He deposited this and the magnifying glass in his pocket.

He leapt up with such athleticism and speed, I jumped back for fear of being overpowered. Below him lay an oilskin of no greater width or length than himself. "Mrs. Gallagher, you are fearful smart, but you don't always, you don't ever pay attention. Maybe if you stop talking, you could think."

A noise came out of me that sounded very much like Dewey-cat's growl.

"I direct your attention to what the road does not show." He waved the oilskin downwind from me. Dirt exited in small puffs. He matched the corners and folded it with geometric precision. As he worked, his gaze went beyond me to the houses. Those blue eyes went back and forth as though he watched a tennis match over my shoulder.

I glanced at the deep rut he had examined.

I raised an eyebrow, tipped my head toward the parasol and said, "I understand why this case is important to you. You've spent months running down insurance claims. It's been lucrative, but low on adventure. This magic box is quite a prize."

He folded the oil cloth into a square even smaller than I would have imagined possible. He put it in an inside jacket pocket. His feet came to a stop on the curb. He put his hands on his hips and peered at me through blue spectacles. "You know, your client was not you in life. You cannot make her you in death." He must have seen the anger on my face, but still stepped closer to me and said in a voice as gentle as the children's choir pretending to be angels at Christmas, "she's not you, Daria. You don't have to protect her."

I shook my head. "No, I do. No one else will."

Teddy leaned her head against my waist.

"Well, we'll be going now." I met the unblinking gaze of those blue eyes surrounded by thick, black lashes and gave a little smile. "Goodbye, Mr. Barker."

I turned and walked with the girls up the broad expanse of lawn toward the medieval folly of the Dorfman house. It appeared to have suffered little storm damage other than shattered glass and a flood line about three feet up the rocky surface. Many of the windows—probably stained glass before the storm—had cardboard over the openings. I spoke to the girls in a voice loud enough for Barker to hear, but I didn't know why I wanted him to know. "We're paying a call on poor Mr. Dorfman who lost his wife." I shot a glance at both heads that bobbed along beside me to make sure they didn't believe he misplaced her.

Teddy gave a serious frown. Jinxie looked as though she would cry. Yes, they understood.

"You've never met him, but you're coming with me because a lady simply doesn't call on a gentleman—even a sympathy call—alone."

Whether or not Viktor the grieving widower would see me, I did not know. Even if he did, I had even less of an idea if he would answer my questions since he was my prime suspect. He was the estranged husband of a wealthy woman. With her dead, I figured he would get her money, but there were even more reasons. He could have been jealous. He also could have risked ruin if his wife's blackmailer went public.

We stepped onto the porch with iron railing around it that made me think of pikes strung together.

I pulled the visiting card I had placed at the top of the basket. "You see, I added your names."

I put the card back before slamming down the door knocker. The house did not have the normal crank doorbell, but a small electric one. Since most of us did not have working electricity yet, it probably would do nothing when pressed for at least for the next few months.

The maid showed us in without waiting for an explanation of who I was or taking the visiting card. I dropped it in a silver tray set atop a table carved with gothic arches. Beside the tray lay the morning addition of the Daily News. Good, it looked to have the original folds from when the newsboy tossed it on the lawn and had not been read.

The foyer was lined with faded tapestries and carved marble bookshelves filled with so many books; they rested atop the rows and piled above the crown molding. Some leather volumes had gold detail that looked hand painted. Others had colors of even brighter hue, perhaps enamel in beautiful designs of flowers or insects. Some had designs, ancient and beautiful.

The maid took my parasol, and expecting a lighter item, almost dropped it. She deposited it in the bottom of a hall tree and did not seem to wonder why it was heavier than most women's.

I perched on the edge of the jacquard settee. Doilies covered the arms and back of this, as well as the chair in the corner. Every wall was covered with oak bookshelves and these were filled with Moroccan leather and gold edged book volumes.

Another maid in the same starched gray dress with black ribbon around the arm and white lace apron tied at the waist. "Follow me . . ." she shot a glance to my visiting card, "Mrs. Gallagher."

The sofa, settee, chaise, and even center of the marble-topped table were doily covered.

On an armless sofa set between two oak columns, a slight young woman swathed in black muslin and edged with lace sat. She stood to slide the lace curtains open. The round walls beyond her revealed this room to be part of the turret where the replaced glass showed the inside of the gardenia bushes.

I recognized the girl: Nina Karparova.

Viktor rose from a stool against a vitrine cabinet full of small, clasped books. I stepped toward Viktor, shook his hand, and said,—well, I didn't ask, "Did you kill Larisa?" no matter how I wanted to do so—"Your house is beautiful. I'd love to live among these books."

"His little masterpieces," Larisa's sister said. I could not tell whether she meant the phrase derisively or with admiration since the nasal Russian accent got in the way. "He binds books. He's always saved a first addition for himself. They are worth a fortune, you know." At this, she smiled. "He probably has more money than my father." She spoke of her parents with a twitch of her head.

Of course, I realized. The twitch was a locator since they lived next door.

"Nina," Viktor said with a slight scold, but his face held a smile.

So, he didn't need Larisa financially.

"Oh, I brought fried chicken." I urged Teddie forward with a pat on her shoulder. I looked around this trove of Roman sculpture, bestselling books, and Persian carpets.

Silence followed, which I filled with the first thing that came to mind rather than the cleverest. "And deviled eggs, of course."

Nina and Viktor looked at me, looked at each other, and looked back to me with furrowed brows.

"Yes." I slid a glance to the girls who looked around the room. "I guess bringing food to the family of the departed is something new to you." And probably not something people with this much money do. I felt my face blush at my own idiocy. "It's a tradition here. Some of the best recipes you'll ever taste are only brought out at funerals. I . . . I'm sorry for your loss."

"Thank you." He gave a smile that made me smile back and looked me in the eye. "Please, ladies, sit down."

The girls giggled at being called 'ladies' and looked at me.

The maid reentered silently and took the basket that I was now glad to see go from my arm that I gushed a, "Thank you".

I gave the girls a rapid set of eye gestures that I hoped looked encouraging them to do what the man said. They took the hint and dropped into their best curtseys before they trundled off to a carved wooden bench that looked like some ancient instrument of torture. I gave my flapping part-the-waters motion, and they sidled over to make enough room for me.

Viktor gave me a little bow before he sat. "I remember you, Mrs. Gallagher, from Mr. Barker's office."

"Why did you go to Mr. Barker's—the detective's—office?"

He stood statue-still for an instant and then blinked. "I wanted to see if she was there." He glanced at Nina.

"To see my sister." She gave a sad look toward Viktor. "I told him she would be there. She said . . . " She stood and slapped at her train of black silk until it was behind her and strolled into the room with us. "I haven't seen her in months."

"Months?" I asked.

She took her purse from the hearth.

"It was silly of me." Viktor shook his head and looked down to the table and an old leather volume beneath a glass cover.

"Silly?" I asked. "Why?"

Viktor shrugged and said nothing.

If I wanted to get information out of him, I would have to coax him to talk about himself, even about his feelings, something I doubted this man in the high collar and tight silk necktie did by nature.

The girls watched her for an instant and then their attention was turned back to the rows of books.

Nina found a chair and sat by letting her knees drop in a carnival-ride plunge. She pulled a cigarette case from her purse that held three lumpy cigarettes. Her big brown eyes narrowed at me in a dare.

I shrugged. "I've never seen a lady do that." I put the emphasis on "lady" so my daughters would know what was expected of them without me nagging. I looked down at them to see if they noticed and doubt they could have seen anything. Teddie looked at her high-buttons shoes and Jinxie had her face pressed against my shirtwaist so hard, I thought the print of the fabric might come off and leave cherries all over her face. They were shy girls, launched by the adoption into a world of everything fearsome and new to them while everyone would seem to know just how to act.

Oh no! I've taken them into a den of possible murderers. Well, the Karparovs couldn't possibly pose a danger to them.

Nina looked at Viktor. With a cigarette in her hand, she fumbled through her purse.

I prayed the Karparovs would not care enough about my daughters to do them harm.

"Damn!" Nina scrounged through her chain purse. "That idiot, Slava, took my matches."

Viktor sat on a couch beside me but angled toward his sister-in-law.

He stared at Nina with a frown that did not start with the swear word, but since she called this Slava person an idiot. I remembered the name that he was a bodyguard. I guess he was tasked with keeping the remaining daughter in line.

I needed to get answers before she asked the big one of: why do I have to answer anything you ask? "So did you and your sister have a falling out?"

Nina laughed at this with a piercing sharp sound. "Matches, Viktor?" Her voice rose in command.

Viktor found a porcelain match holder on the sideboard and carried to Nina.

She struck a match on the emery-covered cup of matches.

I gave Viktor a sharp look. I shouldn't scold if I wanted information from him, but he was helping a woman act unfeminine and doing it in front of my daughters.

"You understand," he said. "I'm sure."

"Perfectly," I said through a smile. "She comes here to smoke and swear because her father won't let her do it under his roof."

Nina looked out the window toward the front door.

Viktor kept looking down at that old book under the glass. Either he just realized it got there or he was embarrassed and didn't want to make eye contact.

I said, "This Slava fellow works for Papa and keeps his eye on her."

"Slava is her fiancé," Barker said from where he brushed the maroon-silk tassels hanging in the archway of the room. He gave the maid his flat straw hat and a smile that showed those angular cheeks had dimples.

"You've met him?" Nina said. With a couple hasty jabs, her cigarette was extinguished in a china ashtray.

"I saw the ring on your finger. It is an engagement ring and of the pinkish tint of gold familiar to Russian mines within the last century. It would be a family heirloom from that part of the world."

"Good work." I gave Barker a nod.

He raised an eyebrow at me. I think I caught a slight trace of dimple before it disappeared, but it was not there when he took a stance beside the oaken column.

Viktor gave a little cough. The gesture was to get my attention, but he had pale skin with red cheeks and a nervous energy that made him sit in one place, get up, pace a bit, and take another seat. I wondered if he was a lunger. I looked down at the girls. They would not be shaking hands with him. Tuberculosis trumped etiquette every time and also meant we would all take an extra helping of cod-liver elixir tonight.

"Mrs. Gallagher, what I hoped you to understand was that I cannot control my wife's family." Viktor's eyes implored mine, and I felt bad for scolding a grieving man.

But how grieving is he?

"Events have made this a tough time for you and your family," Barker said.

Nina looked up at Barker.

No, Mr. Clever Britches Detective, I thought. You will not take over this interview. It's mine.

"I came to offer my condolences," Barker said.

"As did I." I said. *Dang, uttering a "me too" is hardly the way to take over this stagecoach.*

"She brought food," Viktor gave a little flick of his hand in my direction that ended with him straightening his cuff. "Funeral food." He raised his index finger an inch off the doily and then back down in recognition of the strange natives and their customs. His hand then slid over the black band around the black suit sleeve. "Women tend to leave food for the family of the bereaved. I'd assume you'd know even less of this than we do, Mr. Barker, your father being a Duke and all."

I looked at Barker to see his reaction to that statement, was it true or not?

I could not see Barker's face. He stood in the windowed alcove and looked out the window. His hand rested on the latch and toggled the opening on the French doors.

"I wonder what your interest in our family is, Mrs. Gallagher?" Viktor asked.

Yes! He was offering me, well, not a chance to ask him about his relationship with his wife, but at least an opening toward that.

"Your wife and I were friends. I was her attorney."

"Why did she need an attorney?" Nina slapped me with phrase as though it were a punch with brass knuckles.

I fought a frown and sat up straight enough to rival Barker's ramrod posture and please my mother, if that could be done. "She thought she might have enemies." I spoke in a soft voice and only a glance up from the hands in my lap. "Do you know why?"

Barker turned around from the window to give me a wry smile. He had those blue spectacles on again.

"How would I know? I haven't seen my sister for months." She sobbed on the black lace sleeve of her dress.

Barker turned from the display of feminine emotion beside him and opened the lace curtain to look beyond the gardenia bushes to the Karparov home. I could see that their house had part of the back missing and tarps hanging over damaged roof, as well as the servant's quarters/carriage house.

I stared at Viktor and waited for him to answer.

"My wife was gone for so long and now death." Viktor spoke loud, a little too loud for the hushed room, as though he kept so much inside his gray satin vest that he could not also control his volume. And after a cough, retreated into silence.

I nodded. *He must need to get this emotion out.* I know I needed him to get it out to find out if he was upset enough to kill his wife. "What do you feel?"

Barker slid a glance to me.

I held my breath. I hoped Viktor would say more and I did not want to do anything to break the tensile strand of his words.

"She was not the woman I thought I had married." He straightened a wrinkle from the doily on the arm of the couch.

I waited for more words, but none came. I would have to spur them on. "You must feel all sorts of things." Oh, that was leading the witness, not good. I needed to do something. I felt so close to getting him to talk. "You must have feelings you need to let out. That's what mourning is for, let the feelings out."

Nina huffed out an angry cloud of smoke.   She was right. I had overstepped my position as guest, but I needed answers.

I gave Viktor a kind smile. "What happened?"

"I care for her still, but I long ago realized she was not the person I thought I knew."

I knew what Larisa had done to defile the marriage. I considered covering the girls' ears, but that would just make them curious. "About when would you say that was?"

"About three or four years after we married." Viktor's brow furrowed. "We have been living our own lives for about a year." His brow furrowed and his eyes shone.

Barker sat beside her and offered the weeping woman his linen handkerchief.

"My sister left after she and my father had a terrible fight." Nina took the handkerchief, but crumpled it in her fingers rather than daub her face. "I tried to talk to her. I sent her letters through a friend."

I tried not to look too curious and shot only a glance at Viktor. His hands rested loose on his lap.   "Why did you want to see Larisa?"

Viktor shrugged and shifted his weight on the stool. "I don't know, not really." He looked at me. His eyes were welling with tears. "I guess I held out hope that she might come back to me, that we would have what we did in the beginning." He convulsed in a series of sniffs, worsened by the fact he tried to fight them.   "I will never be able to now." He attempted to mask his choked up state with a cough that brought on a series of actual coughs. He attempted to smother these with a handkerchief to his mouth, but they came in waves.

Barker used a reserve handkerchief to daub a tear from Nina's cheek.

"She never answered my letters." Nina leaned toward Barker. "Thank you, Mr. Barker. If my father knew I sent them, he would have killed me."

Well slap me naked, but that's an interesting turn of phrase, considering.

"He cut my sister off. The trust that had been set up for her by grandmama. He stopped Larisa from getting any checks."

"He could do that?" I said. This was my area; I had clients who got checks from their trusts every month. Dissolving whatever trust had been set up for a specific person is much more difficult than writing out a beneficiary on your own trust.

"My father can do just about anything he wants," Nina said. She thrust the handkerchief back into Barker's hand.

"That would mean he got the family attorney to go against the wishes of the trust," I heard myself say.

"My father can be a harsh man." Nina slid a smile to Viktor. "I am fortunate for Viktor's help."

Viktor blinked at me as though surprised to still see me in the room.

"Yes," I said. I stood. "Thank you for your time."

Viktor rose and gave me a friendly smile. "Thank you. Speaking of what is inside the mind helps, even if only to confess to being a fool about my wife."

Barker said his goodbyes faster and was out of the house house—my daughters following him—by the time I was done telling Nina, "Contact me if you need to."

When I said it, she inched toward Viktor when I said that as though I had threatened her.

Barker's fast walk and upright carriage had him halfway across the lawn toward the Karparov version of Caesar's villa before I emerged from the house.

The girls trotted after Barker, but turned back to me. I gave them some coins for the street car and a couple pennies for candy. I would not take them to hear another murder suspect. They dashed away. Teddie, the treasurer for the two, may have even skipped.

"You'll take me in to see your client, won't you?" I asked. "I'd like to ask him some questions."

"And you need an escort." Barker unbuttoned all but the top button of his suit jacket and pressed his hands into his pockets. "That's how all these lady-rules work."

"You notice that Dorfman didn't need his wife's money." I strode—on a few paces, even leapt with a flounce of my white skirts—to keep pace with Barker. "But his sister-in-law seemed pretty sweet on her sister's husband."

"Not inappropriately while we were there."

"But that girl's hiding something."

Barker slowed for an instant, turned to me, and turned back to the trek across the lawn.

I kept pace. "They're sisters. It's a close bond and you don't cut your sister off just because your father tells you to."

Barker's spats hopped the mud between the shrubs and made toward the walkway.

"Larisa's father just recently cut her money off." I pinched my skirt up high over my ankles to keep from tripping in my pursuit. I doubt Barker noticed. "You know she probably got mad about that and stole his treasure."

Barker stormed the walkway. My boots clattered to keep up with his fast pace.

"That would have made her father plumb angry with her." I said. "And there was the lover? I wonder about him."

"What about him, indeed." Barker said this as a sort of Scottish version of my second-grade teacher who had treated us as if we were particularly dimwitted children.

"Don't patronize me, Mr. Barker." I reached out before Barker could and clanked the iron knocker against the plate on the front door.

"And why would I, dear lady? He would have some role in this, no matter how minor." He stepped past the withered black butler in gray morning coat who answered the door. "To see Mr. Karparov, I'm Mr. Barker. I'll keep my hat. Ta." He tucked the straw hat under his elbow. The way he said, 'ta' sounded as though it meant "thank you" rather than "good-bye."

The butler turned away and disappeared through one of a set of arches. I caught a glimpse of him going up a staircase.

"We might as well make ourselves comfortable," Mr. Barker said. "Karparov will show his power by making us wait." He tucked his spectacles into a pocket in the top of his jacket. That thing must be a sort of cabinet of curiosities inside. "I would like a beverage and I'd imagine you would like to talk to a maid who knew your client. These interests might go together."

I gave him a nod and walked through the arch to the left since that seemed the most likely to be kitchen-ward. "Yoo-hoo," I said. "Anyone here who can give a gentleman a drink?"

Behind a bench and a section of carved posts, a coffee-colored head emerged with a lacy ruffle bound by a black ribbon atop her hair of interlocking spins. She started at seeing people in the entryway, but only for an instant before she steadied herself against the hall tree and stood tall of buxom frame with the raised brows, dropped lids, and firm cast to her lips that says "I'm what they call 'good help.'"

Dang, I was hoping for some little blonde wisp fresh off the farm and eager for talk. That, I could get to spill.

I said, "Mr. Barker is here to see Mr. Karparov."

"Yes," the maid said. She straightened a jade carving of a horse that she had knocked askew when startled. "The detective who was here a couple days ago. The paper said you used to be a jungle explorer."

Hadn't heard that one. "He'd like some refreshment. Is that possible? I'm Mrs. Gallagher. I just came to pay my respects. I'm—I mean I was—Well, I am Mrs. Dorfman's attorney and I'm her friend."

"I'll bring you some lemonade."

"We'll wait in the conservatory," Barker said. He put a pair of fingers on my elbow and guided me through a dining hall with a long table of dark wood and chairs carved with gothic spires.

"That's a Gainsborough," I whispered of the painting of a powder-haired woman in a gleaming blue satin dress. "Those dark eyes grab hold of you."

Beside her, hung a painting of a man's face in profile showed the mastery of perspective yet not grandeur that marked the early high Renaissance. There were more paintings. They were here and throughout the house because they were art, because the owners knew art, and not because they matched the drapes.

Beyond this room, sunlight glazed the glass set between columns of a conservatory made to look as much like a Roman patio as a greenhouse could. Barker did not sit on the wood edged couches perched on gnarled legs set between spikes of pink and yellow orchids, but strode to the window. He looked out past the azaleas to the Dorfman house.

Nina had not emerged.

I looked at the azaleas. Broken blossoms littered the earth, some of them raked under until they were partly covered with dirt and had more brown than pink. I thought of Larisa and how she was now part of the earth, no one to mourn her any more than anyone did those flowers.

"Here you are," the maid said. She held out two tall glasses of iced lemonade on a tray.

"I'm sorry for everyone's loss," I said. I took a glass. "Thank you. Did you know Mrs. Dorfman?"

Her eyes filled with tears. She nodded with a shake of what looked to be real garnet and tiny pearl earrings. "Since they first came here. She was Miss Karparov then, only they say Karparova for a girl. I always liked that. She wouldn't correct me like her father. He would no matter what . . ." Her words trailed off into a frown and picked up with another thought. "She said it just all gentle, like."

Barker took the other lemonade.

"Want me to sweeten that for you sir?" A smile slid up to her apple cheeks.

"Certainly, ma'am, what is your name?"

She hid a discreet giggle at being called ma'am, tucked the tray into her apron pocket, and pulled a flask from a pocket in the side of her skirt. "I'm Polly."

Was I the only one without a hidden collection of reliquaries within my garments?

She gave Barker a generous finger of brown liquor from the silver flask. "Yes, she was wild, like the newspaper said, but who can blame her? Her father married her to a man she didn't know. She was young and smart, wanted to be her own person. That's what she used to say."

Wow, this was easier than I thought. "Did she and her father argue often?"

Silence. A tightlipped, silence that burned through me and made me want to fill it with chatter.

I swallowed a little lemonade. It was good. I would have made it a bit tarter, but this was certainly good.

Polly said, "Mr. Karparov should be with you shortly."

"Thank you." Barker said an instant before I did.

She started out, but before she reached the door, she turned and said, "Tuesday night was the night Miss Larisa would have passed on?"

"Yes," Barker said. "The time of death was put sometime Tuesday night."

Polly looked at me. "I know what you were trying
to ask, but there's no point. Mr. Karparov and the whole
family—well, except for Miss Larisa—they were here
Tuesday night. They couldn't possibly get down to the pier
without all of us noticing."

"The whole family?" I asked.

"Yes, Mr. Karparov, the Mrs., Miss Nina, and even
Mr. Dorfman."

"Oh."

"Miss Larisa was there earlier in the day, but she
left." Her eyes filled with tears again. "Then maybe she
would have been alive."

I put a hand on her starched shoulder, "We just
can't know what would have been."

Polly smiled and opened her mouth to say
something to me, but Barker gave an "ahem" and said to
her, "I'd like you to show me again where the relic, this
magic casket, was before it was taken."

A shadow of a frown passed over her face."

"Please." Barker had that smile with the dimples
pasted on his face.

She smiled again. "This way, sir." She walked to
the hall with vaulted ceiling. Just before the great room of
columns and marble, she stopped in an alcove with an
arched niche. "Here it was."

The niche was empty from white plaster walls to the
shiny surface of dark wood.

Barker put the blue spectacles. "And when exactly
was it missing?"

"Like I said to you the other day." Polly looked at
the niche, not at Barker. "Sometime during the night. I

saw it before the party and I know it was gone in the morning." She folded her arms over her large chest and pressed her lips together so hard, her mouth veered to the side.

Larisa had been here in after the casket had been last seen and before it disappeared. She then died later that night. I murmured to Barker, "Somehow, the casket must have led to Larisa's death."

He nodded, but his head went sideways at the end.

At the sound of footsteps, Polly glanced behind her. "Your guests, Mr. Karparov." With a rustle of black taffeta, she was gone.

The old man flicked his conductor hair back with both hands. His brow was furrowed with something more like constant peevishness than concern and his bushy brows attempted to hide his eyes. His mouth held tight and looked pinched, especially with a chin thrust always forward with lines showing the muscles had held this unnatural position for many years.

"So, my property, Barker, you get it?"

"No, not yet." Barker tucked his spectacles in his vest pocket. "And I will not attempt to do so as long as you are not truthful with me. I will not have a client who lies to me and keeps part of the house off limits."

Karparov gaped for air with great fish gulps.

Barker strode past the long-haired old codfish. "Not about your relationship with your daughter. Not about the most basic nature of the item I am to find. Not about anything. Consider our relationship suspended until you decide to be honest. You want someone who can find your wee, manky casket, but you will not find a detective in this part of Texas. I am the best. Maybe the Russian consul in Chicago will be willing to find someone for you."

I followed quick behind. Good thing I didn't wear one of those new fitted princess skirts today. I would have split a seam keeping up with that man's long strides.

He turned under the archway to the marble foyer. "If you decide to start telling me the truth, then call on me. Until then, good-bye, sir." He opened the door, but turned to me where I stood an inch from him.

"You wanted to talk to him, lass, go right ahead." He strode outside.

Karparov had gained his voice. In fact, the whole house did since it resonated with the sound of Russian profanities linked Barker's body parts, mayhem, and his family members engaged in depraved and immoral acts, sometimes with deities. Then came the truly ominous stuff.

"If you'll excuse me," I said to anyone in the Karparov house who might be listening. "I think I'll just share a cab with Mr. Barker back to the train station." I tipped my head to the butler who held the door and skidded down the brick steps to where Barker's pace took him halfway to the street.

I skittered down the walkway behind him.

Karparov shouted through the open doorway.

I caught up with Barker and said, "He's saying you are the miscreant son of—"

"I don't think I need a translation."

"Well I certainly wasn't going to go word for word," I said. "Essentially, he's telling you that you're done for." I was thankful for the tiny stays of whalebone in the neck of my shirtwaist that kept me from being able to look back at him. "It's a very expressive language."

Barker put on his blue spectacles. "Are you giving up on all this whole mess as you should or do you want to know what I found out about that wee vial of fluid from her stomach?"

Chapter 9

I tucked the telegram into the envelope, ripped it in half and then rip the sections. I pulled at that wad of paper, but only managed to mangle it. I gave a cry more suited to a wild animal, yanked again, and then threw it in the trash at the foot of my desk.

Behind the typewriting machine on her desk, Evangeline gave a small grimace, but said nothing. She had already read the wretched thing.

All I wanted was to finish the contracts I had to review and get home before my head exploded. I had a headache, probably because I didn't know what to do now that Barker's work in his laboratory determined Larisa had sea water in her stomach, but not any of the mud of the gulf. I didn't know how to investigate her murder. Finding a vase of roses and the newspaper on my desk made everything worse.

The newspaper held a short article describing Larisa's funeral and then this:

A Friend in Life and Death

Mrs. Gallagher is a determined woman. Not only is she one of the handful of women to become attorneys, but she is not giving up on her late friend, Larisa Dorfman. A respectable woman herself, she pays no attention to the wanton lifestyle her friend led, which included much time spent in the lounge of the infamous playground of the wealthy, the Beach Hotel. There, Larisa had been seen in the company of different men but never with her husband. Mrs.

Gallagher denies that the dissipating lifestyle of her friend; a friend rumored to have participated in the Smart Set parties where trays of powders and hypodermic syringes are served with the cocktails. Mrs. Gallagher suspects murder and isn't afraid to say so to the police, the press, and even the grieving family.

"This is your friend?" Evangeline slapped an index finger against the newspaper.

"That's not a word I use, actually." I dawdled a hand over the soft petals of the blood-red roses in a porcelain vase on my desk. I did not take out the card because I felt a funny turn of my stomach. My husband had never sent me flowers, so who would now? Besides, I still felt the effects of a sick headache that had hit me in the morning, had forced me to pull down all the shades, and drink a hearty swig of paregoric to be able to review the shipping contracts on my desk when I felt as though I should be in bed, cradling the chamber pot. I had too much work to do to give in to a migraine.

I smoothed the long sleeve of my olive linen suit with light-green trim swirling through geometric designs. This was a color between the vibrant hues that made me feel sick and the darker ones that made me feel I would never get well.

"'Friend' not a word you'd use for someone like her, I'd bet." Evangeline yanked the sheet of paper from the typewriter, wadded it up, and tossed it into the trashcan painted with ribbons and flowers.

"Not for much of anyone," I said. "It's a quirk. Maybe I was dropped on my head as a baby."

•

Evangeline's scowl bore into me. "You pal on with folks and not like them?"

I shook my head. "You know I was adopted as a kid, from the orphan train."

She nodded, but the scowl remained on her dun-colored forehead.

"My mother wanted a boy to replace the son who died from yellow fever. Going from a family, to an orphanage, to another family, well I never, well, it's a quirk."

"You don't trust people?"

"Yes and no. When someone tells me something, I believe them, but if you're talking about relying on people. I'm not so good at that."

Evangeline gave a little sideways jog of the head. "So, you don't expect Mrs. Quackenbush to treat you any better than she does."

I opened my mouth to argue, but she turned to the typewriter to beat a staccato and I didn't have anything to say. I looked over at the trashcan and the telegram within and gave the brass receptacle a hard kick. That garnered a satisfying "boom" of metal, but did not knock the thing over.

With a quick turn back to my desk, I picked up the pages of the contract before me since looking down to read them made my head feel as though it might topple off. The paregoric had replaced most stabbing pain through carnival-ride dizziness, but sore-eyed ache remained.

The words swam before me. A few blinks may not have cleared them up, but at least set them swimming in lanes.

I read a couple pages, jotted notes, and set the page down to rub my eyes.

"Something wrong, Miss Dash?"

"Tired," I hedged. I didn't like being weak and so I didn't mention the migraine. "And I can't stop thinking about my poor dead client."

"From what you said, doesn't sound like much anybody cares about her."

I frowned and opened the card covered with blossoms in pastel shades. "Her husband cared about her, I think. His life sure hasn't changed any because she's gone, though. Her sister—if anything—is a little happier without the competition, her mother probably doesn't care about much of anything except opium wine, and her father cut her off a while ago. Even if he hadn't, he's too busy with thoughts of some magic casket rather than any human."

Evangeline shuddered.

"She had wanted me to find a detective because she was being blackmailed—she believed I could handle that better than she. She thought I must no someone, what with being an attorney."

"But why did she care? She didn't seem to mind who knew what about her. Why would she care if the blackmailer was fixin' to spill her secrets?"

I set aside the file on a charitable trust I had updated. "I thought about that. She didn't care about her reputation, certainly not as much as I care about mine. But maybe she did care about something that could get ruined if the blackmailer set his plan in action."

"You got a 'such as' for that?"

"Her gentleman friend was married," I said.

"He was married, that makes him no gentleman."

"Oh no!"

"Miss Dash, you've got to see that—"

"Oh that's not the problem. I mean, I do, but that's not why I shouted. It's the flowers, they're from Judge Reams—the one assigned to my adoption—of all people."

"That's, well, friendly-like."

"Unorthodox as well." I frowned at the card, held it far away, then close to make it less blurry, and read it again. "He wanted to make my acquaintance. He doesn't say anything else, but this sure seems a strange way to do things."

Gees, this is going to delay my getting home to a dark room.

I pulled open my drawer and felt for the stack of thank-you notes without looking. I wandered through the basics of a Southern thank you—glowing description of the article, how it delighted, and an anecdote about what you are doing with it—and wondered if I could add something about the adoption. Yes. I wrote, "Thank you so much for getting to my adoption paperwork right away. I know this is a formality, but so important to the girls and me."

I flung the envelope onto Evangeline's desk. "Get that to Judge Reams at the courthouse right away. I might be able to win him over with my manners."

Evangeline's eyes widened to show the black brown pupils stark against the pure white of her eyes.

"What? There are worse ways I could try to win him over."

She opened her mouth as if saying something, but I heard nothing. I felt pain sear through my body and reverberate around my head. For most of the day before, I had felt the tightness in my head and sickness in my stomach, indicating a headache coming on. No, this was something more than that. There was a sound, one coming from outside my head.

Gunshot, that was what I felt and what I heard instead of Evangeline.

"Call the police," I said to Evangeline through the molasses in my head.

Another shot resounded. It was from across the hall in Barker's office. With no thought in my brain other than "make it stop," I ran across the hall and flung the door open.

Until I could see, I steadied myself against the wave of pain. Daylight stretched into the room and through my vision like lightning bolts.

Barker lay face down on the floor, his wrists roped behind him, and a nickel-plated revolver shining in his hands. The plain wall that separated a laboratory from the rest of his office bore a tattoo of bullets in the shape of an "x". "So you can see, someone with hands bound behind them can shoot with accuracy, especially when that person is a marksman, as is your business associate."

He bolted to his feet and flapped away the ropes. Before him stood another man, long and narrow in duck pants, worn jacket, big white watch fob across his vest, and felt cowboy hat.

"I can't thank you enough, Mr. Barker," the man said in the cadence of Texas, but without the twang. "They'd have given me the long drop for that one." He fished around in his breast pocket and pulled out a small white clay pipe. He put it in his mouth, then saw me, tipped his hat, and put the pipe away.

"I told the court the truth," Barker said.

"Well, I'm much obliged." He tipped his hat to me again and walked out. Although his new red and black cowboy boots looked to be of good leather, he shifted in them and walked with wide legs. "If you ever need any help, well, you know what range I'll be riding and when folks tell me something, I keep it dry."

In the hall, he tipped his hat to Evangeline at the telephone.

"Powerful sorry, officer," Evangeline said and hung up the receiver.

I closed the door and turned back to Barker as fast as my headache would let me. "That man is no cowboy." My voice came out louder than intended. I can't control volume or pitch in the throes of a migraine.

"No?" Barker grinned at me while he put emptied the bullets in one desk drawer and put the gun in another. "What is he?"

"I'd guess he's a smuggler."

"Guess?" Barker winced at the word. "Based on what? Women's intuition?"

I gave scoffing laugh that sent ripples of pain through my head. "His pipe, for one thing," I said. "I've never seen a cowboy with one, but a seafarer needs to keep his tobacco dry and would favor a pipe."

"And for another?" He dipped a cloth into the water jug on the sideboard and wrung it out.

I hadn't another, but I thought hard and came up with something, "His boots were new and he had trouble with the heels. His walk was that of a man accustomed to steadying himself on a deck, not wrapping his legs around a horse."

"If I might add, the scrimshaw on his watch chain and the fact that his hands were tanned far more than a cowboy who is prone to wearing gloves."

"Yes, that would have been obvious," I said. "Had I noticed it." I had my eyes closed, so I hadn't seen him walk over, but he took my elbow in a gentle grip.

"Here, put this cloth over your eyes and lie down on the couch. "'Tis for the headache"

Holding my head very still so I did not shake it and cause Vesuvius to erupt between my temples, I stifled a frown at the unwelcome knowledge that he had figured out what I wanted no one to know about me. "No thank you. I have work to do."

His exhale held a slight sigh of exasperation. "You won't let anyone help you."

"I have work to do, but I did want to tell you something."

He held the cloth toward me, but I ignored it.

I grabbed the edge of his desk to keep from swaying. "I remember something Karparov said when he was yelling at you. Something other than insults about you and, um, your family."

Barker reclined on his couch. He might have smiled at me before he draped the cloth over his eyes.

"He said that casket was cursed. He said it will always sow destruction on all—or some such apocalyptic hyperbole, I tell you, I am rusty—until it is returned to the rightful owner, which would be he."

"No surprises there."

"I know you're a man of science and don't believe that hoodoo, but what of these oil speculators he's in with now?" *The ones I think Judge Reams wants me to keep an eye on.*

"What of them?"

"Well, if one of them believed that and wanted the power, maybe he worked with Larisa and bumped her off or found she stole it and . . .You see what I mean." I hoped he did, because forming cogent thoughts hurt like the dickens.

"At last some evidence of logical thinking from you, Mrs. Gallagher."

I gave as much of a smile as I could with the headache. "And those people will surely be at Karparov's ball next Wednesday. That would be a good opportunity to observe them. I could help you."

"I'm off the case," Barker said. "And I've much work to do, so go back to your office now."

I made unsteady strides back to my own office. I wanted to sit at my desk. Maybe drape a cold cloth over my forehead, but in the hallway, I turned back to Barker. "Since you are off the search, that means you can help me with my quest, no conflict."

"Go back to your office and do your work, Mrs. Gallagher."

"Please, Mr. Barker."

"Miss Dash," Evangeline called behind me where she held the telephone receiver. "Telephone for you." She set the brass receiver down on the wood note tray. "It's the courthouse.

Chapter 10

"Judge Reams, thank you so much for the flowers."
I stood straight before the telephone, as if speaking to a
judge presiding over a courtroom. "You're handling my
case?"

"There's really no case." His voice had a strong,
amiable twang, but that still didn't sound good.

"You've wrapped it up already? I'll send my clerk
back to pick up the—"

"Mrs. Gallagher, you seem like a girl who enjoys a
good time."

"Oh, you've been reading the paper. That's not—"

"Since you're in with this Karparov crowd, guess
you know them pretty well."

"I wouldn't say that at all." I shook my head so
hard, a hairpin fell from my pompadour.

"Well then, find out about them. They're having
next week for their daughter's engagement and I'd like to
know who else is there, what it is like."

"Well, they wouldn't—"

"Next day, I'll see you in my office, and you can
tell me all about these Karparovs."

"But why—"

"See you then." I heard a smile in his voice. "Bye-
bye."

The line went dead.

Evangeline stood in the office doorway.

"He wants me to spy on the Karparovs."

"He thinks I'm some sort of giggly Gibson Girl. Hence, the stupid flowers."

"They are rather pretty."

"He hasn't done anything about the adoption. He sounded—I don't know—scared."

"Of you?"

"Of making a decision." I fell against the wall.

"You have to win him over." Evangeline walked back into the office and shouted, "You!"

I peered in the door and shouted, "You!"

Between my padded leather desk chair and me stood Joseph Pulitzer's own debutante, MJ Quackenbush.

I needed MJ. I needed to find out how to get in the ball and she might be invited. While not an honored guest, the wealthy must let the press in the kitchen or something now and then. They must. How else would the newspapers get such detailed stories from who was flirting with whom and what type of beads were embroidered onto the dresses? Still, I needed not to give her any more information than she already knew. I had proved myself to be a big mouth and needed to stop it.

"How could you write those things?" My voice came out in a headache-induced whine. I couldn't control it when I had a migraine, but usually I didn't care if it bothered people. "How could you make me sound so loose and unethical, not to mention mouthy?"

"I thought the article showed what a loyal friend you are," MJ's fingers toyed with the ruffled net scarf hung around her neck. Her suit of a short purple jacket over a blouse and gored skirt, all of it trimmed in bright yellow satin made my head pound.

I closed my eyes and walked around her to my desk.

"I didn't write the article." MJ sat in the visitor chair, crossed her legs, and planted an elbow atop her knee.

"And I'm sure you didn't help a lick with it." Evangeline rose a little higher over her typewriter.

Maybe my headache was affecting my vision, but MJ looked as though her face had started to boil.

I rested my head on the cool surface of the desk. I thought of my Aunt Gladys. MJ knew what a great party-giver she was. Maybe that was how to get to the subject of the Karparov's ball without showing intent. "This is the sort of day my Aunt Gladys would have said 'shined with the gloom of the angels.'"

"Isn't your Aunt Gladys the one they took away in a butterfly net?"

Okay, so Aunt Gladys stopped giving parties when she was taken away to the state hospital. I needed a different tactic.

Evangeline emitted the meekest of "harrumph"s.

"Do you want to know why I'm here?" MJ's skirt fluttered as her foot bobbed in a rapid tic.

"No," Evangeline may have said in a voice too soft to be heard over the typewriter keys.

"You need to leave this Larisa person and her memory alone." MJ raised a warning finger. Before I could do much more than open my mouth, she added, "I've talked to the police. They know it's a murder, but there isn't enough evidence to convict anyone. Besides, a sporting girl like that, you know people figure she got what was coming to her."

"That's not right," I said. "And now that you and your cohorts have linked me with her, that's my reputation gone as well and I never was on the queer."

MJ held her hand to examine her manicure, but would have had a heck of a time seeing it through her kid glove.

"I've already lost clients." My voice was so loud, it annoyed me, but I kept going. "I got a telegram from an old man today who said he would no longer need the services of a woman like me and the Ladies Aid Society suggested I didn't want to come to their meeting. How many more clients will I lose from this? Too many and I lose my daughters. Not exactly something to have a party about."

Evangeline cocked her head at me in confusion. Yes, it was a bad attempt and I'd have to do better.

"Well, dropping this whole Larisa thing until it blows over might help." MJ stood before my desk, hands on hips. "I can't help you.

I knew she couldn't help. She had a kid to support, too, and needed her job as much as I needed mine.

"No, I can't drop it. At this point, it won't blow over for my reputation." My head drooped. I felt as though I would cry. It was the headache talking, I told myself. And feeling.

"You need to stop," MJ shouted at me. Her words rang in the belfry of my pounding head. I think she tried to grab my shoulders, but I flinched away as though pleurisy had got me.

"You just need to stop this now. Stop! Stop! Stop!"

"You stop," I whispered through the pain. "Because I'm fixing to issue some sort of ultimatum."

"Are you threatening to threaten me?" MJ laughed. "Let me know when you get around to the real fireworks."

"Why should she stop?" Evangeline demanded of MJ.

"Maybe she was knocked off." MJ batted her kid-gloved hands against either side of Evangeline's chair.

"That's what I've been trying to say." I spoke in such crisp syllables, that I might have been biting carrots. "She was murdered."

"I mean murdered by political forces of great power, working behind the scenes." MJ said. "And you might get knocked off, too, if you don't stop it."

"Yes I know, the black hand of mumbo-jumbo, it could be everywhere. Making you miss that streetcar when you knew you were on time. Putting lumps in your gravy. Causing the Chinese lady who launders your collars to forget where you live."

"You can't deny a possible political dimension to this." MJ jabbed the air in my direction.

"I can, I will, and I do." *Well, probably.* I had a notion that something more than personal hate led to Larisa's murder, and that notion wouldn't go away.

MJ blew upwards to knock a wiry red hair back into her subtle pompadour. "Politics has an angle in this thing, I'll bet. What do you know about your dead girl's father?"

"He's rich and big at having parties," I said.

"He was some demi-king or something in the old country."

Evangeline's hands wavered over the keyboard, but pressed nothing. "What in thunder is a demi-king?"

MJ stepped before us and clasped her hands like a woman about to give a temperance lecture. "He was appointed by the Tsar to run the railroads in the hinterlands of someplace. That's what our boy was supposed to do, but then he took over a town, the fields, farms, and even the people."

"The people?" I asked.

"They treated him like a king. He had total sway over them. That was, until the Tsar found out and he left a few minutes before the secret police."

Evangeline took the thank-you note and walked out.

"Strange part is that his power had something to do with archeology." MJ tugged at the fluffy boa around her neck to straighten the ends. "That's all I could get from translated newspapers and such. The consul in Chicago was no help at all." Her hands came down on the front of my desk. "Do you know anything about that?"

Yes, there's a magic box, but if I tell you, I can kiss away any chance of my landlord, Mr. Barker from ever helping me again.

Her green eyes bore into mine.

I diverted: "Talk to him at his party."

"Party? What party? A meeting of the angry despot society?"

"Next Wednesday," I said. "His daughter's engagement announcement."

"Thanks for the tip."

"You can get into something like that, can't you?"

She laughed.

I could hear her laughter continue to ring through the building as she walked down the stairs.

Evangeline walked into the office and handed me a visiting card that was larger than mine with an imprint around the edge and the name "Stuyvesant van Rensselaer Livingston" engraved across the center.

"Who is he?" *And is he something else that is going to keep me from getting my aching head home?*

"I can't say as I know much more than you, Miss Dash." Evangeline picked up the stack of folders on her typewriter and looked at them with more interest than in what I said. "A man standing in front of the building when I came back from the courthouse. He saw where I was headed and asked—ever so politely—asked if I knew you. He gave me his card . . ." She flipped a hand toward the card I still fingered. "And asked if you could come outside and meet him in front of the bakery." Evangeline slipped past her desk and toward the front window. "Yep, he's still there."

"Reporter?" I rubbed my forehead and found this caused pain to shoot through my head rather than decrease.

"Don't rightly know, but I doubt it," Evangeline said. "They all lammed it after Mr. Barker had words with them yesterday and nary a one has come back."

Oh no! I was making everything worse for everyone and becoming even more indebted to Barker.

"I'll go see him." I straightened the black, crepe ribbon around my embroidered linen sleeve. "Before people start asking questions."

"He's a mighty fine-looking dude."

Even without Evangeline's comment on his appearance, I would have known which man was my caller. I remembered him as the young man with the waves of pale brown hair from Larisa's funeral.

"How do you do?" I said. My voice quavered with uncertainty.

"I'm so glad to see you," he said. He stepped forward.

I stepped backward and stopped myself when the back of my hat touched Mrs. Hulpke's bakery window.

"I know meeting on the street like this is irregular." He doffed his bowler and threaded the brim through his fingers. "But I figured you would prefer we meet in public. Better for your reputation."

I smiled. I liked that someone was thinking of what little reputation I had left. "Yes, well we can always come up to my office and talk."

"It's a nice day out. Care to dine?" That was a nice smile and came close to making me forget about my migraine. The housekeeper had already planned to get the girls from school and give them a midday meal while I stayed in my darkened office.

My words had been slowed by pain, so I gave a point toward to door of Mrs. Hulpke's bakery. "Sardine sandwiches." I hoped to drag myself back to my office before the little bell rang over the bakery door and thundered through my brain.

He shook his head. "It's such a lovely day. I feel like a brisk walk."

"I don't." Oh no! I had accepted his dinner offer by not saying 'no.'

"Then we'll go to the nearest place."

"That would be the drug store." Oh, I had to stop this, but the headache left me unfit for conversation. "But I'm going back to my office now. Nice to meet you."

"I have to talk to you." His earnest eyes bore into mine. "Please. She—Larisa—said you were her best friend."

"I had no idea." She wasn't mine. I felt a little guilty, perhaps because of the headache.

"One thing she didn't say was how beautiful you are."

"Mr. Livingston." I tried to smile, but my pain-weakened muscles could not manage any more than a lopsided sneer.

"Please, call me 'Skip.' Everyone does. I have a little boat back home that I skipper." He gave a self-conscious laugh that sounded as though it was not such a little boat. "We'll eat at the drug store, then." He extended his arm for me to take.

The breeze on my face eased the pain some. Maybe I could find something out from him.

White iron chairs screeched across the marble floor and echoed against rough plaster over brick walls as a few people sat for a light midday dinner or ice cream, and more people moved the chairs out of their way in the long, narrow drug store to get to the aspirin powder, heroin syrup, and Lydia E. Pinkham's Vegetable Compound.

I sat as still as I could to avoid pain, and feel the cool coming off the ice cream bins.

Skip put his hand on the table. It was a long hand, masculine in the way of one who gets manicures after scraping them on yacht rope. "I can see you are amazingly understanding."

"You are amazingly flattering."

"I'd imagine other women would be . . . " He jogged his head until a few waves fell over his forehead and the word he wanted fell into his mind. "Jealous of Larisa's freedom?"

Was I? My life was work, worry about losing my daughters if I weren't making enough money before that first year was over, and wondering if my life would matter to anyone. If I did envy her, that was blocked out by the knowledge that if I were as free as she, I would do the same things I did in a world full of constraints. With freedom, I would still fill my life with responsibility.

"Freedom?" I turned to the clerk who brought me my sausage on a roll. "Thank you."

"Could I have a coca wine?" He asked. He looked at his oyster pie, but did not touch it.

"We don't serve alcohol here," the clerk said.

"Then I'll a Coca-Cola," he said. He looked at me. "Two."

"Oh, no thank you. I'll have a phosphate. Blood orange." With my sausage roll in one hand, I slowly sunk my teeth into the German sausage, dark mustard, and brown wheat bun. I noticed my other hand that lay on the table as if in hopes he might grab it. How desperate was I for the touch of a man? Very, but he did not need to know. I spooned a little chowchow from the glass decanter on top of my sausage roll.

The waiter brought our drinks.

I took out the straw from mine. I feared using a straw would cause wrinkles around my plush mouth and leave me looking like a shriveled apple doll, like my Aunt Gladys who smoked a pipe. I took a drink.

Skip leaned back as far as he could in the little chair and sipped through the straw.

"So what makes you interested in me?" I took a bite without crunching down too hard and gave it a few gentle chews and waited to see if nausea would overcome me from having something on my stomach other than alcohol and opium.

He set his drink down and raised his hands in a shrug of surrender. "I admit. I'm a man who is very interested in a beautiful woman, and you are perhaps the loveliest I've ever seen."

I looked at him.

He believed what he said. He did not even blink. If he were selling snake oil, he was doing a dang fine job. "I couldn't help but be drawn to you, not just because of how pretty you are, but because of that determination. I've never seen anyone walk the way you do, like you could take on the world."

Did Barker notice the way I walk? Damn, that is the last thing I should be wondering.

I took another bite and chewed with a little more vigor since my head had not yet fallen onto the metal table as it threatened. "That sounds very nice, but you came to my office before you had ever seen me. What do you think I know about Larisa and why do you care?"

He took a sip and smiled at me. "I saw your picture in the paper."

"Picture?" My head felt as though the steel vice around it had been tightened a crank. "The Daily Mail had no picture."

"The Examiner," he said.

Oh no! I had assumed only MJ's newspaper was following me. My mind slid back several months to when I remembered an Examiner reporter with photographer on the morning after the storm. They spotted me as I climbed from my shattered house, a few yards from its foundation. The explosion of the photographer's flash had gone off as I wondered if I had lost everything—everyone—in the world. "Not a good photo."

"But you're lovely."

Dang. He had distracted me from my questions and I was not in best form. Direct questioning wasn't working. I needed another tactic, but none came to my throbbing mind. I sat in silence.

He tossed his head to banish the waves of hair from his forehead. "Larisa and I were close. She was ambitious. I found that exciting and I miss her. I don't know what to do about that."

Hmmm, silence must have gotten to him. I gave him some more. It was the easiest interrogation method for someone with a migraine.

"I was with her the night she died."

"Oh." I remembered the coroner saying that she had multiple men's semen.

"She and I were close." When he said the phrase this time, the word "close" was louder.

"Oh."

"I loved hearing her talk of the world she used to know." His smile at this memory made his face look even more chiseled. "It sounded like a magical place. She planned to go back someday."

"Oh."

His silence this time showed me I needed to change tactics.

"You loved her, didn't you?"

"Loved? Admired?" He ended this with a laugh and a shrug that gave no clue to his feelings. He called the waiter over. "Put this on my tab, Skip Livingston."

"You don't have a tab," the young waiter who had moments earlier been ringing up purchases at the big brass cash register for the drug store. "Nobody's got a tab."

My vision blurred and darkened until all I could see was Skip encircled by darkness. Oh wait, but I did see someone beyond him. Someone outside the door who ducked his hat down and walked away when he saw me looking. Who was that?

"I suppose you will be going to the Karparov's ball in four days, won't you."

"Yes," he said. "Hope to see you there." He followed the waiter to the cash register to continue the conversation.

I made my way to the office. The street was clear of anyone I knew and so I didn't have to affect a smile and say "Fine" if they asked. I did what I hoped was an actual review of a contract for a shipping subcontractor. I had wanted to talk to Barker. Even if he were no longer on the

Karparov case, I wanted to know what Skip had said, but Barker was not there when I returned.

I took my migraine home as soon as I could and blocked the sun attempting to invade the parlor by closing thick curtains. The girls had fluttered around me, brought me a cold drink and not left my side even though I couldn't be much fun prone on the couch.

"On account of he needed help," Teddie said. I could hear the tinkling ice and raised the wet cloth over one eye to see her center her crystal iced tea glass on the center of the tatted coaster and then aligned all three of our glasses equal distant on the parlor table.

"Honey," I said. "Could you start the explanation from the beginning for me?"

Jinxie looked from behind her sister's starched sleeve. She opened her mouth to say something, but then it shuddered closed. Her face was still stained with tears from where our game of "My Grandfather's General Store" had stalled because she could not think of an item starting with 'q.'

I lifted my head up from the plush pillows on the couch and took the wet cloth from over my eyes. I outstretched my arms to Jinxie with wiggling fingers.

She threw herself into my arms and cried in my armpit. I hugged her and kissed her. The last hundred hadn't made her stop crying, but someday, some would. I then opened my arms and brought Teddie into the embrace. She made a sly smile, but entered and slid her arms around both of us.

I kissed their heads and felt my daughters against me. This was good and I would do anything to keep it. I released them.

"Mr. Barker told you, an eight-year old girl, he needed help?"I asked. I pressed the frown from my forehead. "A very capable eight-year old girl, to be certain, but I like to think adult men can see to their own affairs."

From the kitchen doorway, Aunt Cornelia the housekeeper frowned. Her hands astride her waist like a great, aproned Thor coming down from Valhalla to cause a bit of Ragnorok.

"Yes," she looked down at her ruffled skirt. "Well, after I asked him if he needed help, that is."

"Well that was very nice of you," I said.

I gathered what they had said and "So, you looked around in a warehouse."

"No," Teddie said. "She went through the window and let him in."

"It was after we went dancing," Jinxie said. Every week, Aunt Cornelia took the girls to the Garten Verein for a half-hour dance of older children.

"Where was the warehouse?" I asked.

"Over by your office," Aunt Cornelia said. "He was trying to look in. Well, we saw the window open and figured we could help. That Jinxie is a wiry little monkey."

"Don't he beat all, Mama?" Jinxie giggled.

"Yes, he does beat all." I didn't know if I believed that, but I wanted her to hear it in proper grammar.

Teddie took a healthy sip of iced tea and said, "I heard that when he was a vaquero, he stopped a stampede of ten-thousand head, single handed."

I turned to the girls and forced a tiny smile. My short turn of being a mother had already taught me that showing alarm is the best way to get a child to bolt the doors and put a pirate's lock on any information she might have. "What did he find in the warehouse?"

"Stacks of paper," Teddie said. "And lots of nothing."

"He said he wanted to see you," Jinxie said.

"Mr. Barker wants to see me?" <u>Why did that make me nervous?</u> The man shared a building, common conveniences, and a furnished waiting area with me. I shouldn't be scared.

"I was talking first," Teddie said. She started in a whine, realized this was unacceptable, and altered her tone to a more pleasing sound with a smile. "And Mr. Barker said I should let Mama know what we did."

Oh, that got a roll of the eyes from her little sister.

I cocked my head at Jinxie.

"She didn't do that much," Jinxie whispered.

"Did too, I was lookout." Teddie winked one of her slanting brown eyes at me.

"Over by where they're going to be building the canal," Aunt Cornelia said. "I thought you wouldn't mind since you do spend time with the man."

Why did that sound like an accusation?

"Mr. Barker gave the girls money for their little task. Very nice of him to pay for the work, and we used the money to get ice cream after the dancing lesson."

What in the name of all Christ's female cousins? "Golly," I said. "So, do you know what Mr. Barker wants from me now?"

"No, only that he wanted to see you," Teddie said.

"Tonight," Jinxie added.

"No," Teddie said, but the argument was for sport. She turned to me and said, "Yes, tonight."

A series of knocks hit the door with little power, but the unrelenting determination of that black bird in Poe's late-night library.

I covered my mouth before any swear words could come out. I tossed the cloth on the marble-topped table. Before I reached the door, I grabbed a piece of red crepe paper from the hall tree drawer, licked my lips, and gave the paper a resounding kiss. I might look like death on a soda cracker, but I would have red lips.

I opened the door and diminutive Mrs. Kelso, hunched to even look tinier stood there. The bustle on her black dress was probably the biggest part of her.

I had never seen her outside her front parlor, but the lumberman next door and the mercantile owner's wife across the street both said she was the chief source of rumors on our street. Since she was always at that front window beneath the stained glass banner of the Alpha and Omega, I suspected she used semaphore.

"Did you see this?" she waved a copy of the newspaper at me.

"Yes." I stood straight and took a deep, angry breath. "The woman was my friend. Yes, she may have been a tad on the harlot side, but she needed my help. She . . . she had faith in me."

She shot a glance at the paper and then at me. She pulled her head back and frowned as though that made me easier to get a look at me or perhaps figure out what she saw when she did. "She?" Her words had a strong, back-of-the-throat frown to them. "This is all about a man, and those roving bands of negroes that got him." She smacked a bony finger against the newsprint. "We aren't safe, none of us, none of us safe."

"Mrs. Kelso," I said. I spoke fast. I wanted her off my front porch before Barker walked up among the foxgloves. "The newspapers made up those 'roving bands of negroes', wrecking havoc.' They never existed. It was something to sensationalize and sell papers back east." I drew in a deep breath. "News reporters, sometimes I believe they are a vile lot, capable of all sorts of fiction that can ruin the reputation of—"

"Look here," she said. "It's all about those negroes."

I tried to read the blurry text around her finger as best I could and remember what I had seen of the article. I was reading much more of the paper now that my name was liable to end up on the pages. "The dairyman who was murdered was a negro. Seems he lived out on the east end of the island. Vandals or robbers came and tore up his place and stabbed him. Police have no leads on who would kill the quiet loner." I tried to imagine the scene as Mr. Barker would and use his inductive reasoning. "I'll bet he came upon them while they were at their nefarious work. They had thought the place to be abandoned as so many have been since the flood. They killed him so he would not be a witness."

"Yes," she said. "And they'll kill us in our beds. I'm thinking of moving to the mainland. Do you know how much they are going to charge me to have my house lifted up?"

"About the same as they are going to charge me," I said.

"Lift the place up so we will be away and that's when those roving bands of—"

"No roving bands!"

"Now, there's no cause to get all het up." With her arms folded across her narrow chest covered with black satin and beads, she looked as though she was the one about to get angry.

My hands circled the air in hopes of waving a bit of calm around. "We're safe over here. Fact is, no one's terribly interested in us anymore, not even roving bands of any race of hoodoo."

"Well, they just better not." She wielded the newspaper as a club on an invisible hooligan. She did not leave. I did not see any sign of Barker yet.

"I'm sorry I can't invite you in now . . .," I started to say something about the girls, but that would be a lie and I would never lie in front of them. The truth would do my reputation no good. I considered telling her of my migraine, but she might fuss over me, and I didn't like people doing that. "I can't." I smiled. "Bye-bye." I closed the door. I locked it, just in case those sinewy little old hands were pushier than polite.

I turned to face the girls and gasped.

On the sofa, big as a Bengal tiger after eating a Rajah, sat Barker. The piebald Dewey curled up beside him with his head on his leg as though the two of them had been there for hours. "I came in the back way. Teddie said I should sneak in to protect your reputation."

"My neighbors would still see you come through the back."

"Not the way I took. Thank you." He said that to Aunt Cornelia, who offered him a glass of some brown liquor I did not know was even in the house. "I went over a couple fences, crept along the perimeter, and made it across the yard when no one was looking."

The girls clustered in and sat on the floor, silent for the first time all day.

"I'll bet you that's good practice, your line of work and all." Jinxie beamed at him as though he were her favorite beau. I had never heard her say this much to a stranger. I guess he wasn't really a stranger to her, but what was he and what did he want from them?

"That's clever of you to realize, Jinx," I said. "Now what did you want to see me about, Mr. Barker?"

"I'll need your skills at translation. We'll have to go to the mainland, so we'll probably have to stay until tomorrow."

"Oh, that won't be a problem," Aunt Cornelia said from the doorway of the kitchen.

I suppose she figures she can run my life as long as she doesn't venture outside the kitchen to do it.

She looked at me and added, "The lady who cleans comes in tomorrow, we like having Miss Dash out of our way then, anyway. She's messy."

Oh great, just what I want my landlord to know. I gave her a frown I hope she found meaningful.

She smiled at me. "Go on with the man. He needs you."

The girls looked up at me as though witnessing Lady Elaine being asked to come along with the boys and find the Grail.

"I couldn't possibly without a chaperone. My sister lives in Houston, I suppose I could call her."

"I have a chaperone for you. One with whom you are familiar."

"My Aunt Gladys?" My ache-addled brain swirled up an image of Barker and I on the train with Aunt Gladys. Her party-giving days past, she hid within her sunbonnet, only looking out to condemn her neighbors as reincarnated witches or bark out an endorsement of Uneeda biscuits.

"I don't know that woman."

"Good." I pulled the paregoric bottle from my skirt pocket and downed a gulp.

"You'll need to dress differently for the part of town we will be seeing," Barker said. "Less tasteful. You don't want to look out of place in the neighborhood we will be the sort of venue where you'd stand out dressed thusly."

Thusly?

I walked upstairs, packed a small case, and put on a taffeta suit with a sable scarf and a small straw hat with black ribbon, red roses, and black netting over the eyes. If we were meeting the Vanderbilts for tea at the Waldorf, I would look fine.

Barker looked at me as though I gave him hives and not the good kind.

I kissed the girls goodbye.

I don't know how the train journey was because I slept the entire way. I remembered waking for a short time when Barker, chaperone Evangeline, and I checked into two rooms in a brownstone hotel.

Evangeline poked me. I wondered where I was, remembered, and sat up on the bed of black wood. "Mr. Barker wants to take you to supper."

"He doesn't want to take me." I combed the front and sides of my tawny colored hair without taking down my pompadour. I rearranged the swelling and dipping waves at the front, then smoothed the back into the puffed bun. "It's business. He wants me to translate." I felt a twinge inside me. It might have been the sick headache or the realization that he probably didn't need me to translate for some pleasant little babushka.

I leaned back in the taxi seat. I closed my eyes, only opening them for an instant when the cab went over a bump. I saw a glimpse of the red and white stone Houston Cotton Exchange and saw a group of men in what had to be the basement. Too much paregoric had started to work on me and might even be giving me hallucinations.

"Yes," Barker said from the red-leather bench across the cab from mine. "They were in the basement." He must have read some expression I gave when I looked out the window. "The saloon's down there. Probably where most the business occurs."

"You men and your saloons."

"And what do you mean by that, lass?"

I opened my eyes for a moment and closed them again. I thought about how I felt: too drugged to have anything more than the barest awareness of pain. Secure that I had arrived in Houston still in functioning condition and even managed to speak for myself when checking into the hotel.

My suitcase was locked in a room at a splendid hotel of brown stone and white limestone frills that delighted chaperone Evangeline. Once Barker told her she could order anything on room service and he would pay, she opted to stay at the hotel and let us investigate the creek-strewn, swampy lands near downtown Houston.

I attempted a smile, but my lips were thick. "I meant nothing by it. Just a memory that's too far gone to bother me now."

"That your husband didn't come home the night of the storm, but opted to stay in a saloon."

Opening my eyes, I saw that he sat with his normal upright posture that shamed a yardstick. I wondered who had told him and then realized the answer. "Am I so transparent?"

Barker shrugged. "'Tis my job."

I nodded. I put my hand to my forehead to exorcise the pain of that movement. "He wasn't doing anything wrong. Just the sort of thing men do in a saloon, especially on a night when they couldn't make it through the water in the streets and the streetcar had stopped running." I looked down at my hands. The gloves fight better now that I wore no wedding ring beneath. "I shouldn't mind, but I sent a boy with a message to come home around noon. He never even replied. One of many times he never even noticed me."

"You're difficult not to notice." Barker said.

I changed the subject before he could find a way to turn that nice statement into some sort of insult of women in general and me specifically. "So, has Karparov hired you back?" I asked Barker. If they had, getting him to ask me to the ball at their house would be at least a tiny bit easier.

I forced my limbs to stretch until they hurt. I needed to be vigilant, no matter how much migraine or loopy sauce I'd had.

"You're translating." Barker tipped his head to the side to show that firm jaw and taught, tanned skin. "I did not say for whom." Past him, I saw where buildings gave way to smaller buildings, to shacks, and now none at all.

I sat up all the way to see what was out there.

Great steam-powered machines puffed and made jerky motions through the mud and felled trees.

"Then why do you look as though you might break out into porcupine needles?"

He straightened his striped purple vest, buttoned his jacket, and tapped at the top of the cab for the driver to stop. "Nay, they've not hired me back yet, but I am not a man to wait until the last minute."

He helped me down to the street. Not to the street, but to the dirt that threatened to consume the rough wood buildings on one side, but dropped away to cattails and then the bayou on the other. In the bayou, launches and boats sat between the weeds. A steam dredger stood idle this time of evening on the bank. Large planks of iron had been stabbed into the weeds.

He took my arm. "This way, down the bank."

A woman in her underwear—yes, it was her corset and chemise with a thin slip for a skirt—leaned out of a glassless window of a plywood fronted that advertised both "dinner" and "meals" in broad swaths of rust-colored paint. She smiled to advertise something else. She gave me a glance, shrugged at Barker, and smiled to show most all of her teeth still in place.

Barker leaned down to look in the window of a flat-topped houseboat. He stepped onto the gangplank and gestured me forward.

I followed over the board. Below, the green water was opaque and I could not see how deep it was. This was Buffalo Bayou, not the elegant section where the Houston yacht Club met, but a construction area upstream, where work had begun on the new ship channel. This work was only a start, an effort to show the city's hope for the government in Washington to fund an expansion, so the new oil would not have to be sent by train all the way to the damaged Galveston harbor for transport. Spindletop was changing Texas, for everyone from Karparov to that woman in her underwear.

Barker led me through the narrow wooden door.

A tiny woman with a kerchief on her head and the apple cheeks, black-brown eyes, curly hair and milk-chocolate skin of a Creole smiled. "Come in. I can fit two in at a table, give me a minute."

She had that New Orleans sound, almost like when people from New York come down here. I'd heard that before, but never from a black woman.

I looked around.

Kerosene lamps set against tin cast a yellow glow on the fitted planks of the boat. Curtains in the window were dimity festooned with chrysanthemums and dogwood. Tables lay in rows. Men sat so close at these tables that getting between them required walking sideways, rising up, and sucking in.

I leaned against the wall as each of the large men's steps—about thirty of them in this small room—rocked the boat. These were big tough men and every one of them looked at the only woman in the place not the hostess. That would be me: a tall, overdressed blonde with hazel eyes and the high cheekbones of a Gibson drawing.

I flung my fur scarf around my neck. I spent lots of times in courthouses and law libraries filled, venues filled with men. These fellows were the same, even if they wore flannel shirts dungarees, and yes, I could see one with a gun in his boot and another with a bowie knife strapped to his belt.

"We are here to meet someone," Barker said. "A Mr.—"

"Oh yeah, Ivy," she said. "Back this way. He's sort of special. I'm taking care of him while he's having a spell."

We thread between the rows. I walked with Barker behind me. At least I did until someone caught my sable scarf.

"Pretty," he said. A hand with stubs of green and blistered tissue where fingers should be rubbed my scarf.

"Mine." I turned around and saw a large mustache that should have been white, but stained tobacco brown and curling over stained and grooved teeth. A face must have been attached, but my eyes couldn't get past the mouth. "I'll thank you to let go." I tugged. He did not release.

The mouth turned to a sneer meant to intimidate.

Barker turned to the mustache and said, "We don't have time for—"

I stepped before him, I looked the mustached fur grabber in the bloodshot eye—I could only find one open. He didn't scare me. I wouldn't let him, not after I'd looked into the mouth of hell in the form of a hurricane while he slept off a Saturday-night drunk up here in Houston. "I can see why you like it." I remembered to speak in a low voice. A woman can always get a man's attention and take him by surprise when she speaks low. My voice is normally a bit husky, but the morphine from the paregoric had it approaching baritone now. "And I think you're very brave to like something so feminine when all the men at your table laughing at you."

Mustache turned away from me and faced those who, if not his friends, had been his dining buddies moments earlier. Unfortunately, he had not released his grip on my scarf.

A laugh sounded from somewhere at the center of the table.

Mustache lunged for him. His move yanked me forward.

I grabbed some part of Barker and attempted to keep my head from slamming into the table.

Barker pulled a knife from a pocket and sliced through the small pelt between Mustache and me.

I looked at the end of my scarf. Where once dead animal tail and feet dangled, a straight cut exposed seams and stitching. Well, these things always did strike me as odd looking. It wasn't as if the animal was still alive and had draped it around my throat while holding hands with a friend of his species.

Barker's hand was around my corseted waist and he pulled me through the door the Creole woman held open.

Mustache made a lunge for us, but Barker yanked him by the bit of fur he still held and knocked him off his feet. Barker held the fur toward me.

"You keep it." I scrunched up my nose. I know how you've longed to have a keepsake of mine."

He shoved me behind him and away from Mustache who now delivered a series of blows to another man's face.

Behind me, I could hear the breaking glasses and falling chairs of a fight, but I did not look back.

"She does not appear to hold any animosity toward you for a fight having broken out in her place," Barker whispered. "A usual in here, I'd wager."

This back room held a chandelier full of candles, crystals hanging down like small dazzling, spear blades. I wondered if this woman was a pirate who had plundered great ships, but then I figured she was an entrepreneur who liked nice things. The bed was narrow, but had a headboard and footboard of carved pecan with an oval shield carved in place. The feather pillows were dented, but the bed made with a flowered coverlet. At a table of dark wood set with a toile cloth sat a man with thinning brown hair.

He looked down at his ironstone plate, shuddered, and looked up at us through red-rimmed eyes. He was having a bad spell of swamp fever, probably malaria.

"Ivy." Our hostess spoke a little loud, but with a pleasant timber. "These folks are here to see you."

"Yeah, *da, da,*" he said.

"That means 'yes'" I said.

"Thanks," Barker said.

Ivy gestured a yellowed, trembling hand to the empty chair across the table.

The Creole woman brought a small one covered in padded satin from the vanity for me.

"Thanks," I bade her.

"My pleasure. I'll be in with your food in a minute. Y'all picked a great night to be here."

"Thank you for seeing me, Mr. Barker," Ivy said. Swamp fever had left his voice reedy. "I do not travel much."

"Not a problem, I assure you."

"*Nyet*," Ivy said. He drank a heavy draft from the glass of bubbling, clear liquid before him. I imagined it was quinine water. The man was in worse shape than I.

I found myself thankful that I only had a migraine.

"I didn't think it would be a problem for a man fought to protect the Suez Canal such as you." He gave a sly smile that collapsed into fevered tremors.

I had stopped wondering who he was and now wondered if he would make it through an entire interview in any language.

Barker held my chair. "I brought a friend who speaks Russian to make sure I understand everything you tell me. I was sure that would not be a problem."

Ivy gave me a short bow as I sat, "Ivan Dmitrivich Volshikim. I am foreman on this project."

Russian had no articles, so there was no way to tell if this man who spoke heavily accented English meant to say he was the general foreman or a shift boss.

The men sat.

Barker said, "And before that, who did you work for?"

"You know him of whom I am having worked, you asked me before, Karparov."

Gees-o-pete, this guy was hard to understand. No wonder Barker wanted me along.

The Creole woman came up from what must be the galley below, placed a plate of green corn fritters on the table, handed Barker a bottle of a local beer. She gave me a bottle, but also handed me a pilsner glass with only a single chip in the bottom.

I realized I was probably the first female customer she had ever had. Well, the first one who wore more than a set of underwear. I smiled and took a fritter.

She watched me eat a bite.

"Outstanding," I said. It was. I started to set it down, but she smiled and waited to watch me eat the rest.

Barker filled my beer glass and slipped me a grin.

I hoped the meal was light. I would never be able to eat a huge meal with this headache.

"Where did you work for Karparov?" asked Barker.

"Baku."

"So you worked in oil," I said. That was home to most of the world's oil reserves. At least it was until Spindletop hit a gusher. I said it in Russian and then quickly in English.

"I worked for Karparov," he said in Russian. "He was there with the other oil men, but he did not work for any company or any nation. He was above that."

I spoke in a rapid whisper, following his words with the closest I could get in English.

The Creole woman gave us each bowls of gumbo. Was mine heaped with more sausage and shrimp the other two?

I dumped the rice in and took a spoonful. It was savory and spicy. "Delicious." I said. "I don't think I've ever had sausage quite like this."

"Nutria," she said. "I'm so glad you like it. I'll bring your steaks out in a minute. Have some more fritters."

I didn't have long to think of the nutria rat I was eating. Ivy launched into more talk in the language he was comfortable speaking and I had to translate.

"Many nations sent men there—England, America, what have you—to run the operations of getting the oil out of the ground, refined, transported, and all the people taken care of. Big jobs for many people. Karparov, his area was not one of the pretty ones at the sea shore. No, he was back toward the hills, remote, but there, he ruled."

"Ruled?" I asked and then translated for Barker.

"*Da*," Ivy said. "He was an emperor. All who worked there were his slaves. All who lived there only did so at his mercy." He pulled out a well thumbed little brown leather book of ill fitting pages. "I kept a diary. We were not allowed to write things down. Only he and his family."

I stopped my translation for a moment. "That means Larisa probably has always kept one. Once you're trained that way, I mean. . . "

"His daughter," Ivy said. "His princess. He groomed her to be just like him." He nodded to add effect to his words. "He even found a beautiful blond statue for her to marry."

I caught up on the translation. Beautiful, blond statue was not Dorfman.

He opened the browned and stained pages. He read and I translated in a low tone, "Karparov has made me the head of the train station. We need the loaders to work another shift, which they resist. He says I am to cut their rations, but I don't want to do this since they were already weak from the thin stew and piece of bread they ate each day. This would make them too weak to work. They could drop equipment, damaging the train or even the tracks. So, he has another idea."

"Here are your beefsteaks," the Creole woman said. She dropped a beautiful beefsteak, sizzling and smelling of meat and butter before me, before Barker, and before Ivy. Ivy carefully pulled his book away.

Before eating any, I sliced a healthy portion of mine away and gave it to Barker. I had not eaten beefsteak in a very long time. I loved it and this one was rare and tender, but I was already threatening to burst my stays. This was a meal for men who did hard labor all day, not for a woman laced into a tight corset.

Ivy's finger traced the Cyrillic characters, he read, and I followed between bites, "Karparov decided wanted to know who the worst troublemakers were. He did not ask me. He knew. He had spies everywhere." He looked at me. "That was the kind of magic he had."

Once again, magic.

Ivy continued to read. "He found them and had them beaten. They would have died from the beatings, but before they could, he had them tied to the train tracks. When the train came from Moscow and severed their heads and feet from their bodies, these heads were placed on pikes in the train station. The men worked after that. That was one of many things he did to keep order." He stared at me without blinking.

I felt a hatred for Karparov churning inside me, but I showed no emotion. I was sure of that. The old attorney I had apprenticed for would have hit me with a law dictionary if I had shown my feelings when questioning a witness. I took a slow, steady draught of my beer and said to Ivy, "You mentioned how Larisa was the princess. What of the other girl? Her sister?"

Ivy shrugged. "Her job was to take care of that mother who was always sick with this or that. No one ever noticed another girl."

I translated it, but when I substituted the phrase "paid her no nevermind," Barker looked up from his black notebook and stubby pencil to say, "I'll thank you not to improvise, Mrs. Gallagher. You were doing so well."

I smiled. He didn't mind my intrusion about Larisa. I tried another: "Was this blond statue of a man named Stanislav or 'Slava'?"

"Could have been."

"Why didn't Larisa marry him?"

Ivy hesitated. He might have been overcome by a tremor or unwillingness that he was not as close to the Karparovs in the old country as he claimed. He said, "I imagine she didn't care for him. She did what she wanted and her father let her." He smiled. "Like Teddy's daughter, Alice Roosevelt."

I got back to Barker's subject: "Why didn't anyone stop Karparov?"

"Because of his power. They dared not tell the Russian government. He was stronger than even the security police. Karparov said he protected us from the Russian Empire."

"I'll bet the Russian government loved that," Barker said.

"What could they do? He had become more powerful than the tsars."

"How?" I asked. "I've met the man. I can't see how one slightly crazy-eyed fellow is going to be able to make a more impressive fist than the wealthiest leader in the world who has an army three times the size of any other." A nudge from Barker and I translated what I had said.

"Because he had magic." Ivy's fevered intensity might be from the malaria or he might always speak that way about such things. "He started as a bureaucrat. Wealthy man with skills for organizing, to be sure, but that was all. Then, there was an earthquake." He said it in a husky whisper and with a pause as though he expected an eldritch wind to douse the lanterns or a clap of thunder to shake the boat.

I chewed, translated, and vowed internally never to eat again. Beside me, I heard Barker's pencil scribble.

"The earthquake opened cracks within the hills, strange cracks that went deep, opening to great caves. The local peasants knew to probe these with sticks. 'What are you doing,' Karparov demanded when he saw a group of shepherds one day. He knew not to believe their story that they had lost a sheep into a cave." Ivy swirled his finger around his own eyes. "He could see into their lying soul, so he explored. What he found were jewels and treasures beyond measure. What became of those shepherds, well, their family will remember them."

"With jewels, he bought the loyalty of the people?" I ventured.

"Not jewels alone. There was also the Casket of the Crown." He turned to Barker as though the man would understand his native tongue. "In the middle ages, a crown of great beauty existed, such beauty that the common people could not look on it. So, the king of this area had it placed in a stone casket. Whoever holds this stone casket rules this area, the people are totally loyal to him."

"No matter how terrible that man might be," I said.

"You have lived in America too long if you think the world is ruled by nice men." Ivy flashed me as much of a wry smile as he could between tremors.

I translated.

"So why isn't he ruling there still?" asked Barker.

I started to translate into Russian, but Ivy interrupted with a wave of his hand. "I think his claims to being stronger than the secret police were untrue. Russia might have a big army, pretty lady, but she has an even bigger security force, ready to kill her own people or at least keep them in line. In this case, they started spreading rumors that there was no crown inside."

"And he couldn't prove there was?" Barker said.

"The way to open this ancient box has been lost to history, it seems," Ivy said.

"He couldn't just rattle the thing and say, 'see, sounds like a crown to me?'" I suggested.

Ivy frowned. "You are talking about the power and majesty of a god-king!"

"I'm talking about—" I felt Barker's hand on my arm and had to take a minute to translate before I fired back, "I'm talking about an old man who found a stone box and set up one jim- dandy of a magic act for himself."

"You—" Ivy waved a finger at me; at least his tremors did as soon as he pointed. "You do not understand the mysteries of the universe. You walk around seeing only the surface. You have no faith."

"Now just a minute," I spoke English. Until I was standing, I did not realize I had gotten up from the table and thrown my red checked napkin on my now empty plate. "How can any sane person compare that old hoodoo with the sort of belief one has in our Lord and Savior is several steps beyond me. Why . . ." Oh no, all that food roiled within me. A wave of discomfort crashed and then another rose up to my gorge. I feared I would air my paunch, as the men say, any second now. That would be humiliating. Not only would Barker be forced to use a corset knife on my beautiful suit that my dressmaker and I made from a picture in January's The Delineator, but I would dishearten that sweet little Creole woman.

I stood very still.

Barker stood beside me, taking my elbow.

"You," Ivy said in Russian. "You go now. I don't think you deserve dessert, impudent young lady."

The translation had but left my lips when the Creole woman was up the galley stairs with a small bakery box tied in string. "Oh, don't you take no notice of Mr. Ivy here. He needs his rest, but you take the pecan pie with you."

"Oh bless you," I said to her.

"I can also find another way out for you." She set a small glass with a small amount of green, licorice-scented absinthe before Ivy. She set a slotted spoon over the glass and rested a sugar cube on it. She poured water from the pitcher on the table over the sugar cube. As it dissolved, the water mixed with absinthe turned to a cloudy white.

"The green fairy." Ivy cradled the glass to his chest and stretched out on the bed.

She pulled the curtains back from a window that stretched from near ceiling to the floor. I hoped it was wide enough to accommodate both my stomach and me without jostling.

Barker put a buck on the table to cover our three meals and then handed a sawbuck to Ivy. Five dollars was a huge amount of money, especially without Karparov as a client to reimburse.

"One thing," Barker said before Ivy got too far under the spell of his green fairy. "When the jig was up for Karparov and he fled to America, who of his family came?"

"His daughters, he had no sons, those bodyguards, and his wife. He left his mistress behind." Ivy sat up. "And he took me. I was valuable to him. Then I was."

"I'm sure you were," Barker said in a way that neither revealed he meant it or was being sarcastic.

Ivy took it as though he meant it and beamed. "We were alone in a new country and still managed to make something of ourselves. We are proud to live the Strenuous Life." he gave a shrug that struck me as looking particularly Eastern European. "And now you will excuse me, I must sleep the Strenuous Sleep."

"This way," the Creole woman said. She stepped through the open window and then slapped her arm out to hold back the curtain. Barker stepped through onto the tiny deck and then helped me out. The boat was steady, but the water gave a little bit of air, but most of it had the foul smell of rotting vegetation that made my stomach churn harder.

Barker turned back to her with a smile. "Your pies, if only half as good as your suppers, shall be wondrous."

"I do hope they please the gentleman and the lady"

"These bakery boxes show that you sell them to some of the other clientele in town than your own restaurant patrons. Some of the white restaurants and bakeries."

She fluffed her hands about her dress ruffles and beamed with pride.

"You have contact with people outside of this waterfront, aspirations well beyond, and you have a relationship with Ivy," Barker said.

"I'm letting him stay in that room because of the fever," she said. "He's real sick right now and needs—"

"You share that bed with him." Barker said in a matter-of-fact voice and a little less accent than usual. "There are two heads on those pillows and I doubt a man in that shape makes his bed every day."

The Creole woman eyed Barker with eyes a little glassy and afraid.

"We don't care," Barker said. "It doesn't bother us that you are of a different race."

"And you do seem kind to him," I said between swollen swallows.

She beamed a smile at me.

"But we know you were listening to everything we said in there," Barker said. "You were too quick to respond to our needs. You had a full restaurant out there and yet, our meal was brought immediately.

"I do have a boy who helps me."

Barker let a sly smile paint over his face.

"But I may have heard things."

"And so you heard how dangerous Karparov is." Barker grabbed my elbow. I had no idea I had seemed unsteady. "So a clever business woman like you knows there is no business opportunity in going to see him."

She shook her head. "Don't worry."

"Did Ivy come to America with him?" Barker asked.

"Yessir."

"Why doesn't Ivy still work for him?"

"Ivy got sick."

"Lots of people have various forms of swamp fever and that doesn't stop them from working," I said. "They have bad spells when they can't."

She shook her head. "That Russian boss fellow doesn't tolerate anyone who isn't healthy. Besides, Ivy got sick in the heart first. He seemed to think that boss, Mr. Karpar, Karpar—"

"We know who you mean," I mumbled over my rising gorge.

"Thank you. Well, he thought his boss was a bully when everything was all Russian, but when they came here, he expected things to be different."

"Yes," I said. "It is different."

"Maybe," she said. "His boss's got one of those farms, out in Sugarland.

Barker and I both looked at her. Sometimes, the witness tells you more without being questioned.

"A big plantation. A cousin of mine worked there. He got typhoid, they say. He died from it. "

"I'm sorry," I said.

"They all die. Drop like flies. They can't leave, though, because they owe money to the company. The company store makes sure of that. They buy things starting on their first day. Then, by the time they get a pay check, they owe more than they earned. They can't ever get out because they can't ever pay off all the debt they have."

"Peonage," I said. The legal term came to me for working off a debt. "I knew it was done, but I didn't know it was done to enslave people."

"Yessum," she said. "I heard tell my cousin was actually trying to run away and he got the kind of fever you get from a bullet to the head." She shook her head. "That Karpa-Karpa-Karparov fellow is mean and I'll stay away."

"But Ivy?"

"When he saw the plantation overseers were using poor men alongside the ones from prison and that the overseers liked to shoot people, well, he wanted out. You don't get out easy from one of these guy's operations. They left Ivy dead in the marsh one day." She smiled. "He's a tough old Russian, though. He survived, made it out, got a job, and found me."

I smiled back at her. I hoped everything she said was true. She and Ivy seemed good for each other and I wanted them to be good folks.

"Ivy told you what he told you, Mr. Barker." She took a step toward him with steady feet even though the boat pitched at her movement. "It weren't for no money. It was so you could make sure Karparov don't make trouble like that again. He likes it here and doesn't want things going bad."

Cabs didn't come to a part of town like this even in daylight, so we had a walk to where we remembered the last taxi stand. The ladies of the line didn't show their underwear to a man and woman with such a determined walk and my face, which was probably green.

I don't remember much of the walk to the cab or him finding one. I have a recollection of him hoisting me into a cab and then asking for the window to be opened because I couldn't raise my arms to work the one beside me. The most I could do was unfasten the beaded frogs of my jacket, but that did not help.

Earlier, I had found this to be a cold April night. Now, I seemed to be stewing in my satin coat.

The cab bounced along a cobblestone street.

Saliva increased in amounts almost too great for me to swallow. Something wasn't right with me.

"Oh no," Barker pushed me across his lap and held my face toward the open window. "Oh, we have a gusher," I heard him say. I felt him unbutton the back of my skirt and the tight buttons at the bottom of my blouse.

Oh no!

I felt the knife cut through my best shirtwaist and all to my corset lacings. I opened my mouth to protest, but well, he was right. I was a gusher.

I finished and sat back in the coach. He gave me his flask to wash my mouth out with whiskey or whatever was in there. I swizzled, spit in the rutted road, and handed the flask back, but he pressed it back in my hand to have another swallow.

I smiled. "My headache is finally gone." I felt good and full of questions for Barker.

I looped the tattered bits of sable scarf over my elbows, but it was not enough to cover the section where my body spilled from rent corset and was now too swelled to fit within my skirt and blouse.

Barker walked behind me to provide more cover.

I stood in silence on the grand staircase.

Evangeline heard us coming down the hall and opened the door. Her eyes went wide at my disarray with my jacket draped as best I could over the gash in my clothing.

I tugged at the ripped shirtwaist. "I was a bit—"

"I can see what happened." She ducked into the room, grabbed her dressing gown from the bench at the bottom of her bed, and handed it to me. I'm glad she over-packed. I hadn't brought a robe.

"Thank you," I said.

"I'll go down and see if the hotel can do something about a corset by tomorrow morning." She brushed past Barker and me, but turned back to Barker and held out her hand. "I'll need some cash."

He pulled some bills from his wallet and she grasped them in her hand before beaming a dimpled "Thank you" and walking down the hall.

"Time you were getting to bed. We have an early train." He said.

"And I hope I won't be making the journey in a dressing gown." I thrust an index finger at his chest. "You stay in the room until I get back. We have some talking to do."

When I returned, the door was open to show he had pulled an ornate chair of black wood from the hallway and propped it by the little table and the tasseled chair that came with the room. He must have called room service and they arrived during my short absence. A glass of champagne sat before the empty chair as did the bakery boxes, now with the twine sliced from tem. A pair of forks sat before the boxes.

They never came that fast for me.

The hotel room was an attractive confection of lavender striped wallpaper dissected by hydrangea nosegays and purple plush curtains with gold tassels. The high-ceilinged chamber had looked immense until this colossus sat astride a chair that, as large as it was, still creaked under his sinewy thighs.

I wondered why he was still here. I doubted my telling him to stay would have any more effect on him than it did on Dewey the cat.

He must want to know something. I smiled. I had something to bargain with: information. He probably wanted to know about that Skip fellow.

Barker took a sip of his drink from the cut glass. "Mrs. Gallagher, I doubt I should be in your room." He started for the door with his glass in hand.

"Oh Mr. Barker!" I shifted my bundle of torn clothes and corset to one arm. "I admit, I do harbor a crush on you, but I'm certain that's only because of your antagonism toward my gender."

Barker frowned.

"My competitive nature striving for something out of reach, that's all." I gave a wavy little hand gesture. I was glad he had brought it up. As embarrassing as this was to discuss, at least this wouldn't be something unspoken between us. "This will pass, just like a case of indigestion."

"No, I simply thought your headache might come back if you have too much stimulation."

"Oh." Oh dear, I didn't seem to have his gift for inductive reasoning. "You're wrong."

"As I've said, I know very little about women."

I tossed the clothing bundle on one of the large beds and covered the ripped corset and corset cover with the more respectable clothing. "How did you ever find Ivy? Masquerade as someone fresh off the boat and ask the Russians around town?" I pulled the string from one of the boxes and looked inside. Pecan pie. I looked in the other and found peach cobbler.

"Ship manifest when the Karparovs came to America. He was the only other Russian." He said. "I am no master of disguise. A man of my height cannot put on a black goatee, shoe polish his hair, and expect his closest friends to not recognize him. I've taken time to make myself known in different parts of this town as well as ours."

I took a bite of the peach cobbler. "Mmmm, this is delicious." I savored a bit. I was hungry. "I'm impressed that you got him to talk to you."

"No, but he knew me as the type of man he has seen working around here." Barker took the other box and the remaining fork. "I know how to not look like an outsider."

"So, he talked." I drank some champagne. "And he had a line of palaver that sounded true."

"In his condition, the man would have had to work very hard to come up with a false tale."

I sat on the bed beside Barker. Yes, an intimate position with my knees almost touching his and my chemise and French drawers only covered by a robe that was too small for me, but Evangeline should be back at any moment, and he was not the man to get frisky with my virtue. "He told us Karparov is a monster and certainly a man who would kill, even kill someone he loves if they got in the way of what he wanted."

Barker looked at his drink, but gave a little nod.

I took another drink of champagne. "I met a boyfriend of Larisa's. He was with her the night she died. I think he's after the magic box, so that means he doesn't have it."

"How do you know?" He shook his glass so the liquid left in it spun around.

Because I don't see a man being interested in me without an ulterior motive. "Because he asks a lot of questions?"

"You guessed," he said. His voice held an iron rod of accusation in it, as though guessing were right up there with coveting and lying like a cheap toupee.

"I inferred from the evidence."

"Do you have any evidence?"

"I have quite a lot that goes to motive, state of mind. Wait a minute, you didn't ask what the evidence was, just if I had any."

Barker smiled. He pulled a half-empty bottle of champagne from somewhere under the table cloth and filled my glass. "I told the waiter to leave the bottle."

"Thanks," I said. I gave my robe sash a tug to secure it. "Let's start with this. They didn't take the van Dyke over the couch, so they weren't a robber who just found a nice house in the neighborhood. The person was after that little stone box."

"Very good, Mrs. Gallagher."

I flushed and not because of the champagne. "So, Papa might have killed her because she stole it."

"But that limited his ability to get it back."

"And then there's her sister didn't get her mitts in Slava—hey, that's who was watching me through the drug store window at dinner—get her mitts into Slava when Larisa was finally out of the way."

"Work one theory until you're done with it," Barker said. He stretched his legs out and slouched in the chair. "

"Sister seems to prefer Dorfman. Maybe he killed his wife to be with her.

Barker raised an eyebrow in my direction.

"Although they aren't together and I cannot see him doing anything like that. Oh, stop eyeballing me! I'll go back to the first theory. Those were sort of bursting out of me." I savored another spoonful of cobbler. "There's also the one about her lover having gotten jealous and done it. Or Dorfman in a jealous rage because of his wife's infidelity, but while I can see Dorfman cold enough to kill someone, I don't see him having the passion to kill his wife. I mean, he seems to be someone who slumps and sulks, not gets revenge. So, I just can't see him as the murderer."

"Bouncing all these theories around is like seeing someone play tennis with themselves." Barker attacked his pie with a fork. "It cannot be done well."

"Okay, Dad wanted her to be one thing, but she insisted on going her own way. You know, she intended to go back to the old country. I think to take over the family business. That could make him angry, maybe angry enough to kill."

"But Ivy said Karparov trained her to be his heir to the throne he had created."

I felt a bit of triumph and toasted Barker with my champagne glass. "Oh, I noticed something you didn't! But you said women were your blind side."

"And that is?"

I let the triumph linger for a moment. "He wanted her to be a princess. That's very different from wanting her to take control while he is still alive. He wouldn't want her to be the empress who vanquishes him and he could kill her for trying."

Barker gave me such an appraising look, I wondered if he might give me a kiss or a pat on the head and a "good dog." He took another drink.

This seemed a good time to beg. "Mr. Barker, I know you don't have Karparov as a client yet and I also know he is perhaps one of the most pernicious bits of evil in our world today, but he is having a ball next week. Yes, a ball. A big dance with organza, and punch, and 'you waltz divinely, my dear.' I would love to go and you would be the only one I know who could possibly get an invitation." I felt my hands lunge forward to grab his arm, but I saw he was still eating and also realized this would spook him something fierce. I clutched them to my breast. "I'm sure you could find a way to take me."

He looked at his whiskey glass that was now empty. He poured a bit of champagne in and watched it fizz for a moment before taking a drink. 'Mrs. Gallagher, do you have any reason to believe Larisa took the casket? Other than the fact I told you."

I thought. I thought very hard. I had nothing. I could think of no piece of actual evidence, nothing that placed. Oh wait. "Wagon ruts?"

"Excuse me?"

"Wagon ruts that you examined in the street before the Dorfman house. They weren't in front of the Dorfman house. Something heavy left from there. So, Larisa or Dorfman, the occupants of that house, would have been the ones to take the heavy stone box."

Barker smiled at me and I felt as good as I had when I won the fourth-grade spelling bee, but then he shook his head.

I continued: "Occupants of that house took it somewhere. So, I'd say Larisa stole the thing."

Barker's smile crashed and his face, looked like red granite. "When did she take the magic casket?"

"The maid said—"

He pulled those long legs to a standing position faster than I had ever seen a person move. "It is late and I must go. Barker walked to the door and with his back to me said, "Good night, Mrs. Gallagher."

"Mr. Barker," I said. My hands slid over the ties of my robe as I willed them not to soar and dive in my usual dramatic gestures. "I have noticed your failure to answer me about the upcoming ball that the Karparovs will hold. You should know that I would willingly take an invitation to that instead of payment for my assistance tonight."

I stood and turned the key to extinguish the gas lamp so he could not see my face that I knew held a mix of hope and fear.

Evangeline knocked on the open door and came in with an armload of ruffled petticoats, feathered hats, and braid-trimmed gowns. "You wouldn't believe what people leave in the lost and found."

Barker tipped his head to her in greeting, turned around, took his wallet from the front pocket of his pants, and pulled out a bill. He slapped the twenty on the table before me.

"Mr. Barker, I couldn't take this much—"

"Good night, Mrs. Gallagher, Miss Evangeline." He said and walked from the room. He closed the door behind him.

I locked it, not for fear of him coming back, but from general habit. I was deep within my thoughts of what to do and what would happen to me if I arrived at the party without an invitation.

Could I pass myself off as a long forgotten member of the family?

I remembered something.

Something so important, I got up and ran down the hall. Where was Barker's room?

Chapter 11

Barker glanced at his watch while I shot a glance to the marble clock on his desk. Three minutes to nine. He must have a client any second. I was probably in his way, but eagerness to shoo me out of here might make him agree to find a way to take me to the ball.

"She may have called someone an aunt who was not exactly a true relative," I said to Barker, taking a perch on the edge of his desk. I brought this up as if it were a new conversation and not why I had knocked on his hotel-room door last night. Last night, he had said nothing except, "Go to bed," before he closed the door.

Barker stood and looked out the window.

"I don't think Ivy lied about having no other relatives here."

"No, I doubt he did."

"Aunt is a title of respect down here." I kicked my free leg; the other moored me on the floor. Each kick sent my skirt parachuting in an arc of sky blue velvet. At least the bottom part did, the top stayed safely moored with silver soutaches and dark blue welting all the way up the high, tight waist and beyond to the loose jacket. I smoothed the wrinkles from the grosgrain mourning band around my velvet sleeve. "Southern girls have all sorts of Aunts. I assure you, my own Auntie Malvie was a spinster who seemed to have been left at the railroad station Lost and Found."

He looked over his shoulder at me. "I believe you're making that up."

"Sadly, no," I said. I rolled the pen across the blotter between my hands. "The family would have preferred to have her as kin to my eccentric Aunt Gladys and in a way made things harder for me. I don't expect you to understand that."

Barker rubbed his temple where the black hair had started to silver. "Because you were adopted and they worried insanity ran in the blood, a worry from which you were mercifully safe, being adopted?"

I missed my grab of the pen, and it rolled to the floor. Squinting my large eyes until they must have been hazel slits, I stared at Barker.

Barker leaned over and plucked the pen and its severed nib from the floor with one massive hand. He placed them on the desk between my hands. "Your last name is not Russian, but your first name is part of a very Russian naming convention. Your college roommate who is a family friend did not know you are of Russian descent. This sounds as if you were adopted at an age when you were old enough to speak. Learning English must have been difficult."

"I was teased a lot as a kid," I said. "Or worse were the people—kids and adults—who would say, 'Oh, you're the kid from Russia. Say something in Russian, come on say something.' Like I was a trained seal performing in a circus." I felt my leg stop kicking. I stopped rolling the pen between my hands and looked at Barker. "I liked seeing Larisa. She had an accent. I didn't. I've overcome that. Oh, I don't mean I was stronger than she."

"I believe you were."

I laughed. "No, I meant that I was glad to see how she went through life and came here in circumstances that, although privileged, were similar to mine. She was never embarrassed for it. You just have to like that." I smiled at Barker.

He did not smile back. He did not have any expression at all. "Mrs. Gallagher. In the short time I have known you; I have seen nothing for which you should be embarrassed."

Why thank   "

"You comport yourself at times as driven by the impulses of pure logic."

This had to be the highest praise a man of such scientific habits could offer, and so I offered him a smile that made my apple cheeks rosy and sparkled in my large eyes.

He returned my look with a sour smirk and his chin set even higher than normal. "But at other times as though animated by the din of pixies whispering nonsense in your ear. Still, it is your own way and you should be proud of it."

"Oh thanks ever so," I said. I slid from the desk.

"Where are you going?"

"Um," I had a full day of briefs to write, a contract to draw up, another lost client to win back, and a trust to update, but I said, "I figured I would go to my office. The signals from the pixies come in so much clearer there." I fluttered a hand through the damp air to indicate the direction of the ethereal signals.

"Yes." A heavy frown jutted out that full lower lip and creased his brow. "I was expecting you to stay through Karparov's appointment." He glanced at the clock. Two minutes after the hour by that clock.

"Karparov has an appointment?" I spun around so fast, my velvet skirt caught the air and circled to almost knee height with a good amount of red and white striped taffeta petticoat up there with it. "He's come back to you?"

"I'm surprised you didn't know, the phone being between our offices and all." Barker affected a stance of surprise complete with hand to heart straight out of a traveling melodrama, the type of melodrama by one of those companies where the patent medicine features in the script and the ingénue hangs around the saloon after the performance. "And your phrasing puts out an image of lovers running through fields for an embrace that I find doesn't suit Karparov and damn—pardon—darn sure doesn't suit me."

He figured I heard his phone calls. He must then hear mine. What about my one with Judge Reams? Was he not interested in taking me because I wouldn't confide in him why I wanted to go?

"Mr. Barker, I have to go to the Karparov's ball for my girls. You see—"

A firm knock sounded at the door.

"I have no more interest in why a woman wants to go to a party than the latest fashion in millinery or the best way to use curling tongs."

"Your clients are here," I said. I felt my hand point at the door, but none of the rest of me moved.

"They came five minutes late, they can wait." He held my shoulders and guided me to a visitor chair.

The knock sounded on the door harder.

"A moment," Barker called. He turned to me with a soft look in those deep blue eyes. "One thing I don't understand is why Larisa came to you."

"Black—"

"Aye, I know she was being blackmailed. I don't know why she would care. What did she want you to do about it?"

"Larisa had kept saying, kept asking me." I looked to the corner of the hammered copper ceiling where memories formed. "Ever since she came back from seeing her aunt in Chicago, even though I know she probably didn't have an aunt there." I looked Barker in the eyes. "Do you think she even went to Chicago?"

"I'd bet on it," Barker said. "But what did she want from you?" He crouched over the chair and held my arms, not tight, but not in a grip that was going to release any time soon.

"I'm so sorry Mr. Barker, I don't know. She gave me the letter she got, but changed the subject when I would get around to the topic of blackmail. I'm sorry. I figured that since she was paying me, she could talk about whatever she needed to talk about."

"Quite all right."

Those broad fingers on my arms kept me from falling against the plush seats. "Larisa had said that her parents lived here, they're building a big house in Houston, but they're main home is still here. She would mention them and how much she wanted to reconcile with them. She said how she expected me to be their attorney since I was the most prominent lawyer here." I smiled and forced my eyes up to meet his even if it was through my lashes. "I explained to her that I wasn't. She said I must be since I was in such a beautiful office building, the nicest on the island and to share a floor with you. She knew who you were. She even said that if her parents hired a detective, they would hire you." I looked at his desk. I saw he had put that picture of the evil woman back on corner. "She mentioned them and even you often." *Oh please help him not to wonder what sorts of things I said about him!*

Barker stood. "Ta." I'd heard him say that before to mean "thank you." He turned away from me and opened the door.

The clerk Barker called "Clark"—either from accent or the man's actual name—walked in with an impatient looking millionaire whose hair flowed free.

Karparov rounded the young man, looked at me, and said to Barker, "Ah, I see what detained you."

I stood to leave, but felt Barker's hand on my arm. "You've met Mrs. Gallagher."

Karparov lunged forward for my hand.

Clark gave Barker a nod and left. He closed the door behind him, but through the glass I could see he ran down the stairs and away from us.

Karparov held my hand gently and bent over it to deliver a kiss. His lips lingered on my glove longer than I would have liked, and when he released me, there was a spot of moisture on the white cotton.

Barker formed a tall barrier even with his hands in his pockets for a casual pose. "She speaks Russian, so if you are at any loss for words."

"Really?" Karparov raised his eyebrows and smiled with the same enthusiasm anyone else would show when learning someone else spoke their language. "You are from Russia?"

I shrugged.

Barker grabbed one of those large walnut and plush green visitor chairs with a single hand and swung it beside his desk and gave me a look with those thick brows inching up on his overhanging brow. He allowed his eyes to penetrate my being for an instant and then gestured to the chair.

"I learned it in college," I mumbled.

I strode to the chair, smoothed my skirt, but did not take a seat.

Karparov gave me a sideways glance that looked as if he could not be bothered to put on his best scare-the-peasants glare, but he said, "That is excellent! I will have to change my impression of American education. They teach a real language to all classes."

So, I'm a peasant even if he didn't know from whence I came.

"You had the maid open the house for us," Barker said.

"Yes," Karparov said from behind a yawn stifled with a wavy hand. "This is a distraction. I say we—"

"The maid opening the house." Barker strode around his desk and to the window, his hands pressed deep in his pockets and his arms holding his suit-jacket back. "That would be Polly, wouldn't it?"

"Yes, she's one of my many servants," Karparov said to his cuticle.

"The one you're having an affair with."

Standing between desk and chair with my hands clasped together and my voice a near monotone, I translated.

"I know what he meant," growled Karparov. He looked at Barker. "Polly would never say such a thing."

I glided down to the chair.

"No, you did." Barker's face held the barest bit of a smile, no, more of a hint of smirk at me. "By giving a maid unprecedented access to the house including the liquor cabinet and buying a pair of ruby earrings for her very recently. This was obvious because of their modern design. They were well beyond what a maid could afford."

Rubies? I guess I had assumed garnets. I looked from Karparov to Barker and back to Karparov. The men were locked in a staring match.

"Yes." Karparov broke off his gaze and looked at me. He said in Russian with a sneer and I translated with no expression, "She is the only woman able to accommodate a man such as myself." Karparov smiled as though this was impish and adorable.

I daubed my mouth with my lace handkerchief before I tossed it in the wastebasket at Barker's feet.

"But, Barker, my friend." Karparov's words came out through a slight smile in a seductive coo. "This has nothing to do with why I hired you. Find my precious object."

"Aye, the magic casket," Barker said. "Where do you keep it?"

Karparov hesitated.

"Honesty." He gave a gesture toward the door and leaned back in his chair with his arms folded across his chest. "You can leave now if you do not intend to be honest." "In everything you say."

I translated this, more for sport than because I thought Karparov needed it.

Karparov gave a shrug. "I suppose I—"

"I need the truth of where it was and when it was taken." Barker's voice rose to a husky shout with his accent as thick as a tartan blanket. "I have no idea why you would hire me to get the thing back when you do not give me any of the information I need to know."

"I want you to find where the thing is." Karparov also shouted. "Not where it was."

"I need to know where it was." Barker took a paper from his coat pocket. "To see where it was." He slapped the paper into Karparov's hand. "And my price is now double what my earlier quote had been, so say nothing more if you do not accept that deal."

Karparov looked at me, either to take a moment to think or because he knew a contract attorney witnessed this exchange of consideration. "On the second floor of my home I have a room built for it." He scratched the side of his nose as he spoke. "Brick walls. I had to reinforce the floor. The whole house, it is designed to my specifications."

"How nice for you." Barker folded his arms across his chest. "Did you ever take anyone up to see it?"

"My business associates occasionally viewed it." Karparov said. "I host supper parties and tell them of my success in Russia, my success everywhere." He stood. His arms swirled around his head. "The power of that casket is intoxicating. I came to this country and only then has the success of Spindletop matched that of the Baku—"

"Aye," Barker said with the short snap one uses to command a dog. "This will go faster without the histrionics. How long has this been missing? Stand or sit, whichever way is more comfortable for you to narrate."

He huffed down to the settee. "Three weeks."

"So, a couple weeks—not a couple days—before the mur—," I said. "Um—Before Larisa's death."

Karparov turned to Barker. "Was there anything you wanted to say?"

"So, the magic box has been missing a full two weeks before the mur-um-Larisa's death?" Barker said with no expression.

"Yes, yes," Karparov said.

"And you suspected your daughter, Larisa, had taken it." Barker leaned back until the brass fittings of his large, leather-covered office chair creaked.

"Yes."

I leapt in. "That is why you had the family come to supper at your house."

Karparov leaned forward and spat out, "Yes, but she did not come. She was dead in Galveston Bay that night. We have gone through her house here on the island and found nothing, nothing. I do not think she took it after all."

Barker licked his pencil and picked up his small black notebook. "Where is her house here?"

"You will find nothing."

"Very well." He snapped the notebook closed. "I can find it from the city records."

"I can help with that." I gave Barker a reassuring nod, although many Galveston records had washed away in the tide, and Houston lost theirs in a fire the year before.

Barker's smile faded when he turned back to Karparov. "You were saying the address."

Karparov rolled his eyes. I'd seen that from Teddie when I sent upstairs to develop a better attitude. "Broadway, of course." He gave an address amidst the remaining granite and limestone mansions.

"And as for the box," Barker said to the notebook in which he scribbled. "What do the carvings look like?"

Karparov gave a little sneer. "Do you think you would mistake it for another carved stone box from antiquity?"

"Mrs. Gallagher," Barker said. "If you would repeat the question in Russian, perhaps that would aid in cooperation."

I repeated and with only the barest trace of a giggle.

"It has an arch at the top and carved lace bits around that. Then, at each corner there are columns with carving at the top. Between all this, there is lacework; flowers, animals, things like this."
"

"It's an iconostasis," I said.

Karparov's face lit with his smile that revealed his old, yellowed teeth. "Yes, exactly."

"That's a sacrilege!"

In Russian, Karparov said, "You are an old fashioned peasant."

"You make me—"

"Translate," Barker growled.

I translate what Barker said, finished with you, "You make me sick," and repeated it in Russian for Karparov.

Karparov chuckled until I thought he would choke on his own mirth. "You are the smallest of minds, the easiest to control. I can find your heart and crush it. I do it for sport."

I translated this.

He was a bully. How did I tell my girls to deal with bullies? Agree with them. They are never as sure as they pretend.

"Yes." I spoke English, the language of my thoughts. "I'm sure you can. Galveston is full of widow women and breaking their heart for sport would be easier than, say, building an orphans home or—"

"If we could get back to the subject." Barker's voice boomed and his feet rocked back and forth on the Persian rug.

"Swear you will give me find my cask and everything that is in it." Karparov spoke Russian. "Before I tell you any more, swear upon your honor as a gentleman that you will return the cask to me with its contents intact."

I translated in hushed tones.

As a lawyer, I could see Barker was a man trying to find loopholes, but I doubt he could find any since I sure couldn't.

Karparov looked at me and said, translate: "Swear you will recognize me as its rightful owner. Ah yes, and owner of all the contents within."

"No!" I shouted.

Hatred puffed Karparov's chest and swelled out his nostrils. "I offer something people want. I give them security and for those who deserve it, power with me. I help them. What have you ever done for anyone?"

I curled my lip and translated. I stood with my back to the grinning Russian and whispered to Barker. "But you can't do this. Think of what he is. Think of what he's done. He's asking you to make a deal with the Devil."

Barker's heavy brow crumpled into a frown. "Go back to your seat or get out of here."

I spun to face Karparov.

The man smiled, master of all the fires of damnation and a few points north.

I'll bet your daughter showed up that night. I'll bet you murdered her when she wouldn't tell you what she did with your precious magic box. I walked back to the chair and slid down.

He may have read all that in my look. His smile grew wider.

Barker said: "I swear upon my honor as a gentleman that I will return the cask to you. I will recognize you as its and all of its contents rightful owner."

"Oh no, Mr. Barker," I said in a soft voice.

"Oh yes," Karparov said. "I now own you."

Yes, Mr. Karparov. You own that section not used by my other clients."

"That would be your soul." Karparov gave a single clap of approval at his own work.

I mumbled, "Seeing as how you've taken on Satan as a client, I'm somewhat inclined to agree."

Barker caught my elbow and pulled me up near even with him. He whispered in my ear, "This is a powerful man. As a gentleman, I'll protect you as much as I can, but you would do well to not antagonize him so damn—pardon me—goddamn much." He released my elbow and I fell back into the chair.

"Protect me?" I mouthed at him in a wordless shout. I did not see a henchman to this Mephistopheles protecting me from him nor did I want him to do so.

Karparov looked to the transom. I figured he believed the reflected light it lit his watery eyes with a magic glow. "For centuries, that box did not exist except in stories. The old king in that valley was unable to choose between his three sons, so he had them share power; the power was in the crown, not in the leader. Each would take his turn, take the casket with the crown and wear it for a year. One brother was ruling, but he gave his wife the casket and allowed her to rule. He became ill and died when he should have had the crown. The power of the casket, but one brother thought the third had poisoned him. The other brothers killed each other in a sword fight."

Barker leaned forward.

Karparov continued with a smile. "The royal brothers died, but the crown remained. An advisor took it and became the strongest man with the largest army. He was the rightful leader because he had the crown in the casket. Over the years, many fought for it, but the one who could claim the crown ruled the valley. It was lost and the kings were gone." He leaned forward and with a soft voice and finger held up for the great celestial count, said, "but then I found it and I ruled the world."

"And you wore the crown?" Barker asked.

"The magic is too great! It must remain in the casket. Remove it wrong, and the stone will fall in to crush the crown, destroying it." Karparov stood and grasped the air before him. "I had it, that was important. I need to still have it. That is why I am willing to pay you an incredible sum of money to get it back. Do you understand what I will do to you if you do not get it back to me right away?"

"Mr. Karparov," Barker said. He opened his drawer and put away the notebook. "I endeavor to make all my clients satisfied. "Until it is returned, I suggest you tell those you usually impress with it that it is out getting cleaned."

Karparov started. Once again, Barker appeared to have answered a question not yet asked.

"Is there anything else?" Barker asked. He looked at me, not at my face, but at the top of my pompadour. I wonder if my hat had left a dent. Perhaps he noticed that my blonde hair color had assistance with lemon juice and a little peroxide combed through on occasion. "Anything?"

I opened my mouth, but nothing came out. I wanted to go to the ball, but I could not ask Karparov for this. This man used indebtedness as a currency jotted down the ledger at his company store for those poor men who would never leave the servitude of his sugar plantation.

"No," I said. "Nothing else."

Karparov pointed a bony finger at me. "She is upset with you, Mr. Barker. I'll bet you were supposed to remember something and will catch it from her later on. An anniversary perhaps? Or one of her daughter's birthday. Yes, Nina told me you are a mother and still run around doing whatever you want." His growl implied that "whatever you want" was not knitting and volunteering at the veterans home.

He stood. He straightened the handkerchief in his pocket with great care rather than extend a hand to Barker. "Whatever it was, when you get my paycheck for finding the cask, I am sure all will be well. For now, goodbye."

Barker followed him down the stairs.

"Mrs. Gallagher," Barker said when he returned to his office and saw me unmoved from the chair. "Why are you still here?"

I rose from the chair and started to put it back in its original place before the desk, but Barker took the heavy, ornate furniture from my grasp and wrangled it back to its proper place with one hand. I asked: "You know the Karparovs are having a ball to celebrate their daughter — their live daughter—and her engagement tomorrow?"

He walked around me to his desk and looked out the window. "I see no reason why that concerns us."

"What better time to get a good look inside the house."

He did not turn around to face me, but stood in that almost impossibly straight posture with his hands in his pockets. "

"They will be busy," I said. "They won't stand in your way, especially with me there to distract them. Yes, Mr. Barker, that ball is the opportunity we need. I expect you to take me. I will be at my house tomorrow evening, awaiting your arrival."

I kicked my skirt around and walked out.

He was silent.

Well, at least I didn't hear laughing.

Chapter 12

"No," Coralie screeched. "You can't wear that."

My off-the-shoulder dress of green moiré and black organza had been altered for a fashionable, blousy inset of black organza. Feathery designs of black beads scattered over the bodice and skirt. The gored skirt went straight and a little tight through my thighs, but blossomed out into a full skirt. The sleeves and hem were trimmed with what had been remnants of my torn sable wrap, now a narrow band of elegant black fur.

I had felt like this before, but very long ago. When? Ah yes, the tense, but exciting moments before I walked down the aisle at my wedding.

I slipped the thick black ribbon over the sleeve.

Coralie snatched it from my hands. "I said you can't wear that," She wound it around her fist. "If you were in mourning all proper, you wouldn't go to a ball. You're not going to mess it up with that."

I said nothing. I found myself unable to make a sound due to emotion far in excess of what the moment merited.

"The girls are right," Coralie said. She wrapped herself around the door to look in from the hallway. "You do look lovely."

"Thank—"

"Shame you don't have an escort and you're going to end up scandalizing the whole family," she said.

"I'm an old widow woman." I flapped my best pair of kid gloves a few times to soften the thin leather. I had not worn the gloves for, gosh, since I got married ten years earlier. "No one cares about me."

"You believe that?" Coralie asked.

"I want to." I slid the glove on.

The door knocker sounded at the front door.

I ignored it and let Aunt Cornelia answer. Actually, I pretended I didn't hear so I wouldn't hope Barker was there and then end up disappointed.

Coralie came in the room, grabbed a buttonhook off the dresser and wangled first one and then the other glove in place.

"Miss Dash," Aunt Cornelia called from downstairs. "There's a taxi here for you."

"Damn," I said.

Coralie took up an atomizer of perfume and spritzed me in the face.

"Watch my face. Those cosmetics don't come cheap."

"I thought you had those things on. You lips look like you've been sucking on berries." I grabbed my short cape with flounces of organza along the edge and pulled Coralie behind me down the stairs.

Yes, yes, there he was. I had wanted him to be here, but never imagined he would

"Coralie, this is my landlord, Mr. Barker."

Coralie eyed him for an instant and returned the gaze to look up the vast length of him. "I'm her sister."

With his hair slicked back, and muscular form bound within wing-tip shirt, swallow-tail coat, and striped pants, he was elegant enough for a shirt advertisement. His overhanging brow, high cheekbones, and square jaw looked handsome to the type of woman who had no interest in the sort of fellow who spent as much time on his hair style as she did.

"Here," Barker said. He handed me a small pink box. Had Mrs. Hulpke sent him with more cookies for the girls? Then I realized how light it was and the smell.

"Thank you," I said. I opened the box to reveal a spray of waxy gardenias with baby's breath between. "They're my favorite." I smiled at Barker and was still looking at his implacable face when I handed the box to Coralie and pinned the blossoms to my waist. "Our grandmother used to raise them."

Coralie gave a laugh at the memory. "She was always telling us not to touch them. I lived in fear of turning the things brown."

Without any concern for what it might do to my dress or corsage, I hugged Jinxie and kissed her cheek, and I hugged Teddie and kissed the top of her head.

"Oh!" Coralie said. The vowel ratcheted out as a scowling sigh. "As if you won't ever see each other again."

I gave her a hug and then walked out on Barker's arm.

The front door was guarded only by the old butler who remembered Barker and admitted us easily. Now, I wondered if we would get thrown out with élan when Karparov's bodyguards caught sight of us.

The Karparov ballroom on the first floor of the house was roller-rink size and decked out with about as many windows as Versailles. Modern tables of carved wood and couches of brocade velvet lounged around, the edge of the room. Lilies, white roses, and gladiolas hung from the drapery, curved around columns, and languished over the two mantles in the wood-paneled room. Black ribbons attached to the ends of the swags and over the windows paid deference to the memory of Larisa.

Beneath the windows, glass doors opened to a veranda to where a string quartet played a schottische. No one danced, all stood. The dance floor was empty, although this should be the time for dancing. Food was always served later at a ball.

An old woman in a matte, black dress of deep mourning leaned toward a pair of young women in white dresses and laughed at a joke the younger women shared with only smiles. She then joined the other widows in black dresses and veils.

I looked at them. I knew I belonged with those old ladies, but being a respectable widow woman was not my mission tonight.

Several men and a few women sat on wooden chairs to balance small plates. A group of men with flowered swags across the front of their tailcoats drank from whiskey glasses.

I looked at a gas lamp in the corner and took a deep breath. Familiar, almost at least, feelings soothed me and loosened my grip on Barker's arm to where he could probably get circulation in those fingers. Yes, I had once felt like this.

Then, I remembered when and the air slid from my lips, I felt as though my health corset was too tight to admit any more oxygen to my lungs. I was nervous, yet not unhappy. In fact, giddiness came in waves.

My wedding. That was when I felt like this. Ten years ago, when I clung to the arm of my husband and a glittering church full of people watched us walk out to start our future together until death did us part.

Chapter 13

"Steady on," Barker said. His un-gripped arm care around and grabbed mine beneath my sleeve.

The last pieces of my old life fluttered from me in the archway to the ballroom. I had never been in this room before, and it had nothing to do with the husband who died when a building collapsed into the swirling flood waters. Still, I knew in my soul that walking into the ballroom would take me away from that past and to a future that might have adventure, but lacked the one thing I had always thought of with my husband, security.

"It will all be over before you know." Barker stepped forward, patted my hand.

I shot a glance at the widows behind the colonnade, and my hand went to feel the sleek fabric of my sleeve without the black band. Even after my husband passed, I had the protection afforded a widow, a respectable woman. I stepped forward.

A kick of my skirt, and I glided up the three marble steps to the great ballroom. I was to make my way on my own and do what I thought right rather than what was respectable thing for a married woman to do.

I had seen ballrooms in a home before, even if that was only at a Southern Heritage Society ball where we paid a donation to get in, and the midnight meal consisted of little more cold chicken and milk punch. Those long, rooms had been built before the war to accommodate a set of quadrille dancers and a few older folks in seats along the edge. This room, as wide as it was long, rivaled the size of the new ballroom in Harmony Hall.

Straight ahead, a raised podium, not as high as a stage, but enough to keep them dry if minor flooding from the local bayou came in the hall, lay swathed in oriental rugs. A red, brown, and black rug with tassels on the ends rolled out behind a set of four high-backed chairs. Karparov sat beside his wife. Karparova stretched over two chairs because she leaned her elbow on the second. On one side, stood an empty chair, on the other was the blonde, Nina leaning toward a big fellow with dirty blond hair who I remembered as a pallbearer at Larisa's funeral.

I whispered, "They've got a throne room."

"Remembering old times," Barker said. He stepped past the throne, gave Karparov a nod and headed toward craggy men drinking whiskey. He tried to disengage my arm, but I rewound myself around him.

Along the left wall, a colonnade leant extra support to the upper story. In the midst of these crepe-draped columns, about seven or eight women in black ranged from a white-haired, wizened granny sitting in a chair pressed back against the wall to a voluptuous woman with a modern pompadour who stood to show how black suited her. These were the widows. They looked at me as Barker and I entered.

They're looking at him, I told myself. They don't know I should be there with them.

Barker swelled his chest and drew in a great draught of cape-jasmine scented air. "Those gentlemen are who I plan to observe right now. No proper woman belonged there."

I shook my head so hard, I thought it might rattle. I was not going to give in to propriety now. "No, they're the ones I have to find out about."

He detached from me, but stood in front of me with a stare.

"Judge Reams, the one handling my daughters' adoption. He wants me to snoop."

Barker frowned. "I had no—"

"So, there you are," said a voice behind me.

I turned to see Skip.

In his evening coat, he looked like youth, beauty, and a memory of the best Christmas present ever. "I thought I was going to be your escort tonight."

"Oh . . . uh . . . oh my." *Oh my stars and garters! I had two dates!* I had invited both men. I remembered something about this ball when I had that migraine, but I couldn't remember exactly what I said. "I'm so sorry."

I heard Barker's feet march away over the granite floor.

"You look so beautiful," Skip said. "Just stand there and let me admire you."

"Well, standing still isn't my greatest skill," I said.

The orchestra started a pretty bit of Viennese pastry in the form of a Schubert waltz.

"Then let's dance," he said.

I set my empty punch glass on an end table. I looked around. I could not see Barker, but I did not need him right now. With my work finished for Judge Reams, I could focus on eliminating suspects.

I looked at Skip and reminded myself that handsome doesn't mean innocent.

He led me to the dance floor and I raised my arm for him to sweep me away in the waltz, but he did not put his arm around me. He took my hand and strode onto the floor with one arm forward, the other back, as one would for a polka.

"Isn't this a waltz?" I said. My voice held the slight grit of panic in it. He started to move me forward, but only the top half went. My legs stood as stiff as those of a balking horse.

"Yes," He stepped behind my raised arm and slid an arm around my waist, his head over my shoulder turned to me with a smile of straight teeth. "But don't you think a cakewalk is so much more fun and I don't think those codgers can play one, do you?"

The radiation of that smile filled me with a little confidence.

Oh why not? The widow section was already staring at me.

To the strains of Strauss, we strode around the floor. I caught my skirt up and added a step-step-back-step from the Mazurka.

"Now, you're getting fancy!" Skip said. He smiled as though I won the blue ribbon for the prize cake at the fair.

I beamed. "You're very nice. No wonder Larisa doted on you."

"Excuse me?" he said. He attempted a skip.

I did his step, but in double time. "She doted on you. I'm sure she did."

"I don't know." Skip said.

"Where did she spend her last night?"

"At her place, I guess. She was there when I left."

From the dais, Nina stood and batted Slava's arm. He looked at her with a frown that indicated he thought she was nothing more than an annoying mosquito. She stepped down from the dais and whispered to the bandleader.

The music ended and Barker was at my elbow. "Did you have fun?"

"As a matter of fact, I did, but I wouldn't think you cared."

"I don't." Barker took my hand and led me to the windows. "Getting to work now." He nodded toward a one-armed man. "He is the lead engineer for the biggest play at Spindletop. That German man is another. The men with them are owners, major stockholders in the Galveston Beaumont Oil Company and Humble Oil. That information should be what your Judge Reams should want."

"Thank you, Barker." I met his eyes with a smile that he did not return.

Barker spoke in such a soft voice, he had to lean toward me for me to hear. I could feel his breath on my ear. "Reams is up for reelection this year. He wants to know the powerful folks who can help him."

"I hope he hasn't fixed on Karparov."

The musicians stopped their playing and the men went off for cigars and billiards, I strode to the dais where Nina spoke to her mother in Russian. "He's wrong about everything." Nina said. "He has no idea what father means by telling him to take care of me."

Her mother gave a slow nod, but looked off toward the guests.

I smiled and started to walk toward them when a man stepped toward me. I recognized him from the funeral, Arbuthnot. I affected a look of ennui to deny that I was excited to talk to him.

"You aren't with the men in the Billiard room?" I affixed what I hoped to be a winsome smile. He looked as though he liked winsome smiles.

"I would prefer to spend my time with all the pretty ladies." He made a little flourish with an unlit cigar.

"Is that how you seduced Larisa?"

"I seduced her?"

"You came to her funeral." Although so did many men I'd bet she had never met. "I assumed you—"

"Oh, I had a relationship with her." His smug smile suggesting a cat that made off with the fisherman's entire catch. "But I was not the seducer." He reached out to my gloved arm.

I should have told him to get his muck forks off me, and I could not stop myself from sliding a glance at the widow ladies under the colonnade who watched this breach of etiquette, but I wanted information.

He leaned close and whispered to me, "She was a devil, she stirred up trouble beyond anything I could imagine, she drew me in, and made me believe things no sane man would dare to dream."

"I'll remind you that you're speaking of the dead," I said in a soft voice. I gave my arm the rapid jerk learned in the Self Defense for Ladies class at the YMCA and got his hand off. "And a woman who was a friend of mine."

"I assure you, she was a much closer friend of mine." Arbuthnot put his cigar in his vest pocket and smoothed his hand over waves of hair that looked as soft and gray as chinchilla fur. "But I am a realist about what she was. You are the lady with the detective, Barker."

Arbuthnot leaned toward me, I felt myself back up until I was against one of the columns. "Do you trust him?"

"I suppose as much as I do any man."

His smile twinkled in his olive-green eyes. "An interesting answer, which tells me more about you, dear lady, than it does about the famous detective." The cigar was back out and jabbed toward the staircase, presumably, the billiard room beyond. "And what is your opinion of our host, Mr. Karparov?"

I looked around and said, "I believe he is a terrible man who killed his daughter."

Arbuthnot tipped his chinchilla head at me. He said, "I think Barker has a fine taste in women. I'd like to talk to him sometime. I have some things to discuss."

"Perhaps you would like me to—"

"I will speak to him myself sometime, my lovely." Arbuthnot took my hand and kissed it. "That does not mean we could not discuss a great many things at our leisure."

A woman who filled in every inch of her princess gown pinched her face to give Arbuthnot the dagger eyes.

Has to be the wife.

He returned her gaze with that of a puppy caught sneaking onto the couch.

He gave me a little bow and walked away toward the billiard room before this woman who gave him the wife-look reach him. She lingered beside the chafing dishes for a moment as he approached, but then with a flap of beaded chiffon, she pulled her skirt in and flounced away from Arbuthnot who pretended he had been headed to the curried beef all along.

Oh, this much emoting in a great hall intrigued me. I gave her a head start since I did not want to appear to follow too closely if she happened to be heading for the bathroom.

I did not see her in the hallway, but I heard the voices within the billiard room. Actually, it was only one voice and no one stirred.

"So," Karparov said. His voice boomed through the room and I could hear him in the hallway of coffered wood paneling with ease. "You now know my story is a simple one. In Russia, in the Caspian, I achieved greatness. Now, that destiny, that magical force I hold from the ages has brought me here to you."

I walked past one door and then the other as if I were not sneaking around. I did not see the woman. I slipped a glance inside the smoke-filled lair of masculinity. Nearly twenty men, most of them in white-tie evening dress, but a few in rumpled suits, stood. Karparov strode to the back of the room and thrust his hands against a paneled wall to reveal a pair of hinged doors. Yes, he had flair, but I preferred George M. Cohan tap-dancing his way out behind the streamers and American flag.

I did not see Barker inside, but I could not see everyone. I saw Arbuthnot make his way in to talk to a one-armed man in a suit. I figured that was one of those Spindletop men.

The men were not taking up pool cues. That meant they would walk out soon. Some had already walked out. I backed onto the veranda. A pair of men walked out, too deep in their own conversation and the last of their cigars to notice me in the darkness. I would watch for Barker without having Arbuthnot's eyes attempt to burn holes through the fabric of my bodice again.

Footsteps sounded close to me. They could not catch me here. Karparov must be homicidal and I was reluctant to displease Barker, who would be paying for the taxi ride back to my house. I stepped back among the azaleas. I leaned out on the veranda to the street where I saw movement around a carriage.

MJ's red head was visible beneath the street lamp. In velvet evening gown and long gloves, she peered into the windows of a closed carriage while the driver slept above.

Well, she said she couldn't get an invitation to the ball.

I took another step into the darkness so I could see her better in the lamplight.

Oh no, she rocked the thing and the driver was waking.

I walked over to an azalea plant, picked up a rock from the container and threw it at her.

She was only three yards away, but it fell short.

I walked forward into the dark of the veranda away from the windows.

I stumbled back against a pillar.

It moved.

Not a pillar, a person.

I turned back to say excuse me, but didn't get any farther than turning my head an inch.

Something grabbed me; someone grabbed me.

I stepped forward, but they did not let me go. I started to say, "you've made a mistake," but a hand clapped over my face and nose before I could get the words—or a scream—out. I started to take a breath, but I got a taste, a whiff. The smell was antiseptic and sparked a woozy memory.

Chapter 14

College, a biology lab, and who was my partner?
We had dared each other to sniff the closer and closer to a
substance into which we were chopping plants. What was
it? I had to think. I held my breath. Chloroform.

I went limp. I would need less air that way.

I slid several inches through the arms of the person,
but arms then caught, held me around the waist, and
pressed the hand to my face.

He was bigger than I, so that's why I would say
"he". He did not let me go and so he was probably
stronger. Assets: I did have my hands free. One, I had one
hand and arm free. Weapons? No, damn, no. Wait. I slid
my hand up my waist and to my corsage.

My lungs hurt. My heart throbbed. I had to
breathe.

I felt the soft blossoms at my waist. Where was it?
Yes, there it was. I grabbed the pin and pulled it free. The
corsage fell away, but my assailant did not seem to notice.

I started to breathe in. I could not help it. The
darkness filled with black and white checks, bright colors
from incandescent lights, and that smell like the dentist's
office.

I was not gone yet. I jabbed, I jabbed hard. I did
not know if I hit his hand or his leg, but I know I hit flesh
and I stabbed the pin in as far as I could.

All I could see was bars of bright orange and
lavender formed a deepening box.

He let out a cry. I don't know how loud it was.

The world went away to blackness.

I opened my eyes to see Barker sitting over me. I knew I had not totally lost consciousness. I had only lost a fraction of a second. The person who did this couldn't have gotten far, but I couldn't move--couldn't speak--to tell him that. I wasn't even sure my eyes were open. They must be. I saw Barker wrap his arm around my shoulder.

"Someone," I managed to say. "Here, now. Someone--"

"Wheesht," Barker hissed to silence me. "Could nay find a body, but you out here. Slippery bug--fellow."

. "Someone wanted me dead," I said "Why, why would someone try to kill—"

"Nay." Barker scanned the leafy garden around the veranda. Before the storm, it would probably have had electric lanterns or even fairy lights. Now, I saw the outline of his up-thrust chin against the black. "A warning. They would not have had time to kill you or drag you away without being seen."

I raised my head and another memory filled me. This time, something MJ had said. "Threatening to threaten me."

"I thought I had time, lass. I'm sorry." He grabbed my arm and pulled me to a sitting position. "I should have protected you. I thought I did by staying with Karparov." He handed me my corsage. "I heard the cry and came." Barker got to his feet and pulled me to mine.

"But Karparov already left. He could have done it."

Barker dusted my skirt with his large hands and turned my shoulders so my face was toward his. He looked in my eyes with a frown shadowing his deep blue eyes.

Barker's grip around my waist tightened to where it was almost uncomfortable. "Let's get you out of this place."

"I'm all right," I said. I put my hand over his at my waist.

"We should go."

"I don't think I'll get another shot at talking to the mama. Besides, I'm hungry."

"Very well," he said with a big smile at me. He patted my shoulder and walked away. "I will not be far."

I smiled at him and glided to the table set with roast beef, salads, and potatoes where Madame Karparova stood with a diadem of diamonds in her hair that was almost entirely glossy black.

"What a lovely party," I said to her. I took one of the fine little green glass plates etched with silver and speared some tomatoes, bread, and then meat onto it. "And so nice to see you again."

"You can make a sandwich if you want," the mother said with her eyelids dropped down so far that I couldn't see the color of her pupils. Her voice was in a high pitch, but still resonant.

"Oh I like it this way." I lapsed into Russian. "Show Americans some bread and they always make sandwiches, *pravda*?"

She followed in her native tongue as well. "Yes, as though there is no other way to eat. It is deplorable. Like the heat. It gets so hot here." She sighed into her gossamer wisp of a handkerchief that, unlike mine, had no black ribbon on the edge. "Things have been so terrible, just so terrible."

"I can imagine how hard it has been for you." I reached to pat her arm, but she twisted away from me. "What an ordeal."

"Yes." She looked in my eyes. Her words came so fast and fluid in Russian that I had to concentrate to keep up. "We had two beautiful homes, one on the mountains and one the beach in the Caspian. Such a lovely place. I could not even bring everything with me and so much of what I did got washed away in that miserable hurricane. Can you believe such weather?"

"But your daughter." I was stunned. My mother could be a temperamental witch to me, but she would be devastated if she ever lost me.

"Yes, she is marrying a fellow from home."

"I'm so sorry for you," I said. It came out in English, but I quickly switched back to Russian. "With the loss of Larisa."

She flinched as though I had come at her with a bat. "Lara was always her father's daughter. They were so close, and I can never change that now."

I set my plate down on the corner of the serving table. Took a small silver-rimmed glass and filled it from the great crystal bowl of rum punch.

She snapped her fingers to a waiter, "bring me a drink." She looked back at me and seemed surprised to see me still there at her elbow, holding a glass of punch in one hand, a plate of tongue, oysters, radishes, and olives in the other. Well, her lapse of memory was my advantage. I could make the past conversation anything I wanted.

"You are right. You have been through such an ordeal with the loss of your daughter. How have you been able to bear it?"

"I don't know how I have managed." She flapped her handkerchief against her other hand. She slid a look from under her lashes. "Although, I would not have been so strong if Viktor was there with me the night Larisa died."

"The night Larisa died?" *Don't show alarm. Don't show alarm. Show alarm, and your witness wipes off her chin and speaks no more.*

"Yes, I could not have withstood it without him."

"Of course, as a mother, I know." What I didn't ask: But they didn't find the body until morning, how did you know that was the night she died?

"I had such a headache. I went to the solarium." She swept a veined hand toward the conservatory where Barker and I had first met the maid Polly. "Viktor was with me, he comforted me when Larisa did not come that evening."

"It was the evening she died?"

She gave an expansive shrug that involved both hands and the lips. She looked toward the dark hallway where the woman I assumed to be Arbuthnot's wife emerged.

Behind Arbuthnot's wife, Karparov slid past her out of the hallway, but his hand remained somewhere behind her for a moment. Mrs. Arbuthnot gave a slight start and a giggle.

Karparova narrowed her eyes at them. "My husband wasn't with me that evening. I did not see him until breakfast."

"And where was he?"

"My husband was wherever he was in the house. This cursed land has taken his most prized possession. He walks the floor up there where that cursed thing should have been." She flapped an arm draped in gauze toward the tiled ceiling. "I expect he was there that night."

"And Nina?"

"With Slava, of course. They are young. They are in love." She gave a gauzy flap of her other arm toward the middle of the room where the girl sat with her hands folded across her chest and back to the large fellow who tried to explain something to her.

So, my original theory of anyone of these people could have done it because they would have lied for each other was not true, but it still meant none of them had an alibi even if all of them did.

Karparov had paced upstairs. A phonograph left to the end of the song would have made the same noise as a man pacing while he was entertaining one of his paramours or killing his daughter. Viktor had been in the solarium with a hop-drunk mother-in-law. She had probably not conscious enough to know if he was there, gone, or transformed into a werewolf. Nina had been with fiancé and possible coconspirator Slava. He would have been strong enough and near enough to chloroform me in the garden a few minutes ago. So the fact that a man had done it did not eliminate Nina as a suspect.

I finished my punch. Mom's the only one I can be sure didn't murder Larisa; intoxicated, she could have done nothing, and sober she and Viktor would provide true alibis for each other.

"My condolences." Giving her arm a pat, I walked off to lean against a column and fashioned the items on my plate into a sandwich, but lost my appetite, so I set the sandwich down on a plinth. I slipped back into the entryway toward the stairs to find Barker.   Although I had not been granted permission to roam the house, I figured that people were distracted and I could sneak away.

My sneaking got me to the newel post with bronze of a hussar atop it.

"Stop!" a woman shouted.

Chapter 15

I turned to see Nina in a filmy dress of the barest shade of pink silk. The silk faded even further until it turned to green around her waist and then back to pink at her toes. I smiled. "You look beautiful. Shouldn't you be dancing at the ball? This is your night."

Nina scowled. On her face of wide-set eyes and plump lips, crunching the features together like this was not a good look for the girl, but it was menacing in the way it made her look more like a big-eyed insect than a normal girl. "I want you to stay away from my men."

I could feel a confused frown take hold of my brow. "*Isvenita*?" I figured she might make more sense if she spoke Russian.

"I want to know why you are taking Slava from me." Nina spoke in Russian. She sprang open a cigarette case.

I shook my head as if she had offered one to me. "I'm doing no such thing."

She stepped up to stand beside me on the staircase.

I backed up until I felt the hussar's sword against my laces. "I saw him a couple days ago outside the drugstore in what I would refer to as loitering. I would not have taken him if he were on sale and half price." I should be nicer. I doubt she knew why Slava followed me, but she might say something that could help me noodle it out, so I gave her my Sunday-best smile. "I was hasty. I mean that I would never have designs on a man I know to be your beau. I'm older than he is anyway."

"You're older than Skip Livingstone." She slid the cigarette through her fingers and tapped it against the silver case, but did not light it. "But I saw you with him."

Not by much. He looked about thirty. "Nina, I am not seeing your beaux." The word translated as a plural when spoken in Russian. "What made you think I was?"

"He told me so. He said he was to spend the day with you that meant we could not go shopping. I need him to help me pick out the colors for our dining room. Papa is giving us the lake house, you know."

"The day? He followed me the entire day?" Or did he just come up with a reason not to pick out drapes?

Her face pinched in again in a scowl, this time with nostrils flaring. "You're crazy to think that? Why would he follow you all day? Why would he care about you?" Her eyes grew wide and skin suddenly paled as agitation overcame her. I got the feeling this was a state in which she probably spent a good share of her time.

If I was going to get any information from her, I needed to calm her. I tried agreeing with her. "Yes, that would be crazy." I gave a moment for my smile to sink in with her. "Did you realize you said 'my men' when you spoke English? What other men?"

"I must not let you keep me from my party any longer." She stepped down from the stairs, but fixed a smug smile at me.

I knew that little victory bouncing around in her head meant I could get at least one more answer. I blurted the first name I could think of. "Viktor?"

She laughed. "Viktor, the righter of wrongs. Viktor the saint. I only think he married my sister because he thought he could change her into something just as noble, destroy my father's influence." She twisted her face up with contempt. "He couldn't and he lost interest in her. He didn't even care when she carried on with all those men, didn't care at all." She covered her mouth, looked around to see if any Russian speakers lurked in the hall, and dashed back to the party.

At the top of the stairs, I saw a maid, not Polly. I whispered to her, "Have you seen that Barker fellow around? Do you know him?"

She nodded. "Oh yes, I heard he became famous detecting murders in the place named after the buggy. Surrey, that's it."

Now that one was just silly. Why would they need a Scotsman there when I'd read that part of England already had Sherlock Holmes, and I imagined the squared-off buggy was named after the place.

"This way, ma'am." She did not lead, but pointed down a corridor covered with faded tapestries of medieval battles, ladies in gardens, and knights on horseback. The only light came from the cracks around a closed door.

I grabbed the knob. I prayed the maid knew who Barker was and wasn't leading me to the murderer. I shoved the door open.

"I thought you were going to stay downstairs, surrounded by people." Barker's voice was loud and accent strong. "Where you would be safe, woman."

I looked past the muscular man with hands on his hips, making his tailcoat flare behind him. Looking up, I saw his face was an angry red. How odd that look gave his well made features a burnish that suited him.

I took my eyes away from him and looked around. "What is this place?"

The windowless walls shone with gold mosaic, the floors with amber-colored marble. The wall opposite the door bore a high niche above a table that looked like an altar, but the carvings of screaming men and distorted faces. Behind it, a high arch curved with a brown trim of formed plaster or stone--I couldn't tell--formed into the shape of skulls, decorated with crossed bones and swirls of vertebrae behind. Within the niche lined with fibulas stood a stone box, as large as the three-story doll house I bought for the girls.

I stepped forward and leaned on the table. I sent one of the burned-out candles to the floor, but I was too engrossed in staring at what was in the altar niche to care about picking it up. "It's a fake?"

"Yes," Barker said behind me. "A bit of plaster on cardboard to fool Karparovs new mates. He must have figured he could get it back from Larisa, but then he couldn't and so he had to hire me."

"So it's all a fake."

"The bones are real enough." He put on his blue-tinted spectacles and examined them.

I shuttered and pressed my lips together to keep them from letting out a frightened whine.

"Old ones. Probably from some unfortunates back in the old country. Yes, they are." He pointed with his pen to a row of femurs making designs across the wall. "Smaller than Americans, you see."

I felt hot, as though I swayed with fever. My stays were suddenly too tight for me to get a breath. "Arbuthnot admitted to me that he was Larisa's lover."

"Thank you, Mrs. Gallagher, that is helpful."

"You look at the Karparovs and think you see normal people." I held my stomach as though my corset was not tight enough. "And they are really the sort of monsters who can live with something like this, who can do this." I rubbed my arms that had grown cold despite my warm head. "They're like the storm. You think the evil is over and then comes another echo, bringing it back."

"These are very old bones." Barker leaned into the niche to get a look from behind. "Probably came up in the excavation with the magic casket."

"Just some more echoes of the storm." I felt hot and slid a tendril of hair off my face. "Maybe, some pre-echoes."

"Pardon?"

"The air before and after hurricane has an oppressive hold of humidity and heat, but it is the stillest air you can imagine. It's like an echo, but on the wrong side. That's what this place is, this whole house. The pre-echo of the horror to come."

"All this mysticism seems to get to you, Mrs. Gallagher." Barker stepped beside me and looked at the altar and then the table. His pen lingered over two long gouges about two feet wide. "Aye, this is where he had that box and this is where she took it from. But, 'tis big, so heavy, a wee girl like that must have had help."

"And that help might have killed her." I straightened the satin of my dress over my bodice, not that he looked at me. "I think it was either Skip or that Arbuthnot fellow. They both admit to being her lovers."

Footsteps sounded along the hall.

"Time I took you home, Mrs. Gallagher." He grabbed me around the waist and hustled me to the door.

"Take care not to do something foolish and get killed on the way out."

The courthouse building was silent, which made my voice seem even louder in the office of oak, plaster, and leather aged to a burnt orange color. I sat on the edge of the chair made for the larger frame of a man and continued reporting what I could remember, ". . . And Arbuthnot, who started as a furrier, but now has some interest in Spindletop." I finished my explanation of who had been at the Karparov ball and set my hands on my lap.

Judge Reams, a man with thick silver hair cropped close to his head in a job I'd bet his wife had done and a small chevron of a mustache that barely made it to the edge of his narrow nose, leaned back in his chair and shook his head. "No, he wouldn't have been."

"I spoke with . . ." No point in being right. I didn't want to win this argument, but to get my kids in the full legal sense. "Do you have any other questions about the ball?" I had left out Barker, getting chloroformed, and that horrible room.

He looked toward the window with closed shades and shook his head.

"Good! Then you've got the papers finished for the adoption."

He looked at me in face-puckering confusion.

"For the adoption of my daughters."

He held a hand up toward me as though I needed to be stopped from lunging at him. "Yes, well, I'd be more comfortable—and I'm sure you'd be—if we do a little more research."

"Thank you, but we've done all the research my family needs. I need my girls."

That hand stayed in the air and flipped around in a sort of shrug. "We have to make sure the real parents are actually dead."

"Real parents?" My hands gripped the walnut arm rests. "I am their real parents."

He gave a chuckle from deep within him. "A lot has happened in the last few months, we need to be sure—"

"People coming back to life isn't part of the aftermath."

His forehead gathered and his nostrils flared. "This will give you a little more time to make your decision."

"I don't need more time. I've made my decision and so have my girls. I'm their mother."

"The time will do you good." He smiled. "I know how women are with decisions." His smile fluctuated a bit to create waves in his gray mustache. "Why, my wife will change her mind back and forth for days before she's sure. And even when she's sure, she isn't."

I don't care that your wife's continued existence is proof the Fool Killer is only a myth. I want my daughters. "Is there, perhaps, another judge to take this case?" One who thinks women are people and not the changeling spawn of the worst kind of fairy?

His face went pale and lips went tight in anger so strong, I was glad he was nowhere near a buggy whip. "I will make the decision when I make the decision, and until then, try to keep your name out of the papers."

"Well." I smiled not because I felt it, but because I knew doing so showed off my well molded cheekbones. "I will be seeing you next week. I'm sure you'll have made amazing progress by then." I extended my hand to shake, but he didn't take it, so I kept it out there until he finally grabbed it. At least, he grabbed three of my gloved fingers for an instant before letting go.

I left the office, walked down the broad, marble staircase, and blinked back the tears as I pushed open the doors of wood with squares inset metal.

Chapter 16

I got on the electric trolley heading toward my house. This was one of the areas where the electric lines had not tangled too badly during the flood and the electricity had replaced mule-drawn cars a month after the storm.

I leaned back against the wood slats of the seat, glad the afternoon sun on this eastward trip shaded my face so none of the other riders saw my emotional state. I was about a mile from my place, but leapt off at Broadway.

I didn't want to go home right now and have the girls ask me why I was upset.

I jumped over a deep drainage trough, and kept my run sprinted down the street of large homes.

I slipped into the alley so I could approach it from the back. A coach house with what appeared to be servant's quarters above stood nearest the alley. The servant's quarters were, empty with no windows or doors remaining and water and waste lines that should be headed toward the ground wrapped around the structure. Inside, debris gathered up against the wall and in the bottom so that no carriage or horse would be there any time soon. The stairs to the servant's quarters had washed away.

Up at the house, I darted to the backdoor.

Locked.

I knocked.

No answer. Good. Okay, now what?

I pressed all the windows that I could find on this floor to see if I could find an open one. Breaking an entering only counts if there is the breaking. Just entering is easier to explain to a court.

Goshdamnit!

I looked up at what was probably a small wooden balcony and a set of French doors on the house. That balcony looked rickety, and I doubted those doors would be held by anything more than a latch.

I spun around and dashed to the carriage house. I turned over boards until I was glistening with a full sweat. Broken planks and rough wood. The debris of the wealthiest was no different from that in my neighborhood, so I should be able to find, yes! The ladder-like construction of a wood in which had gone the lath and plaster of someone's house.

Someone may have sheltered within the confines of a room made of this until it gave way and killed them. Someone may have built this home of their own hands for their family to live. Now, it was debris in a pile and I shook it lose to use as a ladder in a burglary.

My make-shift ladder was unwieldy with some pieces coming free and nails all over that scraped my skin, but kid gloves kept me from getting any deep cuts. I stretched it below the balcony.

Almost. It didn't quite make it, but leaned against the clapboard wall.

I climbed, slipped when a rung broke free, and climbed to the top of the ladder. I could just reach my hands to the railing of the balcony. I reached and missed. Then, reached and grabbed hold of the balcony edge.

Son of a . . .

My ladder slapped to the ground.

Hands wrapped tight around balcony spindles, I dangled in the air from the second story balcony.

All right, I needed to do something soon. I would support my weight on my arms for long and both hands on one side just made my legs dangle beneath the balcony.

Now, with one hand over and one under, I kicked my legs up, just like they taught us girls to climb at Camp Wohelo. I could do this. I kicked again.

I was getting tired. At Camp Wohelo, I had not been constrained by a dress corset, long skirt, or adulthood at Camp Wohelo.

If I fell, I would be on my back on the concrete, and I could die, or worse, become paralyzed.

I thought of Judge Reams and the way he did not think me capable of taking care of anything and how I needed to show him. I kicked, but missed. I thought of my father who always knew I could do more than I thought I did. I kicked once again for all I was worth.

My ankle caught the railing. I slid my leg over the top and the rest of me followed easily. Too easily. I smacked hard onto the balcony.

I sat for a moment, took a breath and shook my head. *No, I don't have time for this. Get in, find a clue, and get out.*

I bounded to my feet and tried the door. The knob turned, but it was latched.

I reached up for my hatpin to slide the latch up through the closed doors, but realized I had lost my hat in the assent.

Hells bells and buckets of blood!

I pulled out a hairpin and straightened it. I slipped it between the white wood doors and slid up.

The door stood firm.

I shot a glance behind me. I was exposed up here since all the trees in Galveston had died. A chance remained that no one saw me since I could not see anyone lurking about the broad street before the house. I pressed the hairpin in deeper and pulled up again, but still no result.

I reached behind me and jerked one of loose spindles. The nails creaked in the wood, but it came free. I smashed it nail-end first into a pane of glass. I smashed and smashed until I could reach my hand in, grab the cold metal latch, and open the door.

The wood grown and shudder beneath me.

Queens have entered their throne rooms with less triumph than I did that upstairs guestroom.

I looked around the dim room. The washstand was bare metal with chipped white porcelain. The bed and chest of drawers were the sort of cheap oak from the Sears Catalogue. This would have been where some servant stayed since the flood took out the servant's quarters. Two more rooms looked the same.

In the hallway, I found a room just before the staircase with an exotic metal ceiling medallion above a tiffany lamp that matched the modern geometric flowers of the stained glass window. Before a fireplace, a screen echoed the design and the painted edging and matched the shape of the Turkish arch led to the dressing room. . The bed sat in a sled of the same oriental artistry. Messy bed.

The dressing room was empty of dresses.

I looked through the drawers. Enough cocaine for several mouths' worth of toothaches, a half empty bottle of laudanum, and a hardcover book in Russian of the Decameron Nights, glued shut with spilled liniment from a broken jar.

Making my way down the staircase, I slid my feet slowly and with care not to lose my footing in the dark on the rug over the wood steps.

I got to the bottom step and started at the shape before me. Tall man, suit, but no other features visible in the dark.

Chapter 17

"Hello," I said. I hoped this tall, dressed-up man at the foot of the stairs was Barker with the same idea I had. I hoped it was not someone who belonged here. I was sure I'd found the right house.

"Well, you're the most cheerful burglar I've ever met," the man who was not Barker said.

Think, I have to think something rational to explain why I'm here.

"I'm sor—" *Don't apologize.* "The door was open." *It was after I broke it.* "Perhaps you should introduce yourself." *Yes, charge forward.*

"Perhaps *you* should." He laughed.

On the count of three? I suggested.

"Whatever the pretty lady wants." He lit the hurricane lamp on the foyer table. Skip. He smiled and looked as though Mr. Edison had come up with a new invention of electric handsomeness. "What are you doing here, Dash?"

"I believe Larisa was murdered, no matter what the police think, and I came here to find clues," I blurted. "Why are you here?"

"I spend the night here sometimes," Skip's eyes wandered around the curved foyer. "Reminds me of her."

I felt shaky from the effort to get in here and what Judge Reams had said. "Oh, excuse me. I need to freshen up."

"Sure." He gave a smile full of kindness and understanding.

I tore myself away to the bathroom. The room was large and modern with a toilet in a closet and a stained glass window over the sink. The first spikes of sun now showed detail of the place. Rust stained the section of the sink below the spigot. The tub was clean with patina on the large, handheld fixture. Between these stood a small bidet and an oak cabinet with drawers on the bottom and a broken shelf at the top.

I closed the door behind me.

The spigot came on, but the water was thick with rust. My white shirtwaist was ripped and soiled, the fabric now translucent with sweat, but Galveston women got used to being soaked, and that water would not make anything better. I shut off the tap.

I opened the small medicine cabinet. Inside a small bottle of heroin cough syrup that looked empty, a tin of tooth powder, and a box of bath salts. I reached into the box and ran my fingers through the small, even crystals. They might be pink and might smell of almonds, but enough of them could make salt water that could pass for the ocean once inside a dead woman's lungs.

Time, I didn't have much time.

I opened the two drawers of the cabinet. Empty. I felt beneath them. Bottom one, nothing. Second. Yes, something taped to the bottom. Might be n advertising bill from the cabinet manufacturer, but might be more. I did not have time to care, but needed to grab it and get out of here. I pulled it free and stuck it in the pocket of my skirt before I walked back out to the foyer.

The lantern was gone, but the shape of a man stood silhouetted by the open front door standing before the open front door again.

"Skip?"

"I can if you insist," said Barker. "Will you take my arm?" He struck a match and lit the lantern Skip had left on the foyer table.

At the back of the house, a great creak sounded and then a crash. That had to be the balcony breaking free.

He looked over me from messy hair, sweaty face, to ripped and dirty shirtwaist and gave the quickest of glances to the window where he must have seen the remains of the balcony and gave me a smirk that showed no surprise. "Hello Mrs. Gallagher."

"I was here with Skip Livingstone."

He gave a sharp little nod that said, "I knew that, now can you get on with important things?"

I walked down and handed him the item from under the sink.

He took it, his large fingers just touching mine.

I did not let go. "I haven't looked at this paper. We'll look at it together."

"Certainly," Barker said. "But first I have an errand." He looked at the paper. "You'll probably want to come."

I took a step toward him and then stopped because I needed to get back to the office. I needed to do all I could to keep the clients I still had happy.

Barker stopped. "Are you coming or not?"

I kept pace with Barker through the millinery section of the Arbuthnot department store and into the stairwell door Barker held open for me. "Do you have an appointment?"

He slipped past me on the stairs and smiled. "Ah, that would spoil the surprise."

I followed him up to the fourth floor. Oh, I longed for the day when everywhere had electricity again.

Arbuthnot's office lay within the carved wood elements of the fourth floor of the office building above his department store. The door had the brass letters of "Arbuthnot" hammered into the light wood.

"Why does a furrier need an office?"

"His business has expanded." Barker grabbed the knob on the great, arched door, but instead of opening it, he looked me in the eyes.

Maybe he knew I had something I wanted to ask or maybe he just wanted to see if I'd preened enough from my adventures at Larisa's to look presentable, but I took the time to ask, "Do you think Arbuthnot was her main fellow or Skip?"

"She might have encouraged both of them."

"Yes." I gave what I knew to be a pretty, dimpled smirk. "I realize 'encouraged' is a euphemism for had sexual relations with."

He turned away to open the door for me. Once I was inside, he passed me again, gave a quick tip of the fedora to the pudgy, bald man behind the desk. Barker said, "I imagine he's expecting us," and opened the inner office door for me.

I did like the man's style.

Arbuthnot looked up from a desk the size of a tugboat. His eyes grew wide and his hand reached into a desk drawer.

Barker rounded the desk, leaping over the final corner. With his face turned toward me, Barker pressed his forearm against Arbuthnot's lapel and shoved him against the wall.

With a smile to the man in the outer office, I closed the door.

Barker took a gun from the coat of the smaller man he had pinned. He tossed it behind and I caught it.

"I too always carry a gun." Barker gave Arbuthnot a shove. "You won't be able to get between it and me, however."

Arbuthnot looked beyond him to me. "Hello, pretty one."

I waved back, with the hand not holding the gun.

"Why hasn't Karparov had you destroyed?" Barker's accent was so strong, I took a second to understand his words.

Arbuthnot attempted as much of a laugh as he could with the arm against his throat. "I am too—"

Barker said what sounded through the heather of his accent like, "No one is too powerful to keep that maniac from making your life miserable."

"He's right." No one needed me to say that, but I wanted to do more than stand against the hat rack with a gun in a way for it not to hurt anyone.

Arbuthnot managed a shrug. "He thought I might still know something."

"Do you?"

"Of course, he—"

"Do you?" Barker's voice rattled the entire office.

"Perhaps a bit." Arbuthnot shrugged.

I twisted the key to lock the door and wedged my foot against it in case the matron outside found a key.

"I know Larisa planned to rule the world. Who wouldn't be drawn to a woman like that?"

Barker, who isn't drawn to any woman.

"Did she have the stone casket?" Barker growled.

Arbuthnot nodded.

"Where?" Barker demanded.

"I saw it once." Arbuthnot shrugged.

"When you helped her steal it." Barker's pressure on Arbuthnot did not relent.

"Where did you take it?" I blurted.

He shook his head. "I took it out of her father's house. We hid it in an old cart behind the servant's quarters. She would not let me help her after that. Wanted to protect my reputation in case this didn't work, she said."

"Maybe you weren't important enough to her?" I led the witness a little, but Barker slipped me a wink that made me flush to my toes.

"I was the most important man in her life." His face grew a smile. "We were going together to take over the land that evicted her father."

I almost asked if he would leave his wife, but realized he would, and his wife wouldn't mind.

"Where do you think she took the casket?" Barker asked.

Arbuthnot shrugged and got slammed against the wall for the movement. "She had a place, a little beach house, where I would never go. It was flooded out, in the water. Crazy to keep going there, but she liked the privacy."

Barker pulled away. His hand went inside his jacket. I would bet he wasn't kidding about that gun. "Give me the address."

Arbuthnot stepped to his desk, grabbed a pad and pen, but turned and shook the pen at Barker rather than writing. "You have to protect me from Karparov if I help you."

Barker leaned back, but didn't take his hand off the gun. "I believe I will neutralize him."

Arbuthnot stood for a moment without moving, and what may not even have been breathing. Then, he scribbled something. "This is directions from what she told me. You need someone who knows the area to tell you where the place was, since it is now in the water."

A new day left me feeling a bit better. I had enough time to get my work done, to please my clients. I sat at my desk in silence. I shot a glance to the pink and yellow blossoms in the vase at the end of my desk. Evangeline had told me that Skip brought them while I was home having dinner with the girls.

Evangeline typed at what might have been sixty miles an hour without looking up at our guest.

I heard shoes click across the floor and stop, but I ignored them. "He got those flowers from a wedding this morning." MJ said. She leaned back to stretch out as far as she could in my guest chair. She flicked her index finger toward the bouquet. "Flowers, wedding, morning. I covered it for the paper. Saw him take them right as he walked out of the church."

I looked up with a frown as if I didn't know who she meant.

Jinxie walked through the door of my office, the large bow atop her short hair darted both ways as she looked around, and said, "Why does Mr. Barker have his shirt off?"

Beside her, Teddie said in a soft voice intended for her sister and not the women staring at them, "he's going to fight someone, like John L. Sullivan."

Teddie's life needed logic. She spent so much time not being told what was going on, she filled in what she did not know with logic and sometimes she just made up something that made sense.

"Excuse me ladies," MJ said. Her kid boots skidded around my desk. She thrust an elbow before her competition, but Evangeline was quick and around it, into the hall.

I stepped around my desk and felt the force of my body propelled forward even faster than my feet carried me with Evangeline's hand on my skirt and MJ's grip on my upper arm.

Why did they assume I wasn't coming? Why did they want me to? I guess just because they were friends.

As a group, we skidded short of slamming into my daughters who stood in the open doorway to Barker's office.

"Watch the hoseman for the okay before entering the water," Clark read from a thin green-leather notebook.

'Hoseman?'

He turned toward me to show bloodshot eyes. "You have been a lot of trouble lately," I thought I heard him whisper before he turned back to Barker.

I slipped to the front, put my arms around the girls' shoulders. Teddie was at hip height, Jinxie shorter.

Barker stood shirtless in the middle of the room. With strong arms, dinner plates for pectorals, and a muscular girth above the waist and under his arms, he had the physique of a guy who could take care of himself if he ended up in a fight with a circus weightlifter. My father had once told me that a man needs those muscles at the sides to hit a man. Barker wore the wide belt that must have looked like a boxer to Teddie and what looked like dark long-underwear.

My father had shown me how, when done right, the strength of a blow doesn't come from the arm, but the trunk.

Clark consulted his notes and spoke to Barker. "He will do the final check of hose integrity before signaling you in."

MJ asked, "What the hell are you planning?"

Barker looked up, not at MJ, not at the girls, but at me.

I blinked.

Clark followed Barker's gaze, gave me a quick scowl, and turned back to Barker, "Do you want me to go through it again?" He started toward the door, I assumed to shoo us away and close it until the circus was leaving town.

"Ta," Barker said. "But I'll be leaving now anyway." He walked straight at us and we slipped to the sides. Well, all of us except for MJ who I had to yank by the back of the skirt until she was beside me at the wall.

Barker patted Jinxie's cheek and pinched Teddie's ear, but continued to look at me with a lack of expression that made me stumble inside.

He walked to the edge of the stairs, still wearing nothing but what God had given him incased in boxing tights.

"The view from the back is just as good," MJ whispered in my ear.

Barker walked into the waiting room we shared and pressed a section of the carved paneling. It bounced back to reveal a small cupboard with pegs for three coats. He took a raincoat and donned it.

I glanced through the curved windows over the large doorway. Blue sky and sunshine. One could never be sure what the gulf wanted to do, but I was reasonably sure it didn't intend to rain today. He slipped his feet into a pair of galoshes at the bottom of the cabinet.

I saw his outfit, I thought of Clark's instructions, and I remembered that drawing I had seen in the margin of the paper in his wastebasket.

I caught up with him on the stairs. "Are you sure this is safe? Can you, I mean, can you swim and everything?"

He tossed me a smile that creased those peach-colored cheeks. "As well as I need to for this. I'm fortunate the gulf isn't as deep as some other bodies of water and the current isn't as strong."

"Oh Mr. Barker," was all I could whisper. I turned back and gave a splayed hand of "Stop" to my friends and daughters.

Barker walked out the front door, and I waved to Mrs. Hulpke for the both of us.

I expected him to go straight for the wharf, but he turned to the right. I followed. "Have you ever done this before?"

"In more than theory?" his long strides almost lost me. "I'll have to say no."

"But you have researched it most thoroughly?"

"Aye."

"And invested in the best possible equipment and team?" I hopped over an open trench that drained to the sea and skittered to a stop to keep from smacking into his back.

"Anonymity is important in this operation." He turned to look at me, his eyes darkened with a sternness that willed me to silence. He took my arm and we crossed the street to a marina of salvaged planks and boats left to molder as they tugged their rotted lines wound around pitted and stained capstans. A gull landed on one, found it had nothing of interest for him, and flew away.

Barker released my arm and bobbed his head toward me as if he expected me to leave.

I followed him onto the rickety boards of the creaking dock. We walked past shrimp boats that picked clean long ago, and vessels listing beyond hope. Barker stopped at a skiff with a pair of burley oarsman and a lanky fellow in a cowboy hat waved him aboard.

I recognized him. That was the smuggler I had seen in Barker's office.

"Hey there friend, take a gander." His weathered hands grabbed a stack of oil skins on the skiff and threw them back.

I gasped.

A diver's helmet gleamed in full glass and brass glory. That thing could be salvation for a man under the waves, or a watery grave if there was a slight crack anywhere in the suit.

"Mr. Barker." I clutched his sleeve and spoke in a whisper. "You can't do this! These men are, well, they aren't fellows you should trust, even if they do leave you alive to take home Karparov's casket." I did not take my eyes from them. "You don't have a chance."

"Maybe the wee casket will shed its protecting magic on me." He smirked. Yes, in a situation of life or death—his own—he smirked.

I frowned at him. "Funny, you didn't go through the hurricane."

"Nay."

"But you act like those of us who've had the scared knocked right out of us."

He looked in my eyes and gave a slow nod. "Some things do not scare me anymore, no."

"What happened to you, Mr. Barker?"

"I must be going."

"I pray for your safe return, Mr. Barker." I flung my arms around him in a quick hug. "A real prayer, not some incantation to that box."

He may have patted my back, but that feeling may have been the wind because I released him before I could be sure.

"Ah come on," the cowboy-pirate said. "Give your girlie a kiss."

"She's not my—"

"Aw, come on!" another crewman insisted.

"Please go now," he said to me. He kissed my cheek and I ran away.

I prayed for him all the way back to the office.

Chapter 18

"I would like help," Barker said from the doorway of my office.

The smile I felt beamed from the depths of me. He was alive and well. This was the first time I had seen him since leaving him on the dock yesterday. He must have gone through some underwater change because he had never said anything like that before. Oh wait, he had. "You need something translated?"

He shook his head. "Meet me at the Livery Stable on Mechanic at nine tonight." He walked away before I could ask any questions.

Under the flicker of gas streetlamp light, Barker shot a glance up to my tame pompadour of blonde waves held at the back by a ribbon. Then, his eyes lingered over my fitted blouse, bloomer-style pants buckled below the knee, and the length of black stocking leading down to my boots. He gave a frown and a shrug as though I had passed some sort of muster, but just barely.

Before us stood a garage door of whitewashed wood with a window just below the top rail.

"You can leave your bike here. The brollie, too." He pointed at my umbrella.

He slid a hand into his hand into his jacket pocket and pulled out a set of keys. With a quick move, he unlocked the white door and slid it along the rails. He stepped inside, but before I could follow, pulled a large bicycle from the garage. In the streetlight, it looked bulky even for a man's bike and a shiny shade of yellow orange. A belt wound from one of the boxes on the front rail to the back tire. There was no room for a passenger.

I slipped my umbrella into the carrying case at the back, but he pulled it out. With a yank, I pulled it from his hands, pressed the button at the bottom, and twisted the handle until the top came off. I held the sharp knife before him.

He took the knife from my hands and the rest of the umbrella and tossed them on the garbage heap. "If someone can get your weapon away that easily, then you might as well just hand it to them and avoid all the argy-bargy."

"Okay," I said. I straddled the front wheel and flapped my hand back to find Barker's shoulder. "Give me a boost, and I'll ride on the handlebars." I flailed my hand behind me. I could not feel him and he gave no assist.

"This one's a wee bit faster than the bikes you're used to."

"Yes," I said. "I'm sure you pedal like a demon. Now can you give me a hoist and get to it?"

His large hands came around my waist and lifted me up until my behind slapped onto the handlebars.

Beneath me, an engine roared to life and then puttered.

"A motor?"

He leaned forward and whispered in my ear, "Motorcycle."

We stuttered down the road, wobbled, Barker slowed to get his bearings, and tore into the night. We curved around the alley at a steep angle.

I bit my lip to keep from screaming since that wouldn't seem right after that "pedal like a demon" thing. I shut my eyes, but opened them when I realized this could make my equilibrium off kilter. We flew over the ground at twenty miles an hour or more. I pulled my knees back so my feet would not entangle in the flying wheels.

We hit the street, bounded over a puddle. I felt Barker behind me stand on the coasting brake. We bounced over the tar-covered surface; he pumped those strong legs over the pedals until the motor outpaced him.

Through gritted teeth, I asked, "From whence did you acquire such a beast?"

"Fellow owed me a few bob."

"At the livery stable?" Since the flood, Hank's livery stable hadn't had many horses. He was said to make most of his money from gambling on bare knuckle fights late at night. Was that how Barker honed such a physique? *Oh no!* Now I had joined the ranks of those with fanciful Barker stories.

The bike hit a rock. It swerved. I wobbled. I tried to steel my muscles against the narrow handlebars to steady myself, but I knew I would topple. I screamed. I pitched forward into the night.

Something stopped me. Something caught my breath inside me; it held me atop the bike, Barker's arm around my waist.

The bike slowed to a stop. Its insect hiss of a motor went quiet.

Barker engaged the kickstand and rounded to face me. He offered an arm.

I grabbed it and jumped free of the contrivance. "Frightening yes," I said with a smile. "But most definitely exhilarating. Where to now?"

Without a look to me, he retracted his arm and walked down a seaside road that had once been a quarter mile away from the shore. Black water lit only by moonlight lapped against piles of wood that had not yet been scavenged since most of it probably spent times of high tide soaked with briny brown water. Even now, the area smelled like dead fish and kitchen rot. This smell haunted Galveston. It had for seven months now, but had eased in most of the town, but here, the smell wrapped its hand around my throat and choked.

Each pungent breath drew in a memory: a buckboard bounding down my street, full of bodies; a pair of feet with no shoes protruding past a coffin because he must have been tall; children's toys broken in the rubble of houses

Here, whole families would have been submerged and died with no trace that they had ever lived as bodies and everything they owned washed out to sea. Tonight must be a night when the moon pulled the tides to a spectacular low.

I tread after Barker into ankle deep water. Broken pylons and whittled piers showed that once houses and wharfs stood out in what were now stacks of debris and the occasional leaning shack. In the water, a chimney rose as Nemo's periscope from the brine.

I thought of chimneys with no houses between except for one warehouse held rows of bodies, some wrapped in cloth, some their faces and most of their bodies exposed. People walked past with no more garments than the bodies. If they had retained more clothing than their underwear, they could not bear to wear it in the hot, still air that followed the storm.

Barker stopped. He took out a compass and a map that I could not make out in the moonlight except that it held a grid. I guessed it was an old map of the city. I didn't need to see what it was. I figured out what he had and what he was doing.

The smell of stale sea and what was probably death, but smelled like a roast left too long outside an icebox.

I remembered water coming in the light fixture on the second floor bedroom where I huddled with my neighbors. Water slid down the chandelier, but most of the house held together even if it had been knocked free of its foundation. A later memory came of stepping over the stones that had been the marble façade of the great newspaper building looking for the remains of my husband or any of the tycoons with whom he had met that afternoon. I had found nothing of him and the militia man had told me I was foolish to try.

"Please look over the map," he said with a gentleness I may have imagined. We stood in water over our ankles.

I knew my vision clouded as I looked at the map. I blinked. "Yes, we're here on the map." I pointed. "There used to be a tea shop on that corner and the sea was back three blocks"

"Damn," Barker said. He looked into the distance raised his brawny hand in what was an obvious count of missing land parcels and then did it again. "Damn," he said with greater ferocity under his breath.

"I think the water is pretty shallow," I said. "We could wade for it." My boots were not swimming shoes, but they were nearly as light and my bloomers the same cloth as my bathing costume. I could swim in this. I looked to a row of three leaning houses on stilts.

"I think it's that second cracker box there." He stretched his arms and rolled the sleeves of his sweater up to show arms sinewy with muscle beneath the fine blond hairs. "You may notice that of the few places left, none of them have staircases intact."

I swiveled around to see. "Son of a bitch." I caught the corner of a blue eye and gave him a little shrug where only my shoulders moved.

He started forward and I waded after him. Water only to his hips was well past my waist. I worried it would go even deeper. Yes, I could swim and do so well, but I wondered what else might be under us. The ground was uneven.

I trod upon a door and slid off into murk that generated an even stronger smell of sea death. I ran ahead of Barker to get away from what I suspected might be what was left of a beach home dweller under that door. I caught Barker's arm.

He held my arm as if we walked to a church social until we were beneath the seaward side of the address he had counted out. He unfastened his belt, stood tall and flung the buckle toward the back of a house on uneven stilts. The belt hit the underside with a ting.

I jumped away before it could come down against me.

He stepped back to the seaward side of the house and swung his belt buckle side over the rafter. With a leap, his hand caught the short end over the rafter. He swung his leg up and over the porch.

The house creaked.

His hand reached down for me.

Chapter 19

I grabbed the brawny arm and scrambled up the post as I reached to what of the balcony railing that remained. It gave way beneath my grasp. My hand flattened on the deck. I felt Barker grab me by the back of my bloomers and pluck me to the deck.

I scrambled to my feet and shook my boots to get the water from them.

In here, the smell was not as bad. When I set my foot down, did the wood move?

Barker stepped through the broken French doors.

With my gloved hands I smacked some of the remaining glass free and followed. I blinked as if this might help my eyes adjust to the dark.

Plaster slid away like melting cake frosting showed the wood beneath. Taffeta had hung from the ceiling in what was probably an Arabian Nights fantasy of opulence, but now dangled in tatters and tangles against the walls. Only the far corner of fabric still swooped from the center shreds with beads and crystals. At the center of the room, a bare wire showed someone had been here to claim whatever chandelier had hung. A mattress was either tossed aside by the storm or looters. A headboard of curved wood stood against gathers of rich material. A nightstand bore only a triangle of what would have been a square of marble.

Barker felt inside the nightstand. He withdrew his hands, empty.

"Scavengers," I said. "The family doesn't know about this place and Arbuthnot didn't like coming here."

The shack, that would once have been a cottage, shifted. I leaned my hand toward the left wall and stumbled.

Barker caught me.

No left wall, at least not where I reached.

I looked. Tattered fabric billowed and the dark water of the ocean below. I looked into the blackness of the interior of the place next door. The surge of the storm had chewed great holes in these shacks and showed that the sea would claim them soon. No wall remained on my left and floorboards bristled in uneven lines.

Although this place may have become unstable within the past few days of storms at sea, Larisa must have been in love with danger to boat out here for privacy.

I breathed in and my nose again filled with memories: I saw the boy down the street who had survived the floodwaters, but tore his foot on a rusted length of barbed wire; I saw him for an instant on his bike; then I saw him in bed with blood poisoning moments before he joined is parents in death.

I swallowed hard. "What are we looking for? Do you think anything is left?"

"Answers," Barker said. He shot a quick glance of those blue eyes back beneath that weathered brow, but they searched my face for only an instant. "Your client Mrs. Dorfman knew things that in death she can't tell us. Finding evidence of her can tell us those memories, those thoughts."

Were her memories like mine?

He pulled a silver cylinder—one of those flashlight things—from his pocket. He cranked it and arced it around the room to light the crevice of shattered glass, seaweed, and partial picture frames. "Her ambitions."

He stopped.

I stretched my hands through the dark and held them before me like a sleepwalker. I walked over the uneven, unsure floor to where he stood in a corner.

He shoved the flashlight at me and I grabbed it.

Barker tore taffeta and gauze from the wall. He reached down and kicked.

The structure rocked.

"Careful," I said in what sounded like a cat's warning growl. "We can swim it if we fall in the water, but not if we're trapped under all this debris. "I don't want to die like people who ended that way."

The building jittered. I stumbled, but then found my footing on the slippery floor.

"The tide's coming back." He shoved his shoulder against the wall. He stepped back, and then kicked at the wall like a locked out bridegroom kicks a hole in the door of the bedroom suite. He then kicked around the edge of the hole. "And we'll have to hurry." He flicked a hand toward the ceiling. "The sway of this place is worse than the cracks and missing spots."

I cranked the handle at the side of the flashlight and a yellow circle of light emerged.

Yes, the ceiling had a pronounced sway, as though a giant sat above the roof.

"Back here is the most dangerous even if it is the most intact."

"How could you possibly know that?" I crept toward the area he said was dangerous.

"Because I am a trained engineer."

The flashlight gleam faded to blackness.

This was the first thing he had ever told me anything of himself.

"Keep the light on. There's a girl."

"False corner?" I asked. "Could be for the pipes and whatnot since these aren't expensive-built . . ." I steadied myself against the rocking and bent down to light the opening he forced in wood.

He yanked a gossamer length of sodden fabric from the wall to clear his view.

I peered at the metal box I illuminated with a few cranks. "A safe."

Yes, he nodded. He kicked away more wood.

I knelt down beside him with the light close to the combination.

"It's bolted to the floor," he said. "Hence the metal plate beneath the building."

"Oh, that's what you hit with your belt." I wagged my hand. "When we were down there."

The flashlight dimmed and the face looking at me plunged into darkness. Able to ascribe any expression I wanted, I figured he smiled at me.

"It hasn't been opened." He leaned his head down toward the safe. "Sea water makes this easier. The rust knows the numbers." He spun the large old dial.

"I'll not ask how you came by that skill, trained engineer that you are."

I felt him bat the air to silence me. I heard the dial click through its rotation and then stop.

He turned the bar at the side. It gave, but did not open.

"It moved," I said.

"Yes, I noticed that." His teeth gritted with exertion. He tried again.

"Put a little English on the ball."

He glared at me, "Hardly that." He gave it another pull with both hands and the small black safe shuddered open.

The room swayed. I looked down and saw water close below the floorboards.

I cranked the flashlight back on and held it close to the safe. Some jewelry. I could not make out details, but no sparkle of great diamond necklaces or tiaras. Small pieces, like a watch pin, belt buckle and a couple flower broaches. Also within, some papers, photographs and a thick book. I unbuttoned my bloomer pocket, grabbed the jewelry and shoved it in. "I want out of here now. We can figure out what this is later."

He looked at the photographs with a smile and tucked them into the top of his sweater. He leapt to his feet and then pulled my arm up. He bent his head down to mine and whispered in my ear. "Don't be alarmed when you turn around."

The house gave a creak.

I turned and cranked the flashlight back on. I gasped.

"Hiya, dearie." Skip held a match to his thumbnail and lit it, then a kerosene lantern. The room glowed in orange and rotted shades of green.

"Howdy Skip," I said. "We'll talk outside." The structure skittered again on its remaining pylons. "We all need to get out of here now."

"Yes, give me your hand." He smiled with a twinkle of straight teeth and clear eyes in the kerosene light.

I stepped toward him, my hand outstretched. I handed the flashlight to Barker.

His fingers closed over mine and slid the flashlight from them.

Skip caught my free hand. "Now, precious, you get out of here." He pulled me past him and toward the French door, but never turned his eye away from Barker.

I slipped and hit the wall with my shoulder. That knocked the boards free and I wheeled my arm to gain balance.

"You just go." He said in a tone he tried to control, but still screeched with panic at the end of the sentence. "I'll take care of this."

I didn't like his sound. "What's to take care of?" I shot a glance back at Barker.

He stood without moving.

"Find anything interesting in there?" Skip said.

"Let's talk about this outside," I said.

Back in that dark corner, Barker's head bobbed to urge me outside.

Another jolt of the house moving smacked me against the broken wall. I pulled from the splintered slats and looked at Skip.

"I . . .I need to deal with something first." Skip set the lantern on the floor and took a series of gulps to empty a glass flask of some patent medicine and tossed it through the broken window into the sea.

"Certainly," I said. "Come, Mr. Barker."

"Oh, Mr. Barker and I have things to discuss. Like what he got out of that safe." Skip turned to me again and stroked a tress back from my face. ""I wanted to keep you from harm, dearie. You are my girl now. So go."

Skip extended one beseeching hand toward Barker, while he kept the other wedged in his pants pocket.

Chapter 20

Dollars to doughnuts, he wasn't doing that thing in his pocket that tended to get the creepier eighth-grade boys in trouble, but fingered a small gun in there. Barker probably figured that as well since he had not moved since he stood.

The house creaked and I threw myself farther than the momentum had taken me. I fell to the ground beside the French door. I felt around. Yes, I got what I wanted.

Is there really danger? Should I do this or calm down?

Skip turned to me. "But sweetheart, you know you should do what I say. This man isn't someone you should listen to. He's been a bank robber and a murderer, haven't you heard?" Skip put his hand on my cheek and placed a gentle kiss on my lips. "Don't I mean anything to you?"

Thank you, thank you, for saying what I needed to hear.

"Of course," I said. "Of course I'll do anything you want." I stepped closer to him so my body was against his, but one arm still behind me.

"Yes," Skip said. "He's trespassing, my dearie. He's here illegally. I've got to deal with this, but don't you be afraid."

Oh no! He grabbed my shoulders.

I held my breath.

I dashed the shard of glass to Skip's throat.

.

He screamed and whacked my shoulder with a few blows.

I tried to shove the blade glass through soft tissue of his neck into the brain to kill him, but I only managed to shove him against the wall and press the end of the glass into his neck.   "You think I could just let you kill a man?"

The shack fell off the seaward pylons, but I was too angry to leave.

"Just because I'm lonely and you tell me a few pretty things?"

He said nothing. His eyes widened like a spooked horse and blood dribbled down his neck.

"My husband was not a great man, but he would never have done something so . . . so debased, so horrible." Tears streamed from my eyes. I blinked them away. "He, well for all his faults, he cared about more than himself." The floor jostled, but I kept the knife against his flesh.

"I'm thinking of you," Skip said. He managed his top-dollar smile even with the knife at his throat.

"Oh please! You make this easy for me to—"

"Mrs. Gallagher," Barker said. He had slipped past Skip to stand behind me, near the opening chewed in the side of the building. "Daria—."

"And you left out the fact that I am a man of power." Skip's head tilted at an awkward angle around my blade, but not so far that he suffered deep injury. "I will ruin you for this. The two of can go nowhere to find quarter. Do you think that my name, my connections, my money will not prevail?"

"Do you think I am without resources?" I hissed. "Feel the blade at your throat and wonder what kind of woman would have that."

"A bitch," Skip said.

"A woman who came home to the family apartment in Russia and found my mother's blood all over and my drunken father just sitting there." My voice came out as an angry cat squall. "Someone who survived in the sewers under *Nevski Prospekt*. I'm someone who survived when my husband decided he would rather pursue a crazy business proposition than be home to face the flood waters and you—you waste of time and money—you don't scare me." I took a deep breath to plunge the glass in far enough to kill.

Skip slid the gun out and aimed it at me. He shot. He missed. Why did he miss? Because the room slanted until I almost dropped to my knee. Almost. Why didn't I? Rage. White rage for every injustice, every lack of love I had ever faced in my entire life kept me at his throat with the blade. I would show him and everyone all the way back to my mother, that I was just fine even without them caring about me.

"Daria," Barker said. His arm around my waist was why I had not fallen. "Leave him."

A beam crashed across the bed.

I fell through the opening. No, Barker pulled me through the opening. He caught the edge of the deck.

My glass shard fell from my hand.

Skip fell onto the bed. I caught a glimpse before the shack fell around him.

Barker crouched on the deck, reached down, and caught something on the underside. He held tight to my waist and we swung. A ladder. Yes, we hung from a rope ladder. It must have been Skip's. We fell.

The cold water stung my body and made my movements underwater sluggish. I felt my bloomers tear over the leg, but I got free.

Pain. Some part of the now shattering house scraped my arm.

I needed to surface. Where was I? I hoped no more shack was left to fall before I ran out of air and had to surface. I pulled to the surface.

I drew in air and looked. I screamed. Just beside me, boards splashed.

I tucked my head down and crawled through the underwater frog swim my sister and I learned as kids at camp.

Arms grabbed me around my chest. They grabbed from above.

I did not struggle. If I needed to fight with Skip, I could only take him by surprise if I went limp now.

I looked up. They arms belonged to Barker. He sat in a small rowboat. "Skip seems to have brought this with him." He pulled me in.

I turned back and saw roof planks break off and fall into the water.

"He didn't make it out, then."

"I could grab him or I could grab you."

"Thank you." I shivered in the cold, but did not dare say anything.

Barker dove back into the water.

I shouted, "What are . . ." What was he doing? I knew. I didn't like the way it made me angry, though. I watched for his shape, but he disappeared through the black water. I knelt in the boat and craned to get a better look.

"Leave him," I called out to the night. "He's probably dead." And don't we want him that way? Skip wasn't just a waste of time and money. He was trouble for Barker, for me, and I would imagine a whole bunch of other people.

I saw Barker's head bob up. Something weighted him down. I saw the arm of the man he carried.

I groaned, but stretched forward and took hold of his unwieldy burden.

Skip was still.

The back half of the house rolled into the water.

I held him steady against the side of the rocking boat while Barker climbed in.

He hoisted Skip's limp form into the boat, held his head to the side, and pushed the dirty water from his lungs. Barker grabbed both oars and stroked with Henley Regatta form.

I felt Skip's pulse. "He's alive. I suppose you were right to go back for him."

Barker's muscles pulsed with each alternating jab of the paddle into the water. 'You've seen much death. Don't let that inure you to life." He stopped rowing to look at me without blinking. "The men who let it get to them lost some of themselves that they never got back." He looked down at the oar he drove into the water.

I looked at Barker, at the face with smooth skin and just a few crowsfeet around those eyes, so large and blue with innocent, draping black lashes that kept his eyes from meeting mine. What had those eyes seen? His determined frown and grim mouth went through some internal hell experienced in the past. His erect posture and tense muscles showed he would not let that harsh event happen again when he could help it.

He had known war. He had that tough, distant look of the men in the Civil War home when remembering the worst days when all their friends died. I don't know if the stories about him with the Rough Riders were true or if he had seen action in the Boer War. Maybe Afghanistan. Wherever it was, Barker had seen things that make a man wonder why he was left to live.

"You do what you do—you're a detective—to help people, don't you?"

"Of course." The terse syllables were all that lit on the night mist except for the slaps of the oar into the water.

I felt my lower lip tremble as when I was a small child about to cry. I did not know if I was sad for Barker, sad for myself, or still had feelings of anger and frustration for the man lying at my feet in the boat. I took a deep breath and tried to think of something else. "What will we do with him now?"

Chapter 21

Barker slid the boat with Skip's injured form onto the beach. "He's conscious, just exhausted. A sleep in the sea air will do him good." Barker took my arm and led me up the sand. "My house is closer if you want to make yourself presentable before going home."

I opened my mouth to say that was a good idea, but then he said, "It's on Post Office."

"No."

In the moonlight, I saw he rolled his eyes.

I gave a sad little smile for my lost reputation, but only mourned it an instant before I gave way to chattering teeth. I gave his arm a friendly pat. "I still have some clients I haven't lost. I don't think they'd stay with me if I home before I go to that part of town."

"I'll give you a ride."

Morning sun forced its way through the lace curtains of my front parlor in long streams of yellow and white light.

I sat on the couch and smiled at the girls. Teddie sat on the piano bench and attempted to drag Jinxie beside her, but the younger girl wanted to sit on the floor and watch the patterns the sun made on her white gloves.

We were At Home.

"We just sit here?" Teddie asked. This was not the first time we had been At Home to visitors and not the first time she had asked this.

"What do you think?" I asked with a smile I wished my mother had learned.

"I think we sit here until roving hordes of bandits come to kill us in our beds." Teddie said.

I pulled my tatting from the painted wooden sewing hamper, which sat beside the sofa. "If we are here, then we wouldn't exactly be killed in our beds, would we?"

"We saw the newspaper," Teddie said. "Hordes of—"

"No raging hordes!" I slipped the needle from the white thread and picked out the stitches I had made that looked more like a spider's web than the lace I'd seen in the Ladies Home Journal.

Teddie whined, "but they strangled that drayman."

"No, it was just a bunch of, well, robbers. That doesn't mean . . ."

"That poor man," Jinxie said.

A knock at the front door startled the three of us. Aunt Cornelia noticed because she shot us a glare as she answered.

"Good Afternoon," MJ said as she strolled in past Aunt Cornelia's glare. "Don't mean to keep you from your biscuits, Eula."

Aunt Cornelia blew out a sigh the length of her walk back to the kitchen.

I tucked my tatting back into the hamper before MJ could see the errant stitches and give me a "tsk" or worse, show me how it's done. She was always better at feminine craft than I. For someone determined to make her way in a man's world and sometimes in a man's way—at one society event, she had insisted on going out behind the

cotillion hall to join the men who were smoking cigars—
she was a girly girl. I thought of that and said, "MJ, you're
just like the rest of us girls who dream in our heart to wear
a beautiful ball gown and be crowned a princess."

"If all the queen positions are taken, I suppose." MJ
gave the girls a wink and sat on the couch beside me.

Teddie shook her head and then joined Jinxie in a
giggle at the thought of getting to be a princess.

MJ pulled her pencil and pad from her draw-string
purse and licked the pencil tip. Her green eyes bore into
mine. "Skip was found dead" in the same tone she might
have used to ask for a cup of tea with milk. "What was in
that note you wrote to him?"

"I don't know what note you're talking about," I
said. "I've never written anything to him."

"Just checking. They found a note on him. Said,
'My darling, Never doubt I'm yours.' in a squirrely hand
with no signature."

I glared at her. "Where did they find him?"

"In his room at the Tremont."

I stood, grabbed my knitted shall, and kissed Teddie
and Jinxie. "Keep your white gloves on until five. You're
hostesses while I'm out."

Teddie nodded. Jinxie saluted.

I dashed to the street and fumbled in my purse to
pay a streetcar.

Chapter 22

"I'm his attorney," I said to the man at the front desk.

The desk was more a state of mind than actual furniture since it was formed from two sawhorses and a piece of plywood. Behind it, ornate mahogany carving held a cracked mirror. At desk height, an unstained edge showed where the original wood had been yanked out by the waters of the storm.

Water had filled the first floor of the Tremont Hotel, but it had not given way to the storm and hundreds had found shelter here. Now, workmen strove to turn it back into an elegant hotel. New plaster adorned the walls and painters now added a pale green color. Comfortable couches and chairs in the smoking lounge had been replaced by wood benches, but the mahogany bar was stocked with sparkling bottles and glasses. I wanted to go up that wide staircase that sported stains where once a carpet runner had been. This bearded fellow at the desk could get me there.

I smiled.

He frowned.

"We need to make sure nothing, oh, sensitive gets sent back to his parents in New York." Yes, this was true and there probably wasn't anyone else to do it. I handed him my card.

He looked at it as if reading were a skill he had yet to master. He made no move to help me or shoo me away.

"I don't know his room number. Oh yes, and I need the key." I slipped a dollar across the makeshift counter. "Is there a special fee for that?"

He started, with a shake of all that facial hair, and turned away to busy himself with a box of uneven file cards. He looked up from that only to give a nod to someone in the offices behind the desk.

I hoped that person was not employed to drag unruly women from the premises.

He hadn't told me to leave, so I wouldn't. I opened my mouth to say something, but remembered the last time I complained to a clerk and became known to the press as someone harassing the police. He then wandered to the cubbyholes at his right.

I cleared my throat to remind him I was not going away.

After a few moments, he turned back to me and slapped a key on the counter. "Room three-twenty-six."

He waved me away with an extra wave toward my attempted bribe. "Just box it all up and let us know where to send it."

Oh no! Yes, I could get the address from MJ, but then she would be all over me with questions and publish the answers. I would have to think of something. In the meantime, I grabbed the key on its large brass tab and bolted for the stairs.

The hotel room was big, with curtains around the bed that held a white crochet bedspread over a mauve satin comforter, a bow-legged desk, a bone china vase set on what would have once been a washstand, and a modern armoire of carved wood.

I opened the cupboard the marble-topped nightstand. Nothing. I walked around to the other side and opened that one. An inkwell, stack of paper, and a city directory. I looked behind and felt beneath the nightstand and found more nothing. I did this to the other with the same result.

I opened the armoire. A suit and several shirts had been hung up, probably by the maid since the celluloid collars stacked in an unruly pile beside the bed showed Skip not to be of the tidy mold.

"You should not be doing this."

I jumped and turned around to see Barker sitting on the bed. "No kidding! I'm not even sure what I'm doing."

"So you didn't have a plan."

"I have an idea," I said.

"Which is?"

"That there is something up here that would tell me why he died."

Barker shrugged.

A chill slid up my spine. "Have you been following me?"

Barker's blue eyes sparkled and his face pulled around his cheekbones with a smile that did not make it to his lips. "Nay, the hotel detective called me to check out the nosy *bissom* of an attorney."

"That would be me," I said. "Even if I don't know what it is." I sat beside him on the bed. "So, do you think I'll find anything here?"

Barker shrugged. "It's where they found him." He pointed toward the open door to the hallway. "In the doorway. That's why they got him so jolly quick."

"What do you think? Was it murder?"

"What do *you* think?"

"That you are a frustrated geometry teacher who wants me to work things out for myself."

Barker's smile spread all the way to his lips. "Trigonometry, now there's math for you! But I'm honored that you find me a mentor of sorts."

I closed my eyes and let it fill with images of a smiling Skip. "He drank coca wine, but so does the pope. I think he took other drugs and suspect he did more than he should, but that leads to a slow, dissipating death. He seemed in good shape." I opened my eyes. "I also thought he was poor."

Barker gave a confused frown.

"That he'd been cut off by his parents and couldn't pay for anything."

"And yet, he stays in a deluxe room."

"So he had someone else." I swung my purse around my arm. "And he wanted to make a big score to, I don't know, not need his parents or something."

"He may have had an immediate need for big money," Barker said. "He was certainly desperate last night." He raised his eyebrows to will me to get the extra meaning in what he said.

I couldn't see it because my mind had wandered. "Could a murderer get up here unseen?"

"Aye," Barker said. "Hotels always have a way for—shall we say—visiting ladies to get in and out without being seen."

"The sort of ladies on Post Office street?"

"Similar." He craned forward toward the hallway. "This room is next to the stairs and no room directly across the hall. Those exit to the alley behind the dry-goods warehouse. Someone coming to this room would not be seen." He looked up to the crown molding. "Looks as though the room was picked for that purpose."

"Do you think the ladyfriend killed him?"

He rolled his eyes and made one of those very Scottish sounds. "Killing someone with drugs requires a fair degree of premeditation, not passion from one who gave him a note so recently, that it is still in his dead hand now on the coroner's table."

"I keep coming back to it probably being an accident and not murder. I mean, why would someone kill him and not you?" I shrugged at his frown. "I would think his quest for the casket was nothing compared to yours, but probably what got him killed."

"That's simple. The murderer does not see me as trouble, but did see him. Your quest requires you to figure out why."

The candlestick phone on the nightstand rang.

I jumped, but did not move toward it. "Maybe, he got too close to something else."

The telephone rang again.

"They know you're up here," Barker said. "It's probably for you."

I frowned at him, but answered the phone.

"Mrs. Gallagher?" said the voice on the other end. He did not wait for a reply. "Your friend is on the way up." He hung up before I could ask anything.

"Oh no!" I said. "MJ wouldn't have had to figure much to figure out where I am. I'll bet that's she." I made wide, shooing motions to Barker sitting on the bed. "You have to get out of here. You'll ruin my reputation."

He gestured to the open door and said in a voice louder than an American gentleman would use toward a lady, "I came here to help you and now you accuse me of being . . . I don't know what you think I would do."

"Oh trust me! I know you can't do anything where a female is concerned." I folded my arms over my chest so tight that I could feel the beading on my dress pressing through corset cover and chemise to my flesh. "But that doesn't mean you can't ruin what is left of my reputation."

"You go too far, Mrs. Gallagher. But figures that a woman would be more concerned about what people say about her behind her back rather than why a man was murdered."

"So, you can tell he was murdered." I fought the satisfied smile tugging at my lips. He was right, I did care more about my reputation than this man who I had left for dead once he exposed himself to be a parasite bent on manipulating women.

"I believed that obvious," Barker said.

I may have rolled my eyes because Barker let out a huff.

"So, the husband of whomever his, um, sponsor," I said. "May have done it. That type of jealousy can be premeditated." I gave a knowing nod, as if my extensive legal experience meant I knew this, rather than how much grease a connector manufacturer can be reasonably expected to use in shipbuilding.

Barker's eyes roamed to my foot, which tapped on the thick floor cloth.

"Hello, Miss Dash, are you there?" Evangeline rounded the corner into the room. She carried a large cardboard box. "Mr. Barker said I should bring these up to you."

Thanks." I stood and stretched. "Put them by the armoire." I walked into the bathroom of large, yellow tile.

Shaving soap in a cup, a razor and strap beside the sink.

I opened the medicine cabinet and found a tin of women's powder, a lady's syringe, a hypodermic syringe, and four bottle of heroin, all but one empty. I leaned against the tile wall and found it warm, rather than the cool I expected. Maybe all my worry had brought on a fever.

Heroin is supposed to be non-addictive, but like any drug, it could kill when overdosed. Since he had the equipment that showed he regularly took a large amount, someone he knew would have little trouble helping him to just a little too much.

Barker's big hand grabbed my arm. "Get out of here."

I smelled smoke. I looked at the armoire and Evangeline grabbed my hand. We ran toward the door, but I looked back.

Barker went to the phone and pumped the hook to get the desk. He saw me and said, "Go on! I have to warn the desk."

Evangeline held my hand and we ran from the room.

The hallway had even more smoke and tongues of red flame at the stairwell door.

"Front stairs!" I yelled. Evangeline followed me in clutching her skirt up high to keep it from catching fire and ran down the hall even faster than I.

Chapter 23

I watched the fire department pull the black steel and brass engine to the side door and charge up the stairs with the hose.

Evangeline gave me a hug and walked back toward the office.

"No one hurt," Barker said. "But you won't have to be mailing any property to his parents now."

The man lighting the streetlamps was up and streetcar mules would have gone to bed already, so Barker flagged into a cab outside the hotel. The office was walking distance, so I clambered in to find out where he was going. The horses pulled away before I had my skirt in and the door closed.

I straightened and tugged my sleeves down full length. "I didn't hear where you told the driver to go, but I figure I know."

Barker sat in silence.

Silence always brings the talk out in me. "Karparov. He did this. He killed his daughter for taking the magic casket, he killed Skip for getting too close and then he set the fire to—I don't know—do you in or keep us from finding evidence."

"You seem very sure."

While I was still deciding whether or not I was so goshdog sure, he said, "And what proof do you have?"

"The man is a loon, for starters. He spoke of her as if he knew she was dead."

"But you even stated that Russian is vague on such points."

"Yes," I agreed. "But he's had that henchman fellow of his spying on us. And, well, he hired you to find the magic box, but not to find out what happened to his missing daughter. To me, that says he knows."

Barker said a lot more nothing until lit to the street before the Karparov house.

I leapt from the cab while Barker finished up with the driver. He was beside me when I got to the front door and he slammed the knocker against the carved oak.

A butler answered, Barker nudged him aside, and I followed Barker through a hallway filled with boxes. Barker stood tall and still for an instant, and then darted to the left.

Barker plunged past the butler.

Polly gave a scream and ran through a hall lined with packing boxes into to the recesses of the house.

"She's probably gone to get Karparov," I said.

"Good," was all Barker got out before Slava, his face screwed up with rage, thundered toward Barker. Barker stopped him with an arm to the throat. He then pushed him against the wall of the entryway. Slava hit the coat closet door with a snap and punched Barker in the stomach. Barker pulled away before the blow could land with full force.

I looked around for something to grab and on the hall tree, found a bronze statuette of a rearing horse. I hadn't seen a fight since elementary school and those were more dog pile than anything.

Barker blocked a punch with one forearm and sent a blow to Slava's head with the other.

I wondered if I should plunge in to break it up, but Barker was doing fine and I didn't want to interrupt.

Slava landed one on Barker's cheek, sending him sideways.

I lunged forward with the bronze, but careened to the side when I saw Nina in the doorway.

She screamed toward Barker's back. I ran toward her and hit her in the gut with my elbow. She scrambled to catch hold of me, but I batted her hands away with the bronze.

Barker looked over his shoulder at us and gave a sniff.

I threw through the doorway behind me rather than toward any combatant. I doubled my fist and punched Nina in the face. I had fought before, but only against my sister. Coralie was smaller, but she always won.

Nina lunged forward to scratch me, and I dodged it, but then she kicked me in the shin. She fought like my sister.

Well, so could I.

I dropped the bronze on her foot, pulled her head back by her hair, and punched her in the stomach.

"That'll teach you not to wear real stays," I growled. I punched her again in the stomach.

Beyond her, I saw Barker shoot a glance at me and then lean over, barrel himself into Slava and use the momentum of his movement to toss the big blond man over him and onto his back on the floor.

I feinted letting go of her hair, but then grabbed it with both hands. I rocked back and flung her around to the floor atop her fiancé. She tripped, but before she fell, Barker caught her around the waist.

I gasped. "What the . . . ?"

Barker grabbed her arm and pressed it to his face. He made a sniff.

Slava raised to a sitting position.

"Stay down," I growled as if I were armed and just as dangerous as anyone else in the room, but I made sure I was not close enough for him to catch my skirt.

Slava's face grew purple with anger and white with—that stuff the scientists found coursing through a body when excited—adrenalin. He did as Barker commanded, though, and lay back down.

Barker pulled her arm past his nose, and shoved her away.

She stumbled back with a whimper.

"Slava!" Karparov shouted from the archway. "Get up and do something."

"Tell your father and Slava to give us a moment alone," Barker said to Nina.

She hesitated. She shivered with tears that reddened her eyes, but did not spill down her face. Barker pushed her shoulder forward and crouched down so she would see his face. Even though I couldn't see him, I knew look on his face showed a whole netherworld of anger. "Papa, leave us." She spoke Russian between her gasping sobs. She darted her eyes a few times to the man on the floor, swallowed, and then whispered, "Slava, you as well."

Slava rose, but walked toward Barker with a look of premeditated murder on his face.

I sneered at him in Russian, "Act like a gentleman and listen to what a lady says."

That mother thing must be working for me because he let out a growl and walk down the hall.

Karparov held a splayed hand out toward us, but also went down the hall to the main parlor.

Barker caught Nina around the waist and scooted her into a wood-lined study. I was at their heels and closed the door behind us.

"I don't know," she said to Barker's gaze. "I don't know anything."

He stared at her, and for a long time, she did nothing but sob.

After a few minutes, she wailed, "What do you want? I didn't do anything. I wasn't there."

You weren't where? I said nothing; this was Barker's bailiwick.

"Then where were you?" Barker asked.

She struggled against him in what looked like an attempt to avoid eye contact rather than get away. She trembled and didn't even seem to notice that her nose ran and mouth drooled. "Please."

"Nina," he growled. "I can smell the kerosene on your sleeve. What if people died?"

She vibrated with tears. "I just don't know what I was doing." Her eyes darted around the room. "I think he mesmerized me."

I couldn't keep myself from talking any longer. "Who did?"

"Skip." Her voice came out in a whine. "I loved him." More sobs wracked her slim frame.

"So, you know he's dead?" Barker did not wait for an answer. "You have a clerk at the hotel who keeps you informed about him, don't you?"

She looked at her feet.

"Don't you?" Barker shouted through grit teeth.

"He leaves notes for me at Viktor's firm down the street. Viktor would never open them." She looked as though she would spit at Barker. "Viktor is a gentleman, not like you."

Karparov spoke from the doorway. "Nina, you can go now."

"I just didn't want anyone to get my letters." She walked past him into the hallway. Her body jerked with each tear.

I looked at Barker and he at me. Neither of us told her that there were no letters in the room, that he did not care enough to keep any and only happened to still have the one she just sent because he hadn't had time to throw it away before he was killed. I looked at Barker and saw what I assumed to be pity clouding his handsome face.

"She is not well since the casket has gone missing it is what we expect." Karparov's voice was rich with feeling, but still soft enough that it was not much more than a whisper. He glanced down the hall to where Nina had walked away. "That is why she is to marry Slava. He will take care of her."

"Prison would probably be more compassionate than that," Barker said. "But you want to avoid scandal, don't you?"

"There are many things I wish to avoid," Karparov said. "Paying you for nothing is one of them."

"You need not worry about that," Barker said.

"Oh, I don't worry about that." Spittle hissed through Karparov's bottom teeth. "But believe me, I could make you worry if I must."

When I got home, I found Evangeline had dropped off a message for me that Judge Reams wanted to talk to me in the morning.

Chapter 24

At the courthouse in the office of Moroccan-bound volumes and orange-leather chairs, I sat before Judge Ream's desk. I gave him my most engaging smile and willed myself not to shift on the uncomfortable wooden chair.

He furrowed his brow and let out a sigh as though he hesitated to tell me something.

You only have to process the paperwork, you old windbag.

I sat straight without slumping thanks to the corset beneath my cheviot suit. I held my purse so my hands would not fidget and reminded myself every minute not to grip the handle so tightly that the steel frame torqued.

"I don't know, Dash," he said. "You've been consorting with some unsavory types."

"Types?" Never volunteer information under cross examination. It is what I tell my clients when they have to go to court.

"That Russian friend of yours."

"Ah," I said. "That would be a single dead person. As for her associations, was she not a member of the top society of both Houston and Galveston?"

"And do you think it's appropriate for a mother of young girls to spend all of her free time hobnobbing with people that could only look down on her and laugh?"

Another deep breath, another count. The only time when I would come across people such as this is when I do charity work. I believe all of us have been called to do such, no matter how humble we are."

"I just don't know," Judge Reams said with a shake of his head. "You seemed such a quiet woman and now I find you have all sorts of friends."

"I'm sorry, sir, but I can't help wondering." My hand escaped from its grasp of my purse and flapped around over my lap. "The ordeal I'm going through isn't because I'm a woman, is it?"

"A man all alone wouldn't be considered for adoption at all," Judge Reams said. His face contorted into a scowl and his eyes rolled. "Men are such sexual creatures, you know."

I held my breath and looked at the toes of my yellow satin shoes. I didn't want to give him any reaction.

"I'm going to have to look over everything again," he said.

My heart sank, but I was not surprised, so I did not react.

He added, "I just haven't seen you demonstrate any ability to take care of yourself, why should I believe you could teach your daughters to take care of themselves?"

He shouldn't have said that, not if he wanted to keep me from exploding like a pyroclastic surge all over his office.

"How dare you think I can't take care of myself," I said. I've always taken care of myself. I'm the best there is at teaching girls to take care of themselves. "I have taken care of myself in situations that would make you cry whimpering in the corner. My daughters will know how to survive."

"I'm wondering if the children might be better off back at the orphanage. At least for a while."

I stood. I had to move to keep from crying. This was about power and him exerting power over me. Anything I said or did had no meaning. None of my skill as a speaker could make anything better or worse.

"Take a seat, Dash," Judge Reams said with an expansive wave of his hand.

Judge Reams face turned a shade of maroon that came close to purple. "Mrs. Gallagher, you had better sit down and—"

I put rested my weight on my hands on his blotter. I looked in his face.

He pulled back.

"I can't imagine you'd do something so evil as to deny my daughter the mother they love, the only family they have. So, we are done here today and with you trying to rip off parts of my soul in these interviews. Good day, Judge."

I opened the door and strode out. I dared not close it because I couldn't do it without slamming it. I did not see the clerk in the outer office. I had probably scared him away.

Stupid, stupid, stupid, I told myself as I trotted down the grand staircase of the courthouse. I may have ruined my adoption, but I would carry out my threats. I would also do everything I could to keep Reams from taking my daughters away.

A pair of men had just reached the large double glass doors, crossed with brass strips and cabochons.

Without waiting for them to open it for me, I pushed past and through the doors.

I strode through the street. I was almost to my office and on Mechanic Street before I realized where I was. I took a deep breath and turned toward my office. I realized I had walked all the way to where Viktor's printing warehouse stood.

Chapter 25

The warehouse stood towering three stories of brown painted brick. Every yellowed window set within the massive array had been broken until they looked like a Jack O'Lantern made up of only teeth. This was the lee side of the building. That was why the windows had not been blown out entirely.

I stepped over the trenches of hose in the road, these extra wide ones taking in sand to shore up the whole island, and around a mound to the sidewalk. Inside, stacks of I assumed to be books sat wrapped in paper, within crates. A pair of men with his shirtsleeves rolled up slapped paper through the flat plates of a huge printing press. No, they would not be printing the books. These would be labels for the boxes.

This was a successful business with a man standing at a desk beside a working press.

"What are you doing here, Mrs. Gallagher?" Viktor smiled as he said it and walked out from behind the equipment to where I stood on the street. Always a gentleman, he stood on the outside of the fragmented boards. "Still trying to find my wife's murderer?"

"I don't know." I backed up. "I don't know what I'm doing. So you too think she was murdered?"

I heard the whir of the press behind me and smelled the paper and books that had already turned stale and dusty. I loved that smell and it took my mind off my troubles.

"I have not thought about it, I simply remembered that you do. To be honest, I had not thought about Larisa in so many years. But what can I help you with? I cannot be away from my work for long, but I will help you. Please, we will come in off the street."

"Of course, I actually didn't have anything. I . . .well . . .I had a difficult morning and happened to be walking in the area. I knew this warehouse was here, but had never seen it. I thought I would just poke my nose in." I was spending way too much of this interview talking about me. "So, how are you holding up?"

"As I said, it has not affected me."

Does that bother you?"

He laughed. I suppose it does a little. Oh, Mrs. Gallagher!" He grabbed my skirt with one hand and wrapped his other arm around my waist.

I gaped at him. I pulled my arms to my chest. I readied to shove him away if he, well, he was not the sort I could imagine taking a liberty, but I would be ready if he had gone insane.

"Your skirt!" He yanked at the skirt behind me.

A length of skirt wound in cog at the side of the printing press.

He pulled hard and shredded bits of skirt free, and I stumbled forward. I could have been maimed even by this small bit of industrialization.

I could tell by Viktor's wide, frightened eyes that he realized what could have happened. I found myself patting his arm to comfort him.

Two of the men in shirtsleeves came over. One checked the back of my skirt while the other held my elbow as if I might get loose and stampede another machine.

"I'm fine, truly." I told them.

"You can get back to work," Viktor said in a soft voice.

"How embarrassing," I said. "I'm sorry and thank you." I extended another, "I'm sorry," over my shoulder to the two men.

Dorfman folded his arms across his chest. "Did you have anything else, Mrs. Gallagher?"

"I was just wondering how far you go back with your father in law."

He frowned.

I don't think he understood the expression. Yes, his accent was perfect, but there was always something very precise about it—an overemphasis on the' g' in an 'ing' ending, working a little harder at saying an l than anyone else around here—as though he was always trying to make it perfect.

"You are from Russia, like the Karparovs?

He walked a short way up the sidewalk. I gladly joined him to get out of the gaping maw of machinery. "My family was a long line of ethnic Germans living in the area. We had always been Germans. We were merchants and artisans. From before the time of Peter the Great, my people were in that land practicing democracy and freedom very similar to the American way."

"That sounds wonderful," I said. I smiled at Viktor. I found I liked this stiff man with the fussy mustache. Did I think he could kill? Yes, but the reason would have to be more than rage or fear. I realized I should tell something about myself so he was more comfortable giving information. "I'm also from Russia originally. That's how I could hear that your English was a bit too good to be from around here."

"You knew from just that?"

"Also, your mother-in-law said how she had depended on you for so many years."

"Ah," he said. He looked down at his arms. "I do miss her. She is such a frail thing, but I am not comfortable going there now that my only link is severed. I have not been to their house since . . .I was going to say the night Lara did not come to supper, but I should say it was the night she died."

"Yes, you were with Mrs. Karparov, weren't you?"

"Yes."

"All that evening?"

He smiled. Apparently, I wasn't as subtle as I thought. "Yes, until well after midnight when I gave up, got my hat, and went home. Slava and Nina can verify that I was in the solarium all that time."

"Oh, they were with you?"

"No, they were not with us. They were in the music room just beyond and the solarium's only door leads right through the conservatory, so Mrs. Karparov or I would certainly have disturbed their musical efforts had we walked past."

I nodded. I felt my face blush with such obvious questioning.

"If that is all," he said. "I have a business to run." He made a sharp turn on his heels toward his warehouse.

"Yes," I said. "And thank you so much for your time."

He turned back to me. "It was a pleasure. Sometime, we can talk of pleasant things."

"Like books," I said. "I would like that very much."

"Thank you."

"Who do you think could have killed Larisa?"

"I fear her own actions lead to her death. She was a tortured soul in many ways. Her father was not a kind man and I do not think that helped."

"Do you think he could have killed her?"

His eyes grew wide at my boldness. The two men on the printing press came to look because they had never seen their employer show this much emotion. He said, "The man can do a very many things and I would like not to think about that."

"Yes," I said. "Of course. Good-bye and thank you for your kindness."

I strode back to my office each step away from the smell of books and back to the smell of Galveston with the lingering hurricane rot of animals left behind and fish washed ashore brought all the anger and unrest back to me. I felt powerless and that made me even angrier.

I trod up the stairs to my office and saw the door open. MJ, with a hat even wider and more feathery than my own, spilled out all over the place without even leaving the doorway of my office.

"What happened at the courthouse?"

You're a society columnist. You talk about whose visiting whom. How do you know about the courthouse?"

"I also talk about who may have lost it and how. Some of my best leads come from the courthouse. So, Bo Peep, spill."

"Your skirt's all ripped," Evangeline said. "How did that happen?"

"I fell into a printing press."

"You could never make it in newspaper."

I took my shoe off and threw it at her with a major league slopdollager. "Get out of my way!"

"Hey," she said as the pump smacked into her chest. If she wore a bust enhancer as she should, it wouldn't have hurt. She wound up to hurl it back at me.

"Miss Dash," Evangeline said. From over MJ's shoulder, she plucked the shoe away. "Perhaps you could let us know what happened at the courthouse and keep your shoes where they belong." She fielded it around MJ's flailing hands and to me. I missed the catch, but turned to follow it into the hall before MJ could get her mitts on it.

Barker stood in the doorway, holding my shoe.

I extended my hand, but MJ's skinny arm, devoid of any cushioning fat, shoved mine out of the way with a stinging intensity.

Barker looked MJ in the eyes and handed me the shoe. "I think we can trust Daria to keep her shoes on her feet from now on."

MJ smiled at him and gave her head a saucy waggle. "Sit down, Barker. Dash was just about to tell us about her day among the rich and famous."

"I—"

MJ gave me a frown. It might have been one of her concerned ones. "Look I'll see if there's anything I can find out about Reams." She patted my arm and left.

Barker still stood in my office. I wondered what he wanted. He seemed in no hurry to tell.

"Daria," Barker said. "May I speak to you a moment." He gestured toward his office.

"Is this like going to the principal's office?" I said.

"Principal?" He opened the door to his office for me.

"Headmaster," I whispered.

He gave me a wink and a chummy grin and closed the door after we walked in.

"I gather you've taken care of all your other business this morning and had some free time now to come with me on an errand," he said. "Yes, I know of what went on. Mrs. Quackenbush told us. The court clerk to Judge Reams was in the anteroom the entire time listening to what you and the judge said."

"For someone who has irritated and even right honorably infuriated as many people as MJ has, I'm surprised at how many friends she's got."

"Now, the reason I need you is perhaps unorthodox, in that . . . what are you doing?"

I felt tears burn at the back of my eyes. I thought I had held them in check, but I guessed they spilled out.

"Please, should you not save this in with your friends? Your female friends?"

"I don't want them to know how I ruined everything." I leaned my forehead on his chest, my eyes dry for a moment. "And that I'm broken like this without any real plan." I thought of how I had to pay Evangeline out of my savings this week, and tears sprang to my eyes again.

"He gave me a pat on the back. "You assessed a situation, realized Judge Reams was never going to act, and confronted him with the truth." He clapped me on the shoulders and withdrew his hand.

"Trust your friends," Barker suggested. He pulled his notebook from his pocket and flipped through the little pages. "I'm sure they care very much about you."

"Why would anyone care about me?"

He looked up at me with a confused frown.

"Why would anyone? If they did, would I have ended up on the street in Russia?" Too many years of emotion sanded away at my voice so it only rasped out in a hiss. "When I married, my mother told me I had always been a trial to her and she was glad I would be out of her life. I told myself it was just the moment, but inside I had a sort of satisfaction because a voice said, 'I knew all along. I knew you never really cared about me.'"

"You're daughters care about you," Barker said.

"And I can't let him take them from me."

"I don't see him doing that," Barker said.

I stood. "I have a ripped dress, a blotchy face, and a backlog of briefs to write. I need to go." I pretended I was a strong and tough, although I was sure I had all the internal stability of Jell-O just sprung from the mould.

"Larisa's diary," Barker looked me in the eyes and pressed his lips together in a white line. He tossed the small book from the beach shack at me. That was what he had been excited to find, not the photographs now scattered over his desk.

I slid my hand over the cover of the book bound in red leather and gold trim. I opened to tissue-thin pages crackling with wear and blue-back scribbles in Cyrillic. "Oh, this reminds me. Remember that document I found in her bathroom?"

"Mmmm?"

"From the Russian consulate."

"The one in Chicago?" Barker looked out the window.

"Yes—oh—you think that is Larisa's long lost auntie."

Barker shrugged.

"It said how they had reviewed her inquiry and they could find no fault with it. It didn't say what her inquiry had been."

Barker smiled. That was a nice smile.

I had to shape up. I had to stop staring at his mouth. I must stop looking to see if any gaps in his shirt might show the shape of the man beneath.

If not, I would end up bivouacked outside his office some morning with a fresh-baked pie, explaining how this would help his bachelor digestion. I could not live through the humiliation that would bring. The eyelash batting alone would send me into spasm.

"Something wrong with your eye, Mrs. Gallagher?"

"Uh, twitch, I guess." I slid my finger over my lid. "I'll get back to my office now."

"Hello Mr. Barker." Evangeline gave him a little wave from where she sat behind her typewriter. "MJ went back to her office. She said she'd try to keep you out of the paper."

I smiled and felt all teary again as I pulled my chair to my desk.

Barker grabbed an oak visitor chair with one hand, twirled it around to clear Evangeline's desk, and brought it down before my own. He threw a leg over it and dropped his elbows onto my desk and slapped the diary before me. His blue eyes bored into mine.

I looked at the diary open on my desk. "It is Cyrillic. Normal Cyrillic. Not a code or anything." I smoothed down the crumpled first pages. "Oh my!"

"What is it?" Evangeline asked. Her neck and torso lengthened from over her typewriter.

I laughed a little, not at the diary, but at my own silly little notions of what was interesting and how no one else would ever find such things of any merit. "This diary dates September 11, 1900. She was here during the flood. She survived it at a friend's house—a friend I presume who did not lose property to the flood—and she started a new diary when everything she owned was washed away."

"Oh my," Evangeline said.

"That is interesting," Barker said.

My chin fell toward my shoulder and my eyes could only meet his through the curtain of my thick lashes. "There's something in here about the friend she stayed with, a man. They, um, were quite involved with each other."

"Daria," he said. "You need to tell me what she says. Her exact words, translation, not interpretation."

Chapter 26

"But these are horrible words." Shame stung my eyes. "I heard them before, years and years ago. I heard men say them, never women. From the context, I can tell what they mean in English, but I . . . I can't say them."

"I'm sorry, but I need to know." His big, muscled frame dropped into my small guest chair opposite the desk. "This also helps your case. I am an investigator. This is the first real clue you've gotten about her murder."

"I am very uncomfortable saying them in a room with you and Evangeline."

"I understand," Barker said. He patted my hand, that limp, dead mackerel. His hand on mine pinned the book closed. "Evangeline, if you could go take a walk or something? That would help."

Evangeline nodded. "Cert—"

"Not her!" My voice whined through my nose more than my mouth. "I wanted you to go away." My hands pushed a little of the wet, Texas air away from me. "Evangeline can type my findings up, and we can—"

"No." The blue eye stayed open, unblinking, trying to mesmerize me. He held my hand tighter and then set it free.

My fingertips pressed so hard on the desk, I felt the wood pattern molding into my flesh.

"I need to hear it directly, to ask questions. I'm sorry for this ordeal, but this helps your quest to find the killer as much as—"

"I'll go get some pastries from Mrs. Hulpke," Evangeline said. She was already standing and untied her work apron to put it on a peg. From another peg, she took my chatelaine purse of chain mesh. "And some tea, too. You drink tea, don't you Mr. Barker?" She opened a drawer in the sideboard and took out the pot.

"Uh yes," he said. He did not turn to look at her. "Have Mrs. Hulpke put it on my tab. Leave the cups, please."

Behind Barker's back, Evangeline winked at me.

I scowled.

She plunked the pair of cups and saucers on the table beside Barker's elbow and stalked from the office.

"You're just quoting," Barker said softly. From his hip pocket, he took a flask and poured a bit in a cup passed it to me and then poured a small amount in his own. "These aren't your own words."

I sipped a bit of the liquid, and it burned my throat. "'We fucked. Oh, he filled me right there in the men's room. He wasn't usually that good, but he loved when I pretended to be a cheap little tramp—a maid, a whore.'" I took another sip and looked at Barker.

He licked his pencil and stared at me. He and his notebook waited for me to speak again.

"I wanted him to eat my . . . my . . . " I mouthed the word, "cunt.'"

"Opting for the word which goes back at least to Chaucer," he murmured. "Fine choice."

"I can't do this if you make fun of me."

"Go on."

"'. . . To work me there in the men's room with his mouth. Yes, I would have loved to have felt his lips on me there right in the men's room of that restaurant, but he said he thought I had too much wine and he knows that interferes with my. . .'" I frowned and sounded out the next word. "'orgasm.' Huh, how about that? It's the same word in Russian."

I looked up, my finger on the word, looked at the smile percolating through Barker's lips and cheeks and could feel myself blush a hearty shade of boiled lobster. I dropped my head back toward the book.

"'It's all so simple. He makes it sound so simple. I know I'd do anything for him. He believes in me. He believes in my plan. He believes they will accept me.'"

"They?" With a frown, he eyed the still ceiling fan over my head. Far from me, he sat lost in thoughts of this dead woman.

"'They.' Russian word for 'they.' The woman was writing in her diary. She presumed she would know to whom 'they' referred."

"Testy, aren't you?" he said. He looked at me with a smile that showed dimples below his masculine cheekbones. "I thought you only got your nick—ahem—your nose out of joint about rogering."

"New entry," I announced. "'I would never have known that stone thing had any value if Papa hadn't been that way about it. He wouldn't leave Galveston before the flood. I was smart, I knew that meant that stone box was very important.'"

Barker held his pencil over his notebook, but I shook my head.

"'My darling, I think he just cared about his own pleasure. He is such a bastard. I think that is why I like having him take me so. Viktor was always so eager to please me when I was with him. I would start beneath him and then he liked to roll me on top while he slid his hands over my breasts while I slid onto his prick.'"

"Once again, you go for the classic word."

I gaped.

He blinked slowly. "I do not for an instant believe these words come from you. A little levity might make it go faster for you."

"You scare me," I said. "No, that's not in the diary. You, you scare me."

He leaned back and folded his arms across his chest. "Why should I intimidate you?"

A knock wrapped the door.

"Oh do come in, please," I shouted.

One of Mrs. Hulpke's girls in a stripped pinafore brought in a tray with my teapot and a selection of cookies, fruit tarts, and miniature cakes covered with powdered sugar. She was a pretty blonde thing who bobbed like a village maid at the local squire before Barker. He turned a smile toward her, but his eyes came back to bore into me. She almost missed when she lowered the tray toward my desk.

I grabbed her hand to steer the tray onto the blotter.

The girl flounced from the room and closed the door behind her.

I poured some tea over my whisky. I hovered the pot over his forget-me-not trimmed cup until he nodded and splashed the thick brown liquid in.

"I asked you a question," he said.

"You always stare at me as if you're about to shake your head because I've done something idiotic." I took a sip, then took cookie and wedged it next to my cup on the saucer. "Whenever I start to speak, I feel as though you fight the urge to look at your watch."

"But I never have."

I lunged forward, holding the diary just below my dotted green bowtie. "And the fact that you know you never have is telling, indeed."

He raised one of those thick eyebrows.

"It demonstrates you've wanted to."

"I like you." Barker took a drink. "Is that what you'd have me say?"

"If you mean it and that's the best you can do." I took a shortbread cookie from the tray and bit into it. I ran my tongue over the creases in my lips to get the crumbs. "Respect me would be better."

"I do." Barker set down his cup hard enough to slosh liquid onto the saucer. "You insult me not to know that. Would I be here if I did not? Would I bother with you if I believed you to be a fool?"

"'I slid my hand over his prick right there in the audience at the opera.'" My words started in the prim elocution of a spinster first-grade teacher, but descended into a husky near whisper. "'In time to Tosca, I was pinching the head and feeling the delicious warmth of his hard, hard member.'" I only paused for a sip and a bit of cookie. I read faster now. Still shocked, I was curious and wanted to see how far she would press a life so different from my own. "'I don't know if he really loves me, but I know I make him stiff and that makes me so happy. He's so strong, so powerful and can do it all night no matter how many times he reaches an ecstasy. Sometimes, in bed, sometimes we don't even make it to bed, but standing at the base of the stairs, I feel his power claim me, run through me and I look at him to see the power I have over him. I know I can do anything and no one could stop me.'"

"Hmmph." Barker voiced his scowl. He slid lower in the chair and shifted in the small chair. "Although I can't dismiss anything, clues everywhere, you know, but I tire of this woman's self-absorbed pornography."

I pressed the book closed around my finger and said, "Was she something of a simple creature? I don't mean simple as in stupid, but not complex. Everything is sex to her. She saw men for sex—first her husband, now this guy—and she saw sex as power. She saw sex as the power she had to attract them and the way she has of gaining their power to . . . to, I don't know, rule the world."

Even with the cup raised almost to his lips, he could not hide his snicker. "You got all that from 'he ripped my bodice and pumped me ragged at the newel post'?"

I smacked the book onto my desk and spread my hand atop it. "You distrust what you think of as the workings of the female mind as if we are all a bunch of passionate boobs." I bit my lips to fight the grimace at my poor choice of words, but Barker had the grace to hide his smirk behind a hand. "These are hardly the girlish ravings of a lovelorn woman with stars in her eyes about some fellow. This is a sex-driven maniac. The sex gives her confidence, bless her heart. I think she needed to feel that to feel she could accomplish things in life."

"'Poor thing'?" Barker's index finger flicked his forehead and then tapped against his thumb. "Have to like her, don't you? Even if requirement is to explain away her libertine ways to appease your good-girl notions?"

"I'm not terribly sure I like the way you sat up straight and primmy to say 'good girl'." I sipped the tea. It bubbled against the cup and my brain was a bit swimmy in my head from the whiskey in it.

He smiled at me in a way that did not look prim.

I twisted an errant curl around my finger and tucked it into my pompadour. "'He likes to hear the stories I tell him about being with other women. Barbarian. I tolerate this. Sometimes, I like all the attention, but when we are there, when we are back home, I will not put up with this sort of thing. He can indulge in whatever vice he likes. God knows, my father did. The stories that old man told me himself!'" A wince creased my nose. "'But when my lover is my consort, when he is my Potemkin, I expect him to be discreet. Hiram has to understand that I will be the ruler.'" I looked up at Barker with eyes wide. "Hey, that's Arbuthnot, isn't it? His first name."

"Aye."

With a tired sigh, I turned the page to the next day. "'I will be a ruler my father never dared to be. One no one can ever set aside because I know so much more than he will ever learn.'" I closed the book around my hand again, drained the last of my tea cup, and held it out for him to refill.

His expression changed to an amusement that dimpled his cheeks and brightened his eyes, an expression which warmed me through the torso more than any whiskey could. He poured a couple fingers in.

With a careful hold on the teapot lid, I drowned the whiskey. I ate a small tart full of raspberries. I read: "'I have it now! I slipped into the old fart's office'—that's a word I admit I remember in Russian '*puka*', strange the way your mind works."

"Yes."

"' When no one looked and took the precious burden out with the clothes for whatever that foolish charity was.' Oh, oh my!" I always read a few words ahead of what I spoke. I looked at Barker through blurry, wet eyes. "She didn't like, well, I'll tell you."

"You can take a break, my dear, I can—"

"'Beautification society. She just wouldn't shut up'" I looked at Barker for only an instant before my eyes dropped. I pretended to find a bit of lint on bow at my shoulder and swiped away imaginary crumbs from the chest of my celery-colored suit. "The fool woman has some sort of man's job and speaks the Russian of a peasant. She bats her eyes around and thinks she is so pretty, that everyone loves her, but she is only an annoyance. I don't understand why anyone speaks to her, but all the other little hens cluck around her."

I steadied my gaze at Barker, careful not to blink or do anything that appeared as eye-batting. *Do you see me as an annoyance?*

"People lie to their diaries," he said. "That was probably what she wanted to think, not what she knew as fact."

"'She's all smiles and dimples. She probably never knew how wonderful it is to act the whore. To want to strangle her lover to watch him die in her arms, by her hand . . .'" I blinked at Barker. "Well, if that's the best measure of romantic intensity, I'll see if the Baptists want nuns, thank you." I scowled back at the diary. "'. . . I need her, though.'"

Barker leaned closer, his elbows on my desk.

"'She knows him.'" I frowned at Barker. "I wish she'd say names rather than just pronouns."

"No one else but Larisa matters to her," Barker said. "So you and I have no names."

You and I? Barker wasn't the only man I know. Why should she care about him?

"'He is certainly who my father will go to find the treasure. That old man is so predictable. I am always one jump ahead of him.'" I looked up with a smile tugging at the corner of my mouth. "She uses English-language idioms translated into Russian."

"She's forgotten some Russian."

I took a swig and then a butter cookie, bit it, and started to speak when my mouth was almost empty. "'I made up a story about a blackmailer—as if I would care about a blackmailer—and she was stupid enough to believe.'" My eyes opened wide at Barker. I wanted him to realize I'd come across something important, something more important than her opinion of me. "I have the thing. Yes, I have it." I brushed the crumbs of my cookie from my chin and into my mouth. "Can you just see her throwing back her head and laughing like one of the villains in a melodrama at that?"

Barker's large-knuckled hand patted the desk an inch from mine.

I read, "'I have the thing and I almost have it open.'" I stared with open mouth at Barker. The thing? She had the magic casket?

He nodded. "Yes, she did."

With a shudder at his words, I pointed to a section of text and pivoted the diary beneath my index finger for Barker as if he could read it. "She has a rhyme in here. It's in very strange, I think old, Russian. I'll give it a try."

"Yes," he said. He grabbed the notebook from his vest pocket, licked a pencil and hovered the pencil over the small, blank page. "Go."

"But it won't rhyme in English."

"Yes, go, go." His hand brushed the air in some form of encouragement.

"'A drink from the cup gives wisdom, a second gives foolishness. The ruler. He is suspended between heaven and hell. Greatness is his and keeps him alive. He is alive as long as he is victorious.'"

Barker scribbled.

I leaned back and took another sip of the fortified tea. "That's the end. This is all how you open it, isn't it? How you get into the magic box?"

Barker wrote to the end of the page, dotted the line with a period, and looked at me. He narrowed his eyes until the only thing visible of them was a steely glint.

Back in the diary, I read, "'The words are literal. I know what my father never could figure out. Of course, I have got it open.'" I took a deep breath. All the crying and anguish behind it today had made my head hurt. "End of that topic, she's back to, um, athletics: 'We fucked on the window sill of my cozy little apartment. First, I sat on his lap, and then I took it like a dog, no, we are wolves.'" I whipped my hand on the ruffle of my other sleeve and covered my mouth to laugh. "What do you think? After they finished, a brandy, a fine cigar, and a howl at the moon?"

When his squint failed to silence my laugh, he said, "Mrs. Gallagher, when you're ready."

"You know, I rather liked it when you called me Daria. No one ever does." I rolled my free hand in a gesture a couple yards of ermine from being royalty. "You may continue."

"As may you."

"Ah yes, the Dearest Diary." I turned it to show him the redundant characters. "'I needed to take the thing from Papa. He didn't know how to use it. I got that strange little man who came with us from Russia to make a fuss.'" I closed the book on my thumb. "Ivy. She got him to escape from the plantation; it wasn't because he was heart sick."

"I'm sure he wanted to do so. Larisa seems to have been very good at knowing her marks."

I pointed to the date. "That's three months ago. She had it for all that time."

"Yes, her father lied to us. Can you be surprised?"

I shook my head and regretted the gesture when it sent sparkles of pain through me. "She relates when she asked me about you—my landlord is what she calls you— and that I told her I didn't know you."

"Daria, you were doing so well, you know, at giving a clear translation. Now, you've lapsed into summarizing."

With an eyebrow arched high on my forehead, I said, "I figured there weren't any clues there."

"I believe that for me to decide." Barker showed he could also raise a single eyebrow.

"'How much longer can I abide her company? Hasn't my father visited that detective by now? The silly woman says she hasn't seen him there.'" I looked at the white enamel paint gleaming over the ceiling tiles. "Yes, I do remember Larisa telling me about her father. It did seem queer when she asked if I'd met him. I didn't realize she meant he might be your—"

"If I give you a whole silver dollar, do you promise to go back to reading without interruption?"

"If you promise to go to hell."

Barker reeled back in his chair, eyes open wide and a smile spreading from one lean, tanned cheek to the other.

I looked back down at the diary. "Foolish woman says she doesn't know her landlord. She says he passes her in the hall with a nod and a gruff word that could be 'good morning' in some sort of accent. Still, idiotic bitch said he was broad and handsome in a raw-boned way she found quite dreamy." I shoved the book across the table at him. "Now I ask you, can you see me calling anyone dreamy?" Before he could answer, I grabbed the book back and said, "Oh goody! We've got a change of pace from her: 'I took a new lover. In the closet of my father's office. He's a fool, but he has a useful tool.'"

Barker's large teeth did violence to a chocolate cookie.

"'Tonight,'" I read. "'I asked my new friend along. He amuses me and he might be some help.'" I turned a page. "Next day, oh, the night she died. There's still more written here." I pointed a finger at him with the enthusiasm of a sideshow weight reader sure of his guess. "From editorializing, to summarizing, to explaining. You see, my asides have evolved." I leaned back in my chair and pulled the book to me. "'I will bring my friend tonight. We will have fun even if my lover despises me for it. He is a brute, and I adore that.'" I flipped through the next section of empty pages. "Thus ends the reading, Mr. Barker." With my fingertips, I slid the book across the table to him. "Perhaps after all that . . .after everything I . . . well, perhaps I should call you by your . . ." Pain filled my head until I could not speak and light seared my eyes closed.

Chapter 27

Where is this? When is this?

Semidarkness surrounded me. Curtains pulled tight so I could not see whether daylight or evening stretched beyond. My own vision blurred. My thoughts wandered through a darkness inside my head.

I believe I finished the contract. I might have drawn ponies in the margin and left it with Evangeline to transcribe. My headache had worsened to the point that I knew nothing but the swords of pain stabbing through my brain.

I could not raise my head. Pain continued and also a dark murkiness that whooshed over me, through my head and through my stomach in nausea. Damn! I was having so many of these. Well, they always came in clusters at times when I was upset.

My vision cleared enough for me to make out a dark wood wardrobe carved in an elaborate shape past a matching footboard.

Home, I'm home in my bed.

Somehow, I had made my way home. Someone helped me home. It may have been Barker. I remembered being alone in the room and removing my clothes. Actually, I remember my clothes scratching against my skin until I couldn't stand the feel of them, so I must have removed them.

I inhaled and felt how loose everything was around me, even if each breath drew in pain and nausea.

So weak. I didn't think I could move my arms. I might, but the nausea would have me in a heap of sweating, shivering retches on the floor if I tried. I didn't have on my corset, I wore my nightdress. I had to call on all my concentration to feel the fabric against my skin and know what I wore.

At the thought of retching and vomiting, I turned my head to the side. I hope I had changed my clothes, not Barker. I could never overcome that embarrassment. I saw the bottle on the nightstand.

Yes, that was why I was in such bad shape. I took laudanum. I must have downed a massive swig.

I thought of Karparov. No, I saw.

Smiling, the grimace of a jack o'lantern.

He was there in the room. I saw him in the semidarkness.

I screamed. At least I tried. *Yes!* The sound gurgled from my throat and then came out.

He's a full sized, healthy man. I need more of a plan than that.

"The housekeeper," I growled. The morphine made my voice low, rumbling, and I hoped menacing. "She's—"

"Out back in the kitchen making cookies for when your lovely daughters come home from school."

Even if I had not been full of migraine and medicinal poison, I would have been sickened at him mentioning those I care about.

"You want to take care of them. That is nice. I want to help you."

"I don't see you as helpful. I stretched toward the nightstand." My movements swam through a sea of pudding.

"I know what you're doing," he hissed. "You think I killed my daughter. How could I kill the person I cherished most in the world? She carried on my name as good as any son ever could have."

"As well as any son." *What was that?* All my faculties seemed to have deserted me except for a grammatical snippiness.

You see such little things," he said with a laugh, and maybe it was the miasma in my head, but sounded full of mirth. His eyes then opened wide and seemed to grow so pale it shined through the curtain-darkened room, but he gave his head a slow, sad shake. "Those people would have starved without me. They are starving now. I put food in their mouths."

"How did you get in?"

"Barker's guard is not here during the day. My man saw you went home, rang me from the drug store."

"Barker's guard?" I had no interest in learning what he meant. I only spoke the words as a distraction while I made my move.

I reached for the drawer pull.

He turned to face me.

I slid my hand up. I grabbed something. I could see his eyes—the whites of them—turned so they looked at my hand.

"Ah," he said. His head jerked toward the bottle I held. "Laudanum. Be careful. You seem young and such a beauty. I would like to say vibrant." The word came out with a leer that made my flesh crawl over my frame. "You do not want to become a slave to the stuff, like my dear wife. She spends most evenings dead to the world by suppertime. The maids have to drag her to bed and undress her."

"Not an appropriate consort to a king," I said. My voice came out in puffs as though I had been doing heavy calisthenics. "Your whole family has embarrassed you. Is that why you killed Larisa?"

"What kind of perverse nonsense do you talk?" Spittle flying, his voice came out as a scream. "That I could kill my own daughter?"

Uh-oh. He sounded as though I'd gotten him angry enough to kill me, but he stopped looking at my hand and came in to crouch over my face. He was so close, that I could feel his hot, rum-scented breath. "She was wrong. I would have changed her mind. I would have made her right. I would have won. I would never have killed her. She was my own."

"I understand," I said. There, I got the drawer pull. I eased it open in a slow move below the sound of my own voice. "I have children." My hand was in the drawer. I felt, but where was it? I couldn't find it.

"You do not have children of your own, you do not know."

Bastard!

Where is the gun? I'd put Arbuthnot's gun in there, but couldn't reach it.

"You've done research on me," I said. "I'd be flattered, if I didn't find you so unpleasant." My hand scurried around the drawer to find something, anything. I felt cold metal and grabbed it.

He smirked. "I do not care how you find me. I care
that Barker seems interested in you. That is why you
merited my attention. I will keep him motivated any way I
can. If that means you and your brats must—" He yowled
in pain. My letter opener slammed into his arm. Not a
deep cut, but it had to hurt.

I pulled my hand back fast so he could not grab the
weapon, as meager as it was. "Get out of my room," I said.
I figured saying it had more weight than shouting,
especially since I lacked the strength to shout.

He slammed his forearm against my neck and my
neck against the headboard of the bed.

I could not breathe.

"Barker is to retrieve that casket and give it to me.
You make sure he does if you want your family to stay
healthy."

Pain filled my head even stronger than the migraine
and created herring-bone patterns in my vision. I thought
of Dostoyevsky and his seizures. Was my brain swelling
within my skull from all the pain? Was Karparov going to
kill me even faster than he could by strangling me?

I blacked out.

As soon as I got to work in the morning, I raced up
the stairs, threw the door open to Barker's office, and ran to
where he sat at the roll-top desk.

"Another time." Barker did not look up from the
notes on his desk. "You look a bit *wabbit*."

I had no idea what that meant and no inclination to
ask. "Answer my question." I gestured wide, which

smacked my chatelaine purse into my leg. It hit hard with the weight of Arbuthnot's pistol within.

Barker leaned forward on his desk. "You make no sense, woman. You have not asked any question."

My knees weakened and in a crumple of fire-colored taffeta trimmed with olive green, I sank into his chair.

"My daughters."

"I know. I'm a detective. Of course I know that the judge hasn't finalized your adoption. I've been thinking of what I can do and I have an idea—"

"Your client. He came to my bedroom. He was there yesterday afternoon." I whispered, "I'm so scared. I'm scared for me and for my daughters. He knows where they go to school and everything."

"What did he say, Daria? Close your eyes, go back to yesterday, and remember everything."

"He was in my room," I don't know how he got there, but he said your man wasn't there. What did he mean?" I could hear my voice mewl and whine like an alley cat. I could feel my body rock back and forth against the chair. I was glad the door was closed, and if Evangeline came in early, she would not see how I had lost all deportment. "He knew where my daughters go to school. He said that. He wants you to finish the job. Why does he doubt you would? What's happened, Barker?"

Barker's face puckered in silence.

I stood. I shouted, "Why can't you tell me? I'm in danger because of this. Because your client's sick mind thinks we are . . . because he thinks hurting me—

threatening my family—will make you stick with your agreement?."

"I'm sorry," Barker said. "I thought I only needed my clerk there in the evenings." He pronounced "clerk" as "Clark."

"You had Clark watching my house?" So that was why he would great me with a snarl in the mornings. I was keeping him up at night and did not even know it.

"Yes, not from Karparov, there are other dangers."

I eyed him sideways. He was blurry through the tears, but I could still see him frown. I waited for a reply, but only heard the pendulum clock. "Karparov is bad. Even if he didn't kill Larisa, one of those close to him did." I sniffed. I was done crying. "Why is he so afraid he thinks he needs to hold my family ransom to make sure you do what you already contracted and vowed on your good name to do? Mr. Barker?"

"I'm sure he could never visit the sort of evil he did in the remote regions of a far continent here just because of some stone casket," Barker said. He tipped back in his chair and looked out the window, not at me.

I remembered back to his trip out with the smugglers and the deep-sea diving gear. "You have it now, don't you?"

Chapter 27

"Aye." Barker got up from the desk and walked to that small laboratory at the side of his office. "But you're not to tell a soul." He unlocked the door.

I followed him inside.

Rather than open the thick, black curtains, he lit the gaslight in the narrow room with a counter along one side.

On the counter, sat the stone box. It was around four feet wide and just as tall. The arches of carved stone had a few chips and the figures carved below have a few noses sanded away, but almost all of it was intact.

The carvings on the casket were crude depictions of leaves and some startlingly realistic people in the drapery people wore through the early part of history. One carved man sat atop a throne with a rounded hat. Another bas relief was of the crowned man standing before a group of stone faces with his arms outstretched. Another had the man wearing the crown walking over the grooved waves of the sea and yet another showed a mane holding his crown toward what I hoped to be heaven, since otherwise, this casket was fraught with blasphemy.

I ran my finger along rows of letters at the top, each surrounded by a square. "I can't read that. It's Cyrillic, but not something I recognize.

"I suspect it's very old."

I turned away from the thing. I did not want to see it now or ever. I faced Barker. "I thought your client was going to kill me."

"I imagine you did."

"Karparov told me he hadn't killed Larisa. I don't believe him because, well, people who lie, cheat, and steal, lie, cheat, and steal."

Barker looked at the magic box beyond me.

"So if Karparov isn't Larisa's murderer, who is?"

Barker's blue eye looked to me. "That isn't important now." His arm lashed out and caught my sleeves in what was more a brace than hug. "Karparov is a threat to you and your family, we must deal with that."

I nodded and pinched my eyes closed to fight back the tears. "Yes, I know that . . ." my voice trailed off to the lump in my throat.

"Your daughters should go to your sister. And do it quietly."

"Yes, I'd like to get them out of here anyway."

"Not you, not me, not anyone Karparov would recognize. I'll speak to Mrs. Hulpke. She's a dependable old sort."

I nodded, but tears filled my eyes at the thought I would not even be the one to take my girls to safety.

Double back, go past the heights, and then to a relative or friend you know in another town. They will have to deliver your girls to your sister."

"Why don't you just give it to him and be done with it."

"Karparov's a bastard," Barker said. "You know that. What will he do if he gets this mystical object back?"

I sank to the window sill. My brain had filled with so many of my own problems and so much of my own pain, I had not considered anything else. My mind filled with the images of the dance at the Karparov's house, the men from the oil fields who had already sought his favor.

"He'll take over oil fields here like he did in Russia and enslave everyone in his domain."

"He doesn't have as much power here. He couldn't."

"Oh what, you don't think he'll enslave people here?" Barker demanded this in a louder voice than I had ever heard him speak. The window above me rattled in its sill. "Recall his sugar mill. He has slaves here now. You want him governing this whole part of the country?"

"That won't happen."

"Why not? Because this is America? A few months ago, you lived in America's most prosperous city. Did you think then you'd see your neighbors starve to death?"

I walked out of the laboratory and felt a small amount of relief when he locked the door between the magic box and me.

"Go, make your calls." Barker held the office door open for me. "I'll see to Mrs. Hulpke and her train tickets."

I tried to thank him, but the words choked in my throat. I gave his forearm a squeeze.

"Excuse me," Coralie said to a pair of giggling women somewhere in the static of the telephone line. "We have important things to discuss. If you plan to stay on the line, we'll need you to be quiet for a few minutes, if you've got that in you."

"Well, the nerve," one said before disconnecting with a loud click. The other created the loud honk of feedback by putting the receiver to the transmitter.

"Nice," Coralie drawled out in a way to indicate no such thing. This was followed by a couple seconds of silence.

"Thank you for doing this, Coralie," I said.

"She wants to talk to you."

"Damnit," I said.

Through the static, someone gasped.

"Please get off this line," I said. "We'll only be a few minutes more."

I believe a short huff was followed by a click. I continued, "I didn't think she had anything she wanted to say to me."

"Well, for one thing, she would have liked to have had the girls stay with her. A grandmother wants to see—"

"Coralie, stop giving details like that," I snapped.

She inhaled in a sort of reverse sigh that must have accompanied a shake of the head and a taller stance. "You had her bring them—um—your package here. You could let her know why she didn't get to keep the package."

"Because I expected her to not care," I said.

"How could you think that?" A voice said on the other end of the line. It was not Coralie's.

"Hello, Mother," I said.

"How can you say such a thing?"

"Because I don't think you count me as your daughter," I said. "Not totally." Oh, I felt a murderous rage right now for Coralie, but I realized I would never carry it out, unlike the person who killed Larisa and then Skip.

"I've always tried to please you." My mother's voice clogged with tears.

I didn't know what to do. I had never heard my mother cry. "Mama, I didn't realize." I don't think anyone would have.

"I never thought you wanted anything from us. Your husband had all the money you need and gave you all sorts of ideas. He even had you go to law school. I sent you to college. Wasn't that enough?"

This conversation bewildered me. "Yes of course it was," I said. "You instilled a love of learning in me." And I really don't have time for your problems right now. "And I'd love to have you spend time with my girls."

My mother gave a little sniff. "I'll send you a dress. You're heavy, aren't you?"

"No, Mother, I'm actually thinner than the last time you saw me. I seem to have to force myself to eat sometimes."

"Good. You'll get a husband with a nice figure."

"Thanks," I said. "Well, I should go."

"Is everything fine?"

I wanted to say, "Oh, everything's terrible, Mama. Someone killed my friend. I'm trying to figure out who it is because, well, she turned out to be a bit of a tramp and it's costing me business. I've got that high-pissed murderer all out to get me now and now I've cheesed off a megalomaniacal loon who actually found a way to make things worse for me than the worry I had that I could lose my daughters." Instead, I just said, "I love you."

She said, "You get back to work."

I turned my back to Barker's office so he could not see my tears at the fact I could not ask her to kiss the girls for me.

I dipped my pen in the well, scraped off the excess ink, and scribbled the final edit to the contract. I jotted a couple notes on what the shipyard should expect suppliers to provide at their facility in addition to what was stated.

I looked at the window. Humidity surrounded the building, but we were not yet to the season when Southeast Texas started to feel as though we lived in a wet gray sock. Later, someone would start boiling the sock.

I turned from the window to find pictures in the rough plaster of the wall.

I remembered the story I had read a couple years ago of a woman, bereft of her child and imprisoned in a room with no occupation, driven insane by her wallpaper. That had been yellow, though, so I was probably safe even if the last two days without my daughters had made me just as sad.

I stood. I would just go make calls on the Ladies Aid Society. If they had a problem with me to keep from asking me to luncheons, if they found my dead friend had caused me to lose respectability, well I wanted them to say it to my face. I grabbed my hat.

The door hit me in the back.

"Oh, I'm sorry, Miss Dash," Evangeline said. She looked as if she would cry.

"I'm fine, dear," I told her.

"Your sister's on the line."

I hiked up my petticoats and ran to the phone. My sister and I had worked out a code to say how well the "packages" were doing.

"Hello Cora. How are the—"

"Oh, Dash, I'm so sorry."

Even through the tinny telephone line, I could hear my sister sob.

"Oh no," I said. "What is it? Are they sick? I'll come right away."

"They aren't here," Cora said. "A man took them. I . . . I let Mama take a walk with them. This morning. We called the police. Have done everything they said to do. I just can't figure it. Mama said you were getting on so well. I'm sure she watched them just fine. She's a wreck."

"Just like her to think about herself in all this," I murmured.

"Oh she feels just terrible."

"Tell her it isn't her fault. It isn't. It's mine. I never told her there was any danger. He was determined. He wanted to take them."

"Dash, you're not making sense."

"Just tell her it isn't her fault. I . . . I need to figure out what to do." I may have said something more. I may have good bye, but I did not recall. I must have hung up the telephone because I heard it ring with my ring. It felt immediate, but I was moving so slowly, I did not know

Could it be Coralie? Could she be mistaken and the girls were just out playing by the barn?

"Hello?"

"Judge Reams here, is that you, Mrs. Gallagher?"

"Yes, but this is not really a—"

"I'm going to interview you again and make my decision right away, just like you wanted. Just bring your girls to my office."

He knew. He must know. He must have been told by Karparov to do this.

My insides roiled with fury.

"Judge Reams," I said in a voice soft enough to barely be heard above the static. "You will make that decision this week and I will not bother my daughters by parading them past you yet again. You will do so and show you are a man capable of making a decision. I have many friends within the Ladies Aid Society and other groups known to influence how men vote. You don't think they'd want to hear."

"You can stop threatening me and call off that lady reporter, too. You women—"

I hung up before he could say anything else. I smiled for a second, touched at MJ helping me when it could cost her a job she needed.

I looked behind me and saw Evangeline and Barker.

"Barker, he got my girls."

"Daria, you just need to sit tight, and I will—"

Rage burned through me. "You need me. Your inductive reasoning is at its best when I point you in the right direction. I challenge you and I've really helped you and all you ever do is tried to get rid of me." My hand balled in a fist I was angry enough to have smashed into his confused face, but I knew I would need my strength later. "I'm going to get my daughters. You can come with me or not, but for all I care you can go straight to hell!"

Barker rose so fast, his chair spun back and hit the wall. He grabbed his derby hat in one hand and my elbow in the other. Barely keeping up with his strides, we made our way through the crumbling streets to the train station.

Chapter 29

Through the dusk, I watched Barker try the knob of the mansion shaped like a Roman villa. Not even a budge.

We had started at the front door, but no answer. Breaking a French door on the patio would have been easier, but he said "more obvious."

He handed me his flashlight and

The door shuddered open an inch.

Barker nodded to me as if I were stupefied and failed to recognize this sign that we were to head off into action and stupidity.

Barker stepped into the kitchen door and through the pantry. I followed his fast steps with my top speed. I held my breath, not by design, but because each attempts to make my footsteps silent stopped my inhale.

No cooks wandered through the pantry and I heard no footsteps or voices in the kitchen.

The sound of flies and the smell of rotting meat indicated no one had been here in a while.

Oh no. Rotting meat smells like death. "My . . . my girls." I shoved my knuckles into my mouth. Pain gripped at my face, probably tears fighting to get free.

"No!" Barker's hand caught both my arms and he raised me up to stand straight and look up to his face. "It's just old meat." He turned from me, and his rapid stride reached what seemed sixty-miles an hour as he dashed through the empty kitchen.

I slid behind him and stepped forward to look around his shoulder. A blow from his long arm sent me back and I scrambled to right myself before spilling into the flour sacks. I caught up with Barker in the shadowy foyer. Empty. They had left, Gainsborough and all. They had probably moved to one of their other places and that was why we had seen all those boxes in the halls when we were last here. Now, nothing remained but white walls, even whiter in the squares where paintings once hung.

Barker started toward the stairs.

I tugged his coat sleeve.

Flickers of the gaslight streetlamps illuminated the frown he turned on me.

I pointed to myself and made and showed my fingers creeping along the downstairs hallway.

He nodded.

You think it's empty down here, don't you? That's the only reason you'd let me do that.

Only a slight arch of an eyebrow gave any indication he knew what I thought. He spun back to the stairs and took them three at a time.

I walked forward in the darkness. I clutched my purse tight in my hand, ready to bring the gun out if necessary.

I heard Barker's steps upstairs.

I walked into the conservatory, toward the long windows. I looked out for an instant, over the waxy green leaves and fragile white blossoms, already starting to brown of the gardenia bushes. I turned toward the door and took a step.

What was that?

I turned back toward the window. I remembered Barker standing before the panes of glass and looking out this window the first time we were here with Polly.

He saw something out there, something that made him wonder who was in here on the night of the murder.

I looked across the yard to the gardenia bushes outside the turret of the Dorfman house. Excellently tended bushes had full blossoms on each side, including the top. Something, or someone, had brushed against them. A line of brown, gardenia flesh haunted the edges of the blossoms in a line from the window.

I looked at the flimsy little clasp of the window, twisted it in my hand.

It eased open.

I felt a chill go through me.

Viktor stood in his study searching a bookcase for a volume. By the lamplight, I could see his face bore a calm lack of expression.

"Like just before a hurricane," I murmured to myself. I knew who he was. I knew what he had done. I also knew things would get worse before they got better.

Chapter 30

I stepped back from the window, from the sight of Viktor. My mind flooded with answers.

On the night of the murder, he walked through the door here and bruised the gardenias as he walked through into his own side door. He met Larisa upstairs. She was full of drugs and had sex with him as well. She would have thought she was in control and he would have let her, until he held her under in a bathtub full of salt water.

After that, he came back here to the Karparov's, rubbed his footprints flat so they would not be seen under the azaleas, why on my first visit, I had seen some blossoms were left half buried. He resumed his place on the couch with his laudanum-filled mother-in-law. He hadn't wanted to kill me, but tried to warn me off the trail with chloroform.

Barker watched me think through this. He must have known what was in my mind, watched my head move from gardenias to azaleas, or seen my lips move since he nodded when I looked up at him.

"Why?"

"Because he was a knight-errant here to thwart the evil king." Barker grabbed my arm. "Viktor killed his wife because she had that casket and would use it to take over her father's empire. He couldn't let that evil happen, not in a land as much of his ancestors as hers. That's why he felt justified killing that Negro dairyman and making it look like a robbery."

"Oh gees, the stories in the paper." I had forgotten all about that.

"Yes, the story in the paper, Daria, and the wagon ruts. Larisa must have got the casket no farther than her husband's house. Late that night, after the party, he and the drayman who had once done odd jobs for him, loaded body and casket into the cart to dump in the bay."

"You think the drayman wanted more than he was originally paid?"

"Aye." Barker gave a nod toward the man reading a book in his parlor. "Skip figured out something, probably that Viktor had the casket. Whatever he knew, Skip went to Viktor to get paid off."

"And he killed him, too." I leaned against a stand and knocked a potted orchid on the floor with a crash.

"Yes, he's good with slipping something extra to a drug hound, a trait Skip shared with Mrs. Karparova, but strangling seems to be his preference. He strangled both his wife and the drayman."

I touched my own throat.

"How I knew the drayman had not been the victim of a bad robbery. What robber takes the time to strangle?"

"And how you knew chloroforming me was just a warning."

Viktor turned toward us.

Barker pulled me back from the window.

Viktor's plant is across the street from Skip's hotel." Barker put his arms around me pressed me to his chest. "He would have seen him come and go and when Nina was not there. Slipping him too much of what he already took would have been easy."

"But he didn't take my girls, did he?" I felt as though I would cry or throw up, I wasn't sure I had the energy for anything more than putting my head on Barker's chest.

"No, that would be Karparov. He knows I have casket and wants to be certain I'll give it to him."

"You're obligated to give it to him. You gave your word."

"Aye."

I turn to face him. "So why haven't you given it to him?"

"Because I have yet to get it open."

"Why is that important? Why don't you just . . . " I didn't finish the question. I knew why he didn't give it to him, because he would use it to hurt as many people as he could, my daughters would be some of those people. "What are you going to do?"

He moved forward and took my arm in a gentle grasp. "Help you. Let me do what I think is right."

I scowled.

"Trust me."

My stomach roiled at those words. I pulled away from him and hugged my own arms. Tears streamed down my face and stung to the point that they robbed me of words. I looked him in the eyes and nodded.

"Thank you." Barker marched from the conservatory and into the front hall. "I'll bring Karparov to my office tomorrow. He plans to call to review my progress and I doubt he would cheat now. He'll bring the girls. He knows our deal would be off if he didn't. But I have to get that cursed box open."

"If Larisa did, you should. You're smarter." I followed him at a trot to keep up with his stride. "What would the lusty wife of a crazy bookbinder think of that you could not?"

Barker turned a sour scowl toward me.

"Come now, something in her experience must have led her to it. What was the key? Perhaps you're not thinking simple enough, you see, as an intelligent person, you may complicate things when—"

He whirled around, kissed my forehead, and said, "Bookbinder."

When we returned to the office, Barker said, "I will be in my office all night working on a solution. Don't go home, you'll just worry. Stay in yours."

"I do have work to get done," I said. I didn't want to tell him I felt safer across the hall from him than I would anywhere else.

My head had fallen on my desk as sleep overcame me. I don't know how long I was like that, but Viktor's voice woke me from my sleep. "I regret that I no longer have the artifact that would get my father-in-law to release your daughter." He stood before my great mahogany desk, the door shut tight behind him. I would bet it was also locked.

I raised my head from where I had used my beaded purse as a pillow. A scream gurgled in my throat, but before I could get it out, he was across the desk and had grabbed me with a hand holding my throat.

"I know your tricks," he said. "I'll take your hat pin." He knocked me to the floor.

My head hit the wood floor with a snap. He jerked the pin from my hat and took a clump of hair with it. I kicked, but my foot went wide. With his grip on my throat, I would blackout soon and then die.

Was that so bad? I had nothing, my girls were gone, and I didn't know how to get them back, but inside me a wavering flicker of trust said Barker would get them back. I had to live.

I used both my arms to shove him. That loosened his grip for a moment when I got air, but not enough time to get out a scream. I squirmed toward my desk. I slid my hand up the desk. I slipped my other arm between his body and mine.

"You'll just take a few minutes and then you'll be with Larisa. You'll like that, won't you?"

Yes, he probably was a lunger, his body rocked with spasms of a cough that eased the pressure on my throat for a few instants. "You see, I know all about losing your breath. It's not so bad. It won't be such a bad way to go."

I pulled my arm back as hard as I could and punched him above the stomach. I punched him again even higher. My other hand stretched, but reached nothing, not even the desk.

His grip strengthened and he said, "That's why I put your business card on her body before the drayman put her in the sea. I didn't want her to have to go alone."

He was crazy. To him, a piece of paper with my name on it was the same as a person. He was crazy and a bookbinder.

Yes, I caught the chain mesh of my purse. I didn't have time to feel inside, but caught what I thought to be the trigger of my pistol.

"I wish I didn't have to do this, but you saw me. I saw you today at the Karparovs. I saw that you knew."

Blackness crept through the room. I didn't have time to aim.

I fired. Time moved all wrong. I heard the shot echo before I had finished pulling the trigger. None of that mattered.

His body fell limp atop me.

I took a deep breath and shoved him away. I crawled across the floor, never taking my eyes from him.

A wound oozed from his midsection, but another tore half his forehead away and exposed blood, bone, and brain.

I looked behind me on the floor and saw that the bullet had come close and from an angle I could not have fired.

I looked up and saw Barker in the doorway. The rising sun shone behind him and gave an orange and purple shimmer to the gun he held. "My shot killed."

I looked at Viktor's shirt and the dark blood from organs within his midsection. "Mine would have eventually."

Barker called over his shoulder, "Call the police. They should understand this was self defense and give us until later today when we have time to make a statement. I have to get back to work."

Chapter 31

"Photographers cost money," MJ said. Even over the tinny phone line, I could hear the whine in her voice. "Especially the ones who do posed pictures for the rotogravure."

"I'm quite sure," said the voice that came out of me. It sounded all wrong because of the pain in my throat after Viktor had tried to strangle me and because it had lost all life. I went through the motions of life, but had no room for anything inside other than to wonder what would happen to my girls.

"This is the sort of thing that could get a reporter fired if it goes to Halifax." MJ and her son needed that job, but her voice held no reprimand. She just wanted me to talk.

"I know."

"Then—"

"But I have much more pressing worries at the moment." One of those was what statement I would make when I went to the police station, but that would be after Barker and I met with Karparov this afternoon. I only had a few minutes before that and Barker had not come from his office, even when the police arrived and took the body. The biggest concern as that, as the sun came up and turned to morning, I still had no idea if Karparov would bring the girls. I didn't even know if Barker had gotten the message to him through his personal secretary in an office in Houston.

"And what are those?"

"My girls . . . " I didn't dare say anything more over the telephone line when anyone could be listening from Karparov to Judge Ream's clerk. I couldn't say anything that would tip anyone off, but I knew MJ hadn't called about photographers or even her job. She knew something was up and wanted to know what it was. Her voice held concern. She was my friend and cared about me. My fear gave way to a little smile. I had friends and no one who has friends is alone. "There's just a lot I don't know, MJ."

"You don't know what he's doing, do you?" MJ said.

"No, I don't know about photographers and about the rotogravure section of the paper. No. And at this moment, I don't care."

She paused for a moment and then her voice came out soft, "Your Mr. Barker suggested it. I figured it had, um, something to do with the girls."

I felt a thrill course through me. Maybe it did. I realized I had never asked MJ for help and wondered if Barker should have. Would she do what he wanted? I had no idea and I doubted this would be a good time to ask her. "Bye," I said as I hung the receiver on the hook. I pushed off from the wall beneath the telephone and bounded into Barker's office.

"I closed that door, did I not?" Barker said. Midday sunshine streamed though the slats of the blinds and jabbed bits of light into the dim room.

"But you didn't lock it." My eyes adjusted and I saw a stack of papers with cruciform writing scribbled on them. "MJ said something about a photographer from the newspaper. Is that to help get my girls back?"

The papers on Barker's desk were slap-dashed in such inexact stacks, I would have thought elves came in to stir up trouble on Barker's pristine work surface. A pair of books, one of them in Cyrillic claiming to be a "Macedonian to Russian Word Book," sat atop the scattered papers. Then, in the center of the desk was the magic box.

I slid my hand over the cold, smooth stone.

Barker eyed me and said, "You might as well stay. I need another pair of hands to work these letters here."

I leaned over to peer around to the front. "Letters? Those aren't Cyrillic." I ran my hand over the squares holding cruciform shapes similar to the letters on the crumpled papers. The shapes covered the top of the casket, above the carvings of designs on the front that were almost sanded flat.

"No, seem to be Old Church Slovonic," Barker said. "Or close to it. Some Greek lurking in here, too."

"Very old," I guessed.

Barker ran his big mitt over the top and pressed the top arch until it went down a fraction of an inch. Barker gave me a gentle smile. "Press the Alpha and Omega there. Very hard."

I looked for those symbols, but saw none.

"The sideways triangle with the line through it and the "o"."

I found the squares with those figures in the collection of shapes on the very top of the box. I pressed. I wondered if these really were buttons that would go down or just carvings. They looked like carvings.

"Harder!" He still held the arch down.

I stood on my toes and shoved down. The result was still as if I pushed down on solid concrete. My hands hurt, but nothing gave.

"Harder! Come on."

I glared at him.

"Come on, a big girl like you is stronger than Larissa would have been and she did it."

"That's why she needed Arbuthnot." My voice came out in a hollow, aching shiver because of Viktor's attempt to strangle me. I took a deep breath and smashed my thumbs into the letters. Holy Cow! They moved, not much, but they depressed a fraction of an inch.

Barker nodded.

I took another breath and pressed for all I was worth. Deep within the casket, a creak sounded like stone rubbing against stone. I started to take my hands away, but Barker stopped me with an "Ach."

He said, "We don't know if it works when you aren't pressing. Keep at it, lass." He stood close to me. Actually, he leaned his body against my side and arm. He pulled at a thing that looked like a sideways "v" with a circle on either end. It came free.

He smiled at me. His face leaned close to mine. He had a slight, pleasant smell of Florida Water about him. "I thought of what you said about Larisa being a bookbinder's wife. She would understand about typesetting. That's what these letters are, ancient stone typesetting. That would have been a miracle at the time." He had about twenty letters removed. He pressed on my thumbs to keep them down.

"Thanks," I said between breaths.

He looked at the stack of papers, and moved his hand away from mine to flick the top layer back to his notes on Larisa's diary. "The ruler, *igemonov* . . ."

No, that wasn't Russian at all.

He lined up a second row of titles. "Suspended between heaven and hell—a disk"

Similar to Russian, but not quite.

"Let go," he barked.

I did. I pulled away from the thing and massaged my white fingertips. I listened. I heard nothing from within the box.

Barker shrugged. He took the letters out and told me, "Press again."

I complied and thought I heard a faint "click" within the casket.

"Greatness," Barker said. "*Velii*—is his and keeps him alive—*zivu*. Unpress."

I jumped back from the box and from Barker. I shook my hands to get blood back to them.

"Larisa wouldn't have figured this out without being married to Viktor. These were his books." He patted the short stack of books. "I figured one of them must have the key and I found the same characters."

I remembered a line from the diary. "He is alive as long as he is Victorious."

He looked over his notes. "How did she find this out?"

"Most likely she tortured a local historian or archeologist" I said. "He father would have liked seeing her in the family business."

Barker frowned at me.

For once, I knew what he was thinking rather than the other way around. "Oh, I always knew she was, well, she could be cruel. She wasn't a nice person. I know. I knew. Still, she died without anyone caring. That, to me is a terrible tragedy. I figured I made things a little better for her and yes, for me, by caring." I shrugged. "I don't expect it to make sense to you." I shoved my thumbs down on the letters. Either the hinges got looser or I got better at this.

"I think I understand," Barker said. "Alive—*zivu*. Victorious—*pobedilivu*." He nodded to me. "Go ahead and let go."

No sound. Nothing. "That's the end. Shouldn't it have opened?"

"I think it is," Barker said, staring at the casket.

"But—"

"Did you think a thousand-year old stone box would spring open like a jack in the box?"

"Well, yes," I said. "It being the source of supernatural power and all."

Barker slid his hands over the sides and then over the center of the box. "I thought you didn't believe all that argy-bargy." He pressed the worn panels.

They clicked.

Barker looked at me, up and down. "Go, hurry, put on your best dress. That thing you wore to the Karparov ball will work."

"A ball gown?"

"Yes."

"And get back by three o'clock. We have guests this afternoon."

I craned to see the front of the box and what happened to the panels beneath his hands.

"Go! You want to see your girls, then go."

I backed out of the office as if the casket had given him the power to curse me. I walked home to put on my red and white striped taffeta suit with the blue-velvet trim.

"Mama," shouted a voice downstairs. I dropped my skirt and ran wearing nothing but corset and French drawers.

"Mama," mewed out the other.

I ran downstairs and hugged them.

"Hey, you don't even have clothes on," Teddie said.

"I'm just so glad to see you."

Outside, I saw a shadow on the porch. I think it was a man, but he moved away, and I didn't care.

"Why are you crying?" Jinxie asked. "Did I do something?"

"I'm so happy to see you. I missed you."

I knew Aunt Cornelia walked into the room because she gasped.

"Of course we came back," Jinxie said with a laugh. "That colored lady on the boat was nice, but this is home."

"She gave us lemonade," Teddie added. "And said we were to tell you that she took good care of your girls."

"She did," Jinxie said. "We got pie."

Sometime, I would explain to them not to go off with strangers, not even a nice colored lady with lemonade.

For now, I had to make sure Aunt Cornelia kept anyone from seeing them until I came back from the office.

I needed to put my clothes on, first.

"When I walked into Barker's office. His desk had been tidied, but the casket remained. Beside it sat something under a velvet drapery. An addition was MJ standing where customers usually sat. She smiled at me. "Glad I could help," she said, and then looked away to let a blush rise as if she'd said the f-word in church.

The couch had been kicked back against the windows and a short man with a big camera on its tripod took its place.

"Thank you," I said. I looked at the casket. "There must be something we can do to keep Karparov from getting that power back."

MJ raised her hands in a shrug to indicate she did not know what was going on, but the fierce frown indicated she expected me to know.

"Thank you for getting my girls," I said to Barker.

"Oh, I'm glad." Evangeline said from my office in a weepy voice.

"Good, he did as instructed."

Behind me in the hall, I heard the phone sound out my ring, but ignored it.

"Who did?" I asked. "Karparov?"

Evangeline edged around the door. "Miss Dash, it's Judge Reems."

I felt my stomach turn.

"She'll call him back in a few minutes," Barker said. "Or better yet, ask him to come by."

Evangeline looked at me. I nodded. I was not eager to speak to the man. Eventually, I would have to let him interview my daughters and they would tell him they were kidnapped and I would lose them forever, but I could hold on to them as long as I did not speak to the judge.

"Go on." I slipped a look to Barker and a smile. "I trust Mr. Barker."

Barker stood before me and said, "Loose the hat."

Women did not have to take hats off inside, but I could do a small thing like this to please the man who got my daughters back. I pulled the hatpin free, jabbed it in the roses and feathers before setting it on the top of the hat rack beside Barker's bowler.

"So when is something newsworthy going to happen?" MJ said. "You just aren't. No offense"

I found the statement less offensive, than the "no offense" tossed at the end. Before I told her this, Barker said in the tone one uses for saying important things and an accent that sounded almost English, "Wait until our guests arrive."

A gray-haired man in a gray morning coat and ascot walked into Barker's office. He was followed by another in the same attire, but with a shiny blond head of hair.

"Glad to see you gentlemen," Barker looked at me. "Are you going to translate?"

Since my German was rusty and my French limited to ordering food, I translated into Russian.

"We speak English," the blond said. He took my hand and gave it a gentle kiss.

MJ's paw was right there in line after mine.

The gray-haired man smiled at me. "But we would love to have you translate everything for us."

"She has something else for you," Barker said. He steered me behind his desk with a hand on my back. He reached both hands beneath the velvet drape on his desk and pulled out a rounded golden crown studded with rubies and emeralds, all of these colored stones surrounded by rows of diamonds and circles of pearls. The bottom of the crown was ringed with a stripe of perfect brown sable.

I reached to the soft, prickly fur. Had the casket truly been magic? How else would the fur have survived so well through the centuries and time at the bottom of the muddy waters of the Gulf?

"Yes," Barker said. "You noticed the fur." He leaned into me and whispered in my ear, "That fur of yours I had to cut the length off to rescue you from the fight in Ivy's restaurant? It's found its way to posterity." Before I could say anything, Barker clapped the crown onto my head.

A brilliant light and smell of fireworks made me look at the photographer. He was hidden beneath the drape and held the bar that still smoked with the flash.

MJ patted him.

"Daria," Barker said. "Meet the Russian consul and his aid. They came all the way from Chicago for this."

"Chicago?" I said. "That means you sent for them before we knew the girls weren't at the Karparov mansion." And long before he got that box open. I extended my hand with a grace that would have made Queen Alexandra jealous.

Barker shrugged.

"A pleasure," the gray-haired man said in Russian. "And we will gladly take that crown."

I looked at the camera and saw a flash before the photographer put the lens cap back on his camera. With held breath and a sense of ceremony, I slid my fingers over the smooth gold and cold jewels of the crown.

Footsteps outside revealed Karparov looking in the doorway.

"Don't worry," Barker whispered in my ear. "We'll win."

Karparov pointed to the crown with a tremoring finger at my head. "You got the crown out." His voice held the same awe his smile showed. "I will take that, take what is mine." He lunged toward me.

Barker nudged a shoulder at the old man.

"No, Mr. Karparov, I'm afraid." said the consul, and I wondered if he chose English because the sibilant sound revealed disdain better than Russian would. "You seem to have forgotten that you gave this to the Russian people, to be on display in your name at a museum."

"I did no such—"

"Your right to this is questionable at best," the blond aid said in rapid Russian that I whispered to Barker. "Give it to us to show in a museum, and you can avoid prosecution." The blond fellow folded his arms and showed some muscles bulging through the sleeves of his suit. I'd bet he was *Okhrana*, secret police.

Karparov's pale face looked as though he thought this as well.

"There is still the casket it came in," Barker said. "I'm returning it to you just as I said. I've kept my word. I'm sorry if the world will now know it contains no crown, and hence, no power."

Karparov looked as though a sudden sunburn overcame him and seared his lips closed.

Another picture flashed.

"Congratulations, Mr. Karparov," MJ said. "You've made the rotogravure."

Karparov said several things I did not need to translate into English. He stomped out without taking the casket.

The consul waved a hand at the casket. "We will arrange to take that as well."

At the doorway, Judge Reams brushed past Karparov. "What's . . ." He called to the fleeing man, but then turned to face us. "What is this? You called me over here when—"

"Yes," Barker said. "I asked you a couple times this morning before you finally showed, but I thought you would like to meet friends of Mrs. Gallagher's, the Russian consul and his aid."

The two men extended a round of handshaking and once again kissed MJ's and mine.

Judge Reams frowned at MJ.

"MJ Quackenbush," she said. "Your favorite society reporter."

He nodded with a sneer.

Barker said, "Miss Gallagher just made the newspaper for her generous gift to the Russian government."

Another flash of powder on the wood t-square the photographer held.

"For which we are most grateful." The consul walked over to face me. "We will take our leave now." With gentle fingers, he plucked the crown from my head and gave me a deep bow. He handed the crown to his companion and kissed my hand again before they walked out.

"Judge Reams." Barker gave the narrow, medium-sized man a chummy pat on the shoulder. "I imagine you are here to say that you will expedite her adoption," Barker said. "What with her repairing a diplomatic blunder that happened on your watch."

"I've got the paperwork," Judge Reams said. "I've signed it." He tossed it down on Barker's desk. The certificate landed on the crumpled velvet that had covered the crown. "Now, leave me alone and I don't want to hear anything else from you." He stormed out of the office and smacked into Karparov on the stairs.

I don't know how Karparov got behind the Russians, but imagined it involved slinking along the wall and not making eye contact.

"We've got to make the evening edition," MJ said. She shot me a single-armed hug and a kiss on the cheek before she walked out. Her arm slid back inside the office to beckon to the photographer.

He tipped his hat to me and marched after MJ.

Barker followed them and closed the door.

I looked at the certificate of adoption on the desk. "This is so wonderful, I can hardly believe it. Once again, thank you Mr. Barker."

"Well, I said I would get your daughters for you. I figured I needed to do it in a way that would not come undone."

I stood for a few seconds smiling at him. I could think of nothing good enough to say. He slipped behind his desk, and I assumed that to be a sign that he wanted to get on with his work.

"Well, I'll be going now. I should get some of my clients back with that in the paper. Nothing says respectable like a royal crown on your head."

I stepped toward the door, but Barker rose from the desk and slipped into my path.

"Mrs. Gallagher," he said with a frown.

"What is—" my words were cut off by his lips on mine, his arms around my waist. This was a real kiss that explored my mouth and even my soul. Ready to kiss him back, I slid my hands around his shoulders, but he pulled from my grasp and was behind his desk before I could make a move. He read a page from a stack of papers, folded it, and threw it away.

I stumbled slightly, smoothed the pleats at the front of my red and white jacket, and said, "Um, I need to get back to work." I lingered at the door for an instant to smile and say, "Thank you, Mr. Barker." I strode out the door and back to my office.

*Dash and Barker will be back in the next mystery
of the Galveston Hurricane series:*

BRIDES OF THE STORM

"Oh, you're in here." Winnie spoke to a woman on a one-armed empire-style sofa covered with maroon and gold stripped silk. Winnie's voice betrayed no obvious emotion, but her pleasant, light sound instead scratched through the air of the room. Her hand gripped my arm tourniquet tight.

The recipient of this comment had youthful features of round eyes, pug nose, and red cheeks. Her wiry brown hair curled around her face and was pulled back into a ribbon and a polka-dot tie surrounded the neck of her white shirtwaist. She looked like one of those actresses who specialized in playing Little Lord Fontleroy. She smiled to show even teeth on the top, and a chipped one on the bottom. "I'm not going anywhere, dearie."

Winnie put her hands on her hips and gave her head a little shake that released even more tendrils from her wavy topknot of hair. "You remember Abelard had a late wife? Well, here she is. Strangely, not late at all. Early, as a matter of fact. As a matter of fact, the first one to arrive at my bridal tea. "

Holy Christmas!

I linked my arm through Winnie's and pulled her back so far, we almost bumped into my daughters. I craned down to whisper in her ear without taking my eye off this woman and her little smile. "Don't worry. Abandonment. Abelard can get a divorce based on that."

"Hardly abandonment." Damn, she heard me. "I've written to him every day since I've been staying with my poor, sick mother."

Winnie's nostrils flared, her mouth slid into a tight grimace, and her long neck grew a little longer. The last time I'd seen her look like that was in elementary school when she punched a bully for making the boy who stuttered cry.

I stepped a foot before hers in an attempt to keep her from lunging for the gamine brunette before her. "Mr. Barker, remember the detective I rent an office from? He'll find out everything. He's the best there is. We'll talk to Barker."

MJ burst through the dining room doors. She held a cocktail glass of clear liquid and plucked a skewer of olives from it. "Barker speaking to you again, Dash?"

About the Author

Amanda Albright Still has held many jobs since she dropped out of law school: journalist, technical writer, editor, online restaurant critic, and risk manager on projects valued in the billions of dollars. Each of these gigs involved writing, creativity, and some even allowed her to use the occasional adjective. Fiction writing was always something she did on the side until her first novel, "Shadow of Twilight" was published by people who even paid her for the privilege.

Amanda has two college-age daughters who make her proud, and a wonderful husband. Ian, whose Scots accent she can now understand, almost. When not writing, Amanda is a compulsive reader in any genre, but sometimes breaks away long enough to knit or make cheese (the enchilada mozzarella, not so good, the goats milk camembert, heaven). She and Ian are in the process of renovating their Victorian home in the historical district of Galveston.